MILLER'S PUB

GEORGE EDWARD MOON

 www.trafford.com

North America & international
toll-free: 1 888 232 4444 (USA & Canada)
fax: 812 355 4082

Acknowledgements

Hurricane Irma struck the entire state of Florida creating havoc and destruction. The category 5 storm forced my wife and me to take shelter in a nearby church basically taking with us only the clothes on our back, a can of soup, and a couple blankets. There we would remain until it was safe to go back to our mobile home park, Lakeside Village. Fortunately, on our return, we found damage minimal compared to those around us who lost their homes completely. Still, we were facing days without electricity, water, and gasoline in the 90 degree Florida summer.

Heartfelt thanks go out to our neighbors whose concern helped sustain us during this trying ordeal. Special thanks must be extended to Kenny Gardner and his exceptional wife Nancy who took a direct interest in our welfare enabling our survival until living essentials were restored. Their actions convince me there are angels walking about here on earth.

PRELUDE

MILLER'S PUB IS A FABRICATED tale. The characters in the plot are fictitious. Any resemblance of people living or dead is truly a coincidence. Certain historical events mentioned during the story's time line are repeated from memory and confirmed by the excellent Internet Site Wikipedia, the free encyclopedia.

Steven Baker, the principal protagonist, finds himself unexpectedly in a mid-life perplexity. Like many entrepreneurs absorbed by the pathways to success and often at the expense of others, he fails to properly recognize the traditional gap in their marriage. In all fairness, Steven may have been blindsided to this customary interval and unprepared to recognize and control it.

Since the nineteen fifties, American culture, if there ever was such a thing, has gradually lost its former values. Now, relativism rules the day. Steven's grandparents lived by the precepts in the U.S. Constitution and their Bible. The Good Book provided the roadmap for their way of life. The changing of society and environment has led to the decay of the old moral significance. Marriage and the family are disrupted and no longer a basic cultural element—it will never return.

CHAPTER ONE

MERRIAM-WEBSTER IS A SUBSIDIARY OF Encyclopedia Britannica and defines a pub as a building or room, especially in Britain or Ireland, where alcoholic drinks and, often, food are served. Miller's Pub is a Chicago restaurant located on Wabash Avenue.

Established in 1935, it is a stopping off place for a business lunch or celebrating special occasions. Huge collections of vintage oil paintings line the walls, along with numerous photos of Hollywood movie stars, professional athletes, Broadway actors, and musicians. It's the loop destination for American cuisine in a nostalgic ambiance.

I believe it all started there. It isn't where I first met Irene, but where the relationship grew wings.

She was in sales with a company supplying a product necessary to my manufacturing business. She was making a sales call to my factory. I remember her having short hair and looking rather uncomfortable in her tight fitting business suit. Assuming it was probably her time of the month, I placed a chair for her in front of my desk. The speed in which she accepted it and sat convinced me I was right.

Back then, a woman making a sales call was new to a male chauvinist like me. Today, women salespersons are probably in the majority.

The visit by Irene was timed to coincide with lunch. Unfortunately, my factory was located several miles from town and the closest place to get a sandwich was a small café populated with local farmers. I'm amazed by how many farmers, patronizing the restaurant, were missing appendages—one arm, one hand, and several fingers. I was told it had to do with corn pickers.

"Do you have time for lunch?" she asked.

"I have the time but the nearest restaurant is back in town. Tell you what, let's drive both cars and you won't have a ten mile return trip. You can go on about your day from the restaurant. I can't see the parking lot from my office. What kind of car are you driving?"

She gave me a knowing chuckle. Her mode of transportation was a 1982 Chevy Citation with a piston rod ping and clatter. Her boss told her it just sounded bad but didn't interfere with its performance. She believed him. She also insisted on driving.

The trip to town was invigorating. I could barely squeeze into the front seat and had to exhale in order to buckle the seatbelt. Seatbelts weren't required yet—more proof her boss knows how she drives. The accelerator must have been floored because the wheels spun and gravel went everywhere. We fishtailed all the way to the main highway. Fortunately, there's a stop sign before you enter.

"Does my driving scare you? I notice you are rather tense."

"Has your boss ever ridden with you?"

"He knows how I drive."

"He must have a big life insurance policy on you," I seriously stated. She thought I was kidding and laughed aloud. I wished I had driven. Once on the paved road the traffic held her in check. There are three places in town frequented by businessmen when the wolf growls at noon. I suggested the one with the least amount of stops and turns on the pathway reaching it. When you ride with a female whose bent leads to Indy racing, it's best to spend as little time as possible alongside her. To her credit, she whipped into a parking space which I would have rejected—to hunt one with more room.

"Is there enough room for you to get out?" she asked, while withdrawing from the driver's seat. For a second, I felt like faking a difficult time. The thought of riding to another space settled the issue.

Businessmen and those wanting moderate privacy entered through a side door over which a canopy stood. Others found the entrance facing the shopping center. With more illumination from the outside, provided by a sweep of large windows, and volume lighting within, the everyday shoppers preferred this part. It was like two restaurants at one location.

Entering from the bright sunlight, it took a while to acclimate to the darkened contour of the room. Irene took hold of my hand as the receptionist directed us to a table. She selected one in the center of the dining area and then paused, saying, "Do you want one more private?"

"This is fine," I replied.

Each table had a candle in the center, giving a weak flickering of light to help patrons read the menu. While Irene studied the *cart du jour*, I asked about specials and soup of the day. When it comes to lunch, I'm a cheap date. Irene settled on something written in French and I ordered minestrone soup.

At that moment, I observed two things. Irene is a pro when it comes to reading menus, and, she wore a wedding ring on her left hand. I can't exactly explain how those made me feel, the wedding ring that is; but, I definitely passed through an emotional veil. Before I could make a self-analysis, the cocktail waitress was at the table. Irene flashed a perfect smile and asked, "Would you like a cocktail?"

"I don't mind if I do. I'll have a scotch and soda."

She hesitated for a second then requested a daiquiri, saying, "One drink won't bother me. You've got to watch out for the drinking and driving thing."

Restraining myself from saying, "Honey, the way you drive, they would never know the difference," instead, I found myself trying to engender her dazzling grin. I've had lunch, probably at this very table, a hundred times, and never had so many acquaintances stop by to say hello. With each visitor and introduction, she flashed a brilliant grin, revealing a dancing light of mischief in her sparkling blue eyes.

"You know a lot of people," she stated.

"It's a curse."

"I suppose being in business and all," she concluded.

Irene opened her purse and removed a package of Salem menthols. While she fumbled for her lighter, I picked up the matchbook with the name of the restaurant on it, and struck a match. She took a short drag and quickly exhaled—the act of an inexperienced smoker.

"Have you been smoking long?"

"Not really. The other girls in the office smoke. I thought it would help my appearance when making a sales call. I notice you don't smoke. Seems like men are giving it up and it's increasing among women."

"If you want my personal opinion, it doesn't look well on you."

She extinguished the Salem, in the table ashtray, and gave me that snow-white grin.

"Would you care for another scotch?" she asked. My glass only held ice cubes at the bottom.

"Yes please, these glasses are very small. And, I don't need to drive back to the office."

"Something tells me you wouldn't have a problem if you did."

When lunch was brought to our table, Irene's plate was large but the servings were small. I only recognized the green things. They had to be vegetables. The rest is anybody's guess. My minestrone soup, however, came in a large bowl, steaming and recognizable. By breaking the crackers into it, I had a feast fit for a king.

We continued our conversation well after the plates were removed. Irene wasn't uncomfortable taking an extra-long lunch and neither was I. After all, I still owned the damn company. It was in the process of being purchased by a foreign conglomerate; however, we'll talk about that later.

I learned Irene was the mother of two boys, passed their teenage years, and she married her high school sweetheart. Several references about her husband made me think all wasn't too blissful at home.

When the restaurant was down to just us and a drunk at the bar, I suggested we call it a day. Hell, she might have stayed there all night. Before Irene picked up the tab and walked to the cashier, she mentioned the upcoming manufacturer's convention.

"Will you be attending the convention next month?" she asked.

"I guess I will. They elected me president of the organization."

"I was aware of that. My company is having a display booth. I'll attend this year as part of our marketing department. I'll have booth duty, but will be able to take customers to dinner. Would you be my guest?"

"Of course, it all depends on the day. This year's convention is composed of three parts. The last day is the president's dinner. I will have to be there for that."

"My booth duty is flexible. I'll call you with possible times. You select the one best suiting you."

The ride back to the factory was less hectic. Neither one of us said much—apparently leaving the conversation back at the restaurant. I stood on the entrance steps waving goodbye as the Citation's noise from the valve lifters slowly disappeared the farther her car traveled.

When I opened the office door, my secretary, Jane O'Connor, rose from her desk, gave me a knowing smile, and handed me a stack of pink phone messages. The other two girls had similar expressions on their faces when Jane asked, "Did you have a pleasant lunch, Mr. Baker?"

"Yes dear, quite pleasant."

I found it difficult getting back in the swing of things. The phones kept ringing until well after 6 o'clock and Jane stayed to manage the switchboard. Paula Stevens/traffic and Beverly White/inventory control shut it down at 5:30, their normal quitting time.

Jane O'Connor was the best secretary I ever had. She was bright, loyal, and protected me masterfully. Recently, I had a new telephone system installed. I put the main console on her desk, giving her control of incoming calls. She also had an intercom to the factory and my office. The other girls had similar systems which allowed them to cover incoming calls when Jane was occupied with her other duties. My accountant, the plant's engineer, and plant manager also had new phones. For the first month we all were like kids with a new toy, learning the basic functions. I never did learn them all. In addition to the two factory lines, I had another number all my own. It was blocked to the other phones so no one could listen in. Very few people had that number—Jane, my wife, and my lawyer. The button on that line rarely lit up, although, I did use it frequently to call out.

After Jane told me she was leaving, the office downstairs went dark. There still was a stack of mail unread. Jane always used a date and time stamp as she opened the envelopes, separated checks from customers and dealers, and then stacked the rest in order of importance. She has been with me for five years and knows the business fairly well.

I glanced through them and saw several required a written response. By now the clock read 7:00 p.m. and I was too tired to compose intelligent correspondence. I put a glass paperweight on top of them, removed my suit coat from the garment tree, and drove home.

My house was on display. It seemed as though every room had a light on. I guess with five children you should expect it, but, I know for a fact most of the rooms were empty. I could almost hear the electricity meter, located in back of the house, buzzing away. Who needs Christmas decorations? The thing which gripes my ass the most is, the driveway was packed with cars and I had to park in the street.

Any hope of the cars belonging to friends of my children was dashed the minute I entered the front door. Coats and packages were stacked on the living room sofa and chairs. My wife's sisters were paying a call.

These ladies were exponents of horrible illnesses, most of which were only found within the family. If it weren't so pathetic, it would make a sane person laugh. While most families bragged about their children's accomplishments, they carried on over their afflictions. All their news was contained inside the family circle. Not one word about the world around them. Elaine must have heard me come in. She climbed the stairs from where the noise was coming and said, "You're too late for supper so I saved a plate for you. It's in the refrigerator. All you need to do is put it in the microwave. Oh yes, my sisters are here, they're in the family room."

"Where are the kids?"

"The older ones are at the mall. The other two are watching television. Come down when you've finished eating."

Elaine and I have been married for twenty-three years. We had two children by my sophomore year of college. The others came shortly thereafter. She is an excellent mother and kept herself trim until the last ten years in which she gained ten pounds each year. Elaine claims it was a genetic thing and there was nothing she could do about it. Wastebaskets full of candy wrappers seem to belie her opinion.

Rather than fiddle with the microwave, I poured myself a double scotch and bounced down the steps to the family room. They were in the middle of a discussion concerning a serious illness another sister might have had.

The family room has one uncomfortable chair. Naturally, it was vacant. I took it and happily sipped myself into oblivion.

CHAPTER TWO

THE FOLLOWING MORNING I TACKLED the stack of mail. Resting on top was the convention package. It listed the schedule of events, workshops, and speakers. Outside of the board meeting, I was scheduled to make the opening address, on the first day, and be present at the president's dinner. That left two evenings to select whose dinner invitations I wished to accept. Vendors, who purchased a booth, desired having the president among their dinner guests. Others took a hotel suite and set up hospitality rooms, in which liquor usually flowed until the wee hours.

The aroma of fresh perked coffee told me the girls were in the office. Our factory has a lunchroom and perpetual coffee; however, the girls preferred to dodge whistles and make their own. The upside was that first fresh cup, hand delivered by Jane O'Connor.

"Thank you Jane, you're a lifesaver," I said. "Did you give me yesterday's receivable numbers?"

"Yes sir, they must be among the mail," she answered, and flipped through the stack. "Here they are, it was a pretty good day."

The slip indicated just over $300,000. It was a sufficient amount and guaranteed our ability to handle expenditures—payroll, insurance, and vendors. Receivables are the most important part of business. Laxity on the part of dealers could put a serious strain on a company's survival.

"Warren deposited the checks during his lunch hour. You should have a copy of the deposit slip with the mail. Here it is."

When I'm in the office and not traveling for the company, I like to tour the facility, usually with Bailey Marshall, the plant manager. A great deal can be learned concerning the general attitude of the employees as well as detecting safety issues. It's an enjoyable time for me, however, not so much for Bailey. He always feels as though he's back in the air force undergoing inspection. I tell him he's doing a fine job; but, I guess, old habits are hard to break.

A tour of the factory is incomplete without stopping by Arnold Pratt's office. The senior engineer has several projects underway, all of which have critical paths drawn and displayed around the room. From start to finish a colored line passes through projected completion dates as the project nears finalization. And yes, occasionally a critical path is delayed due to some external cause—extended material deliveries, down time due to weather conditions, and, on rare occasions, by my interference. I try to keep that one at a minimum.

Finally, if he is in town, I meet with Russell Webster, my marketing manager. He has daily contact with major customers and all of our dealers, from which he learns the competitors pricing. Some of our dealers also represent a competitor's line.

At least twice a month I hold a general staff meeting in which financials and other business topics are reviewed. Managers are encouraged to let their hair down and relate their pressing problems. In spite of a few elevated decibels, the staff meeting tends to unite the team. Jane O'Connor acts as recording secretary and summarizes the meeting's highpoints and assignments, then distributes a copy to those in attendance. Although I try to keep the meeting at one hour, there are times in which lunch is catered from the country restaurant.

While outlining my response to one of the letters in yesterday's mail, Jane's voice came over the intercom speaker, "Mister Baker, there's a woman named Irene Jones on the line. She says it's about the convention."

"Thanks Jane, I'll take it," I answered, and pushed the lighted button.

"Hello, Steve Baker," I announced.

"Good morning Steve Baker, I'm calling about our dinner date at the upcoming convention. Have you decided which day?"

"Looks like it will have to be the second day. Who all will be joining us at the dinner?"

"Nobody silly, it's going to be just you and me," she answered.

That caught me by surprise. Usually there's a great many guests at a vendor's dinner.

"Are you still there?" she asked.

"Sorry, I was distracted by something. The convention activities are officially over around six o'clock. What time do you want to meet?"

"How about seven, in the hotel lobby. We can catch a taxi from there."

"Okay, seven o'clock it is," I replied.

"Before we hang up, would you like to meet for a drink at the end of the first day?"

Now my heart is racing. I took a second to calm down and replied, "That would be nice. What time?"

"I'm tied up with a group for dinner. We ought to be finished around nine o'clock. Is ten o'clock too late? I'll try to make it sooner."

"You try to make it sooner and I'll try to keep awake," I joked. "Where shall I meet you?"

"Same place. The hotel lobby at the main counter. We can either have a cocktail in the Palmer House bar or walk to Miller's Pub. I prefer Miller's Pub, it's more personal."

"It's beginning to look like a very special convention," I uttered.

"I hope so, see you next month."

"The convention is only two weeks away," I said.

"But it is next month. I might give you a call before then," Irene stated, and hung up the telephone.

People often call me a dreamer. At that moment my fantasies were running amok. It was short lived, however, when Jane told me I had someone waiting on line two.

The week went by without major incident and on Thursday, I met Joe Chamberlain for breakfast. Joe is a vice-president at the bank, and had a new service he wanted to talk about. As it turned out, the bank was offering a high interest business checking account based on the average monthly balance. The rate was 7% with a restriction on the number of checks written each month. I mentally calculated, based on an average balance of $700,000, it would render an additional $49,000 yearly or $4,083 a month supplementary income. Since we were restricted to the number of checks written, I needed to talk to Warren Brantley to see if we could live within the limits. In 1985, the prime rates charged by banks hovered around 10%. Home mortgages were over 11% and certificates of deposit stood at 8.5% for one year. By dumping receivables into the account, and delaying payables, we could maintain a hefty balance. At present, I pay invoices in 7 days and receive 2% off the total. Warren is shrewd. Surely he could figure something out.

As the month of October rolled around the leaves were falling and nights became a lot cooler. I've never been considered a clotheshorse, but, for some reason, my general appearance became a new concern. For the most part, Elaine knew my size and bought my clothes. I still could wear things right off the rack. I used to tell people, "I have a suit for every occasion. This is it."

One of the larger malls north of town was having a sale on men's suits, offering two for the price of one. I still had time to take advantage of the bargain and have the pant cuffs altered before the convention. That weekend, I drove north and bought two suits, one dark navy and the other brown with a fine, light blue, line. This year, at the convention, I'm going to look the part.

On Saturday, the twelfth, Elaine and I celebrated twenty-four years of marriage with dinner at the town's finest restaurant.

On Sunday, I raked leaves. There are three large maple trees in my yard—one in front and two in back. They were a wonderful source of shade in the summer; however, prolific furnishers of multi-colored leaves in the fall—demanding at least sixty leaf bags to return the landscape to lawn grass.

You couldn't ask for a more beautiful day—sweater weather with a bright October sun. Apparently, my neighbors had the same idea. By noon, the streets looked like the remains of a war zone. Living on the edge of the city, we were still allowed to burn leaves. By five o'clock the smoke had subsided and we all stood with rakes in hand, watching stragglers making their zigzag path to the ground. Some folks will be back on the battlefield tomorrow. I'll wait until next Sunday, after the convention.

Monday morning found me at the office at seven and planning to drive to Chicago from there. Knowing I will be gone most of the week, Jane O'Connor also came in early. She already had the phone number of the Palmer House hotel, but, since our business phone will start ringing at eight o'clock, she needed an hour before the interruptions really got going. Jane took note of a list of tasks I had planned for the staff, and made coffee. We were drinking it when the others started to arrive.

At eleven, I placed my briefcase in the back seat and drove to Chicago. In less than an hour I was at the hotel and parked in the underground garage.

Arriving around lunchtime, I registered at the front desk and followed the bell-captain to the elevators. My room was on the seventh floor. It was spacious with windows facing the lake. Vertical buildings covered the landscape and the street below was busy as a beehive. I gave the bell-captain two dollars, thanked him for the service, and hung up my new suits.

Having no appetite for solid food, I rode down to the lobby and found the Palmer House bar. There was an open seat alongside two men wearing convention nametags. I recognized one as a supplier's representative. The other was new to me. They both acknowledged my presence and introduced themselves.

"My name is Tony Barnett, with Taylor Manufacturing," said the shorter of the two, with me reading his nametag as he spoke. "This is Larry Quinn. He's new with us in sales—his first time to the convention."

"My name is Steven Baker." My nametag was still in the convention package.

"Hell, you don't need to introduce yourself. Everybody knows who the president is." Tony had been drinking awhile.

I couldn't help overhearing their conversation. It started out praising the exploits of Pete Rose, (the Cincinnati Red's infielder, who recently broke Ty Cobb's record of total base hits), what a great person he is, and a credit to the American pastime. Then they expressed commiseration for Mexico suffering from the earthquake killing and injuring up to 40,000 people.

As they earnestly applied themselves with more bourbon, the dialogue changed to women.

"She's the best looking woman at the convention," Tony slurred. "Did you see her today?"

"Yeah, she sure can fill out a dress. She's better looking than most movie actresses," Larry confirmed. "What do you think she's doing tonight?"

"Oh, probably taking some of the owners out to dinner. I'd give my left nut to be with them. For years, everybody has tried to hit on her. She just gives them her pearly whites and puts them down."

"Does her husband ever come to the convention?"

"I think he came in the beginning, but ended up drunk and passed out in the hall. Since then, she leaves the old man at home. She's got a couple kids."

Tony bought another round and declared, "I'm getting hungry. Let's drink up and find the hotel restaurant."

In Tony's current condition, I was puzzled as to how he could tell if he was hungry or not. Their approval of Pete Rose, being the credit to the game, might be debatable considering old 'Charlie Hustle's' bad boy reputation. Without mentioning her name, the woman in question had to be no other than, Irene Jones. There's no debating that one.

Thanking Tony for the restaurant invitation, I declined and took a rain check. No sooner had those two left, two others took their places. The Palmer House hostelry was beginning to fill up with people familiar to me. I needed to find the men's room but feared losing my chair. A glance at the clock, located behind the bar, read 3:45 p.m., meaning there was about six hours before meeting Irene. I adjusted my position on the barstool and joined in the hearty conversation. It took another hour before Tom Casey announced, "Save my place, I gotta go find the head." I followed suit.

Standing at the urinal, I came to the realization there's not many things better in a man's life than draining a full bladder. After holding it all afternoon, it truly is the pause that refreshes.

When a group of men are drinking at a bar, the endurance game is on. It's a sinister challenge as to who will be the first to humble himself and go to the john. Once someone does, the rest can cheerfully follow.

When I returned to my barstool, it hit me. I'm not meeting anybody tonight. This isn't the first day of the convention. It begins tomorrow.

Carlton Cook, the organization's secretary, shared the elevator when I returned to my room. I had completely forgotten the one o'clock board meeting.

"Missed you at the meeting," he said.

"I'm sorry about that," expressing regret.

"Over half the members were missing. Apparently, the day before the convention is too difficult for most of the officers. I get here the day ahead to make certain the hotel is prepared properly. We need to schedule the board meeting at a better time," he suggested.

"I think you're right," I agreed. "I'd appreciate seeing your notes from today's meeting."

We had reached the seventh floor and the door opened. Carlton held the door from closing and said, "There aren't any notes. The meeting was cancelled."

Once in my room, I pulled off my tie, laid my pants on the desk chair, and flopped on the bed. I lay there listening to the noises outside the room and fell asleep on top the covers. At three in the morning, I suddenly awakened and got up, pulled the bed covers down, and took off my shirt and socks. The next thing I knew the alarm was beeping.

The convention officially opened on Tuesday, October 15, at nine o'clock, with a short welcoming speech by yours truly. This year, over four hundred people signed up for the assembly. As the hotel auditorium gradually began to fill, I sat on the stage with the other delegates and searched the crowd. After spotting her company's group, there was no sign of the lady in question. When the sergeant-at-arms closed the auditorium doors, I rose and slowly walked to the podium, tapped the microphone, and said, "Welcome to this year's international convention."

Vendor display and sales booths officially opened at ten o'clock. A tour of the showroom is a courtesy expected of the president. Today I had a special interest. There are those who like to walk through, alongside the president, thus, forming a small cadre. We started at one end and gradually progressed to the other. When we reached her employer's booth, someone in the group asked, "Where's Irene Jones?"

"We were all out pretty late last night. She's taking her time this morning. I expect she'll be here soon. I'll tell her she missed the president's visit," said her sales manager. We chuckled at that and went on about the tour. Once we had seen every display someone suggested, "Hey, it's a beautiful morning. I'm for taking a walk outside. Let's get our coats and enjoy the fall air." Inspecting his watch he said, "Meet everybody in front in fifteen minutes." I went to my room, took off my suit coat and lay on the bed. I'm no fresh-air-freak.

CHAPTER THREE

THE HOURS SEEMED TO DRAG, in spite of my efforts to speed them up. I watched the weather forecast on television, called the office for messages, and took part in the convention luncheon. Afterward, refused invitations for dinner—they usually lasted well into the night. When asked for tomorrow, I regretfully said I had a previous commitment. It's not good form to ask, who is it with?

That afternoon, I purposely avoided the Palmer House bar, since I had a good idea who might be there. Yesterday's drinking bout was enough to last me all week.

I ran into Carlton Cook in the lobby and accepted his invitation for a cup of coffee in the hotel's café. Carlton is a humorous fellow, small in stature, however, much larger in significance. To his credit he has expanded his job as secretary to one of extreme importance. Not only concerning the convention and all it incorporates, but, also, editing our monthly industry magazine. He is the only paid officer and the board controls his salary. He's no fool. He is well aware the president holds the final power with the board of trustees.

Listening to his complaint about finding the right hotel and setting up a convention lasted for nearly an hour. He had to be surprised over my willingness to remain during his lamentation over his meager salary. I just gave a knowing nod and stated, "That has to be approved by the board; however, I will recommend an increase at the next meeting—probably during December's annual gathering in Florida." He still carped on, but my mind was elsewhere. Finally, Carlton stated he was taking the organization's office girls to dinner.

"I always wondered who was lucky enough to have that privilege. Personally, I believe it should be the president," I joked.

He seemed startled, as if I meant it, until I admitted it was a witticism.

The coffee klatch ended, and I shook hands with well-wishers on my way to the elevator. Back in my room, I lay down on the bed and began recounting the day. I must have dozed off because I woke with a start. The phone was ringing. Clearing my throat before lifting the receiver, I said, "Hello, Steve Baker."

"I'm sorry I missed you this morning."

"Oh, that's all right. I understand you had a long night."

"Yes, pretty much so, and my booth duties weren't scheduled until after lunch."

"You missed my opening address," I jested.

"Maybe you can give it again tonight. You haven't forgotten, have you?"

"No. I wrote it down."

"I bet. I'll see you around nine," she said, then hung up.

Often my heart races when I first awaken. Right now, it's pounding for a different reason. She must have called me before joining her guests for dinner.

I knew if I went downstairs too soon I'd run the risk of meeting overzealous conventioneers and have a difficult time getting away. I decided to wait in my room and watch television until nine o'clock. There wasn't much to hold my attention so I shut it off and lay back on the bed and dozed.

At nine, I caught a rare empty elevator and descended to the lobby. She was standing by the front desk. She looked different from the last time I saw her. Oh, she still had her eye-catching beauty, especially wearing a form-fitting cocktail dress, the color of aubergine. It served to accentuate her silhouette and, with the only accessories a simple gold necklace and bracelet, she made a most flattering addition to the Chicago nightlife.

I noticed she was carrying a wrap and, like her, I had my topcoat draped over my arm.

"It seems as though we plan to go outside," I commented.

"Yes, I have a reservation at Miller's Pub," she replied.

Once we were outside, the doorman tipped his cap and asked if we wanted a taxi. Irene thanked him and said, "No thanks, it's only a block away. We've decided to walk."

Chicago weather in October can get quite chilly at night. As we neared the street corner, a whistling breeze gave us a sample. The walk to Miller's Pub turned into a scamper with our collars up.

The famous eatery was still crowded with late night revelers. It's most popular with show goers and will likely get busier in an hour or so. The minute we stepped inside we were asked if we had reservations. Irene said, "Yes, reservations for Jones."

The hostess gave me a knowing smile and led us through the happy throng to a table in a far corner. "Is this private enough?" she asked.

Irene hesitated for a moment then said, "I guess it will have to do. You're pretty crowded tonight."

"I could keep my eyes open and move you when a more secluded table opens up," the hostess offered.

"No thanks, this will do fine," I interrupted.

Mixing with the common din, a burst of laughter echoed from the front of the restaurant. Irene frowned saying, "Maybe I should have reserved a different restaurant."

"Nonsense, this is perfect. I needed a distraction from the convention."

"Well, you certainly can get it here."

"When I first saw you at the front desk this evening I sensed there was something different about you. I now know what it is. You're letting your hair grow."

"You said you liked women with longer hair," she stated.

"Do you do everything I tell you?" I joked.

"I would."

I wasn't sure I heard her right, due to the commotion; and, at that moment, the cocktail waitress came to the table. Irene ordered a daiquiri and I a scotch and soda.

Our conversation about the convention was short lived. I've always believed women were basically interested in what they had to say—their preconceived notions and beliefs. They could listen to what men had to say, but kept it in their minds no longer than five minutes. Irene was different. She seemed to hang onto my words and digest them. After three daiquiris, the subject got personal. I learned she was unhappy. She had married her high school steady and raised two boys. For the most part, her high paying sales position supported the family. Ron, her husband, was idle and between jobs for weeks at a time. He could play the piano and entertained with a band on the weekends, however, hadn't done that for months. Also, he was a heavy drinker. He could do that every day.

I noticed her makeup was beginning to wear out, revealing a somewhat older woman. Nevertheless, she was a very beautiful older woman. She must have been clairvoyant because she excused herself for the women's restroom and returned younger than ever.

You might say we were letting our hair down. I told her about my wife, my family, my likes and dislikes, and the pending sale of my company. As yet, there was no indication the alcohol had any effect. We ordered another round. By midnight, our table had gradually become secluded without trying. The crowd had thinned to such an extent we were practically alone.

"Let's have one more for the road and get back to the hotel. That alarm clock will give us headaches in the morning," I implied, while thinking, she would stay here all night if I hadn't said anything.

Irene paid the cocktail waitress and we walked back, pressed against each other, fighting the hawk. The hotel lobby was empty. We took the elevator. I got off on the third floor and escorted her to the door, making sure she was safely inside.

"Would you like to come in for a drink?" she asked, a little under the influence.

"No thanks," I laughed. "We have a dinner date later today."

Once I was back in my room, my head hit the pillow and I didn't move until the alarm clock began to jangle. At first, I thought I had a sore throat but it got better once I was moving around. I took two aspirin just to make sure.

The second day of the convention featured several workshops and a fine lunch served in the main dining room. I planned to attend the workshop entitled Better Organizational Management. It was scheduled to begin at one-thirty, right after lunch. Turkey and gravy was posted on the menu and, for a country boy from West Virginia, that's all I needed. I love roast turkey. Apparently, others felt the same since every table was full. The second day luncheon is a good barometer as to how the convention is going. The festive mood of a couple hundred turkey eaters gave the answer.

I expected the workshop leader to focus on the upper echelon of management. Instead, he brought it down to the factory floor and talked about Maslow's hierarchy of needs.

Maslow's pyramid denotes his theory of psychology measuring the stages of human development. For his study, he chose only commendable models, i.e., Albert Einstein and Eleanor Roosevelt, and avoided the stunted, immature, or neurotic types.

He displayed his hierarchy in the shape of a pyramid with the largest and most fundamental needs at the bottom. Graduating to the top by levels, he included Safety and Security, Love and Belonging, Self-esteem and Confidence, with Self-actualization on top.

Though his effort was to develop the best person one could strive for, his pyramid fails to expand upon differences of social and intellectual needs of differing societies. The level in which Maslow has placed some of the needs, especially sexual intimacy, has been debated for years.

After twenty minutes, I had enough and slipped away from the room. At this point, the closest oasis was the Palmer House lounge. There were two or three hours to kill before my dinner date, so I gave it another fling.

Entering the bar, I noticed all stools were occupied. Scoping the room, I recognized Carlton Cook sitting at a table with the girls. Obviously, he was treating them to a cocktail. When it isn't his money, the man is such a little *Mensch*. Of the three females, the office manager was matronly and the no-nonsense type. The second probably blew out forty-five candles at her last birthday party and the third was young, good-looking, and had attracted three men around her in fawning exchange.

After my promise to raise his salary, I've become Carlton's best friend and was eagerly beckoned to join their table.

The young men were Latin types and they already had taken her in their eyes. My intrusive presence foiled the possibility to carry it any further. Dejected, they strolled away and stood at the bar. And then, quickly drank a beer while standing, and were back on the street resuming their pursuit—*Mejores becarios siguientes suerte.*

Having me at their table definitely put a damper on their discussion. Words were stilted, and the subject turned to the convention. We were on the exact track I wanted to avoid. I needed a break and these people were too intimidated to provide it—the downside of being the president. Staying only long enough to be polite, I finished my drink, thanked them for lively conversation, and rushed off for a previous commitment.

Inside the elevator, I pushed the number seven button and decided to wait it out in my room. Looking down at my watch, there was only two hours left to kill.

As previously agreed, at six o'clock, Irene was waiting for me at the front desk. I had changed into my, all business, navy blue suit. Suit pants always feel good when the creases are sharp. Irene added to the hotel's fashion by wearing a dark green cocktail dress and a pearl necklace that wrapped twice around to achieve the desired length. No *belle femme* could top her.

"You look very nice this evening," I said, thinking, *what a stupid thing to say when every man in the lobby was drooling and licking their chops. She was beautiful whatever she wore.*

"You're not too shabby yourself," she replied.

"Where are we eating tonight?" I asked, as if I gave a damn. It could be in the alley between garbage cans for all I really cared, as long as she was with me.

"It's a surprise," she answered, while we walked outside and the doorman hailed us a taxi.

"Lawry's restaurant," she told the driver.

"The one on east Ontario?" he asked.

"Yes, the one featuring prime rib," she replied.

At one time or another I must have mentioned how much I loved prime rib. Lawry's isn't one of Chicago's high-end restaurants located atop the skyscrapers downtown. It doesn't feature a breathtaking view of the city from the 40th floor. It does, however, have the best prime rib.

What is it about urban cab drivers thinking they are the only vehicle on the road? We sped, zipped and zagged, leaned on the horn, dodged pedestrians, and, with nearly a heart attack, pulled up in front of Lawry's.

Irene, unfazed by it all, paid the driver and I opened the door to the restaurant. The bar was full with a few tables off to the side. She confirmed her reservation with the master receptionist (maître d' restaurant) and returned to me saying, "It will be a few minutes before our table is ready."

I motioned toward one of the vacant tables and we moved in that direction. No sooner had we sat down, a cocktail waitress arrived and took our order. Assuming Irene will be announced when our table is ready, I relaxed in the comfortable chair and observed those at the bar, ogling our table. Since this is a hangout for the Rush Street crowd, no doubt they knew she was a movie star, but, just couldn't think of her name.

"Do you ever get tired of all this?"

"By all this, do you mean taking a handsome man to dinner?" she countered.

"No. I mean being mistaken for a movie star."

"Like Marjorie Main?"

"You know what I mean," I stated firmly. "There's a couple gals at the bar looking like they will bounce right over here and ask for an autograph."

"Honestly Steven, I really don't get out that much and when I do, it's either work, church, or the annual IMA convention." She was serious.

Lost in her radiance, I knew her eyes were blue. Yet, the lighting here in the lounge gave them a greenish cast; and, with her matching dress, she was a knockout. She noticed I was swirling a glass containing only ice and ordered me another scotch and soda.

"It's okay. If you're not finished when we're called, they will bring it to our table," she assured.

This time I sipped it until they announced, "Table for Jones." Sure enough, the waiter brought my drink to our table. We were placed in a little cove, by ourselves, with a table large enough to accommodate any hardy meal. Our vision was basically blocked on each side with only a straightforward view. It took me a while to get used to it. There was no chance of being overlooked due to the restaurant staff frequently checking in on us. After another drink, the intoxication of the person next to me began to blur my senses. They say seventh heaven is a state of extreme happiness. Well, I was entering the rhapsody of the eighth. The waiter handing out the menus broke my stupor.

Naturally, I ordered prime rib, larger cut. Irene ordered the same, only the smaller cut. A separate cart brought the baked potato, which was prepared in front of us. The cart had every topping you could possibly think of. I shot the works while she took a pat of butter and a dab of sour cream. I must have been starved because I caught myself unceremoniously beginning to wolf it down. Fortunately, I stopped before revealing what a disgusting food slob I can be; and, then, picked lightly at the salad.

Now came the main feature, the *pièce de résistance*, on a cart pushed by the chef. He sliced the prime rib according to our request. Mine filled the plate.

After dinner, we sipped a Curaçao triple sec and talked about our dreams. Irene's were a lot more sensible than mine and she told me so. It was easy to see how she could deflate and enfeeble a man when she wanted to. She could level the peak of his ego with a few simple words. It was also easy to see she had no intention to do that with me. Instead, she acted as though my words were filled with prophetic wisdom—like a Japanese *sensei* and *gakusei*. I didn't just get off the boat and I know she's faking it. I only hope her reason may justify my fantasies.

Neither of us wanted dessert. So I settled on another scotch and she a frozen daiquiri.

Often, when she was making a point, Irene placed her hand on mine and left it there until I needed it to take a drink. As the restaurant patrons began to thin out, she indicated we should take it back to the Palmer House. When redeeming our coats, Irene asked the maître d' to call us a cab. He spoke on the intercom with the chief valet and told us, "You have a taxi waiting."

The ride back wasn't nearly as harrowing as the first, due to less traffic. It was physically impossible for Irene to sit closer. When I looked into her eyes, she flashed her brilliant white grin. No words were spoken.

After paying the driver, we walked to the Palmer House entrance welded together. Waiting for the elevator she stated, "I want you to come to my room for a nightcap. There's plenty of scotch in my liquor cart."

My watch indicated it was a quarter past ten—early enough to have a drink. Besides, I had no desire to end this magic evening.

Using her hotel key card, she unlocked the door, took hold of my hand and led me inside the room. When she double locked the door, I noticed the Do Not Disturb tag was missing and assumed it now reposed outside the entrance.

Irene found ice cubes in the small refrigerator and mixed me a scotch and water. Handing it to me, she said, "Take your shoes off and relax. I'm going to take a bath."

I've never been a hobbledehoy when it came to women, but I must admit, for me at least, this is a first. Should I bolt for the door or see where this celestial train ride ends up? Why did she look so damn alluring and beautiful? Why did she have to look like Barbara Mandrell? Why couldn't she be ugly? That certainly would help me decide. Did I mention I was a chauvinist? It would take a better man than me to leave now. I took a healthy slug of my scotch and surrendered to serendipity and the pulchritude of my hostess.

Irene left the bathroom door open so we could continue talking. The air took on the aroma of scented bath salts. I have no control over my eyes. She next appeared wearing nothing but a terry cloth robe and sat on the edge of the bed with a bottle of Johnson's Baby Magic lotion. As she slowly rubbed it onto her arms and legs, I began to feel sick with excitement.

We woke three times during the night. And, after each exhaustive passion, returned to a sound sleep. In the morning, as we lay unmindful of the world around us, she whispered, "I love the way you're made."

"Thanks, I had nothing to do with it," I quipped.

"I want you to know this is the first time I've ever done anything like this."

"Why me?"

"There's something about you that turns me on. Something I can't get enough of. I've never met anyone like you. You're smart, good-looking, and desirable—the kind of man every woman wants."

"I'm sure happy you feel that way," said I, thinking, *and I had to wait until I was fifty years old to find out.*

"Darling, I know this is the last day of the convention and you have the big president's dinner tonight. I won't bother you, but remember how I feel. I plan to stay in bed until lunch; so, in case you don't want to be seen coming off this floor, there's a stairway to the left. Just go down one flight and take the elevator up. We probably won't see each other again until tonight."

I took the recommended route and wasn't recognized until on the seventh floor entering my own room. And then, only by well-wishers commending the convention.

The president's dinner was held in the main dining room and a hundred guests took part. A reduced crowd is expected since the scheduled activities ends at four o'clock. Many members skip the dinner to get an early start heading to the airport and eventually home. Irene's company has an offsite dinner planned with their customers, but, will probably stop by the reception before leaving the hotel. I've hired a professional pianist to entertain, as well as set up an open bar.

Her boss, Harvey Finefield, and a half dozen of his customers, took advantage of the bar—still no sign of Irene. His group walked the room, with a drink in their grasp, shaking hands like the ambassador of New Zealand. When they reached me, I was congratulated for the best battery manufacturing convention ever. How could I dispute that? Harvey invited me to join their dinner party, but I graciously declined claiming the final mop up of convention duties. At that instant, the gathering began to murmur, signaling Irene had entered the room. Several men busted their ass to see who could get her a drink. Harvey came to her rescue holding a Tom Collins and told her, "By the time you finish this, we should be on our way. Make sure you thank Steve Baker. I invited him to join us, but, he has to stay here for the convention clean up."

Irene, wearing the famous little black dress, couldn't suppress her contented grin.

I moved to a place where she could easily reach me. The grip of her handshake was intended to send a message. It was received loud and clear.

Later that evening, while I was in the arms of Morpheus, the telephone rang me awake. I accidently knocked the receiver off its base trying to pick it up. Feeling under the bed with my left hand, I found it and put it to my ear, "Hello, Steve Baker," I said, still drowsy.

"Did I wake you up?" It was Irene.

Clearing my throat I answered, "Not really, I was reading," I lied.

"I'm glad you're being a good boy," she said, knowing she woke me up.

"What time is it, anyway?"

"It's eleven thirty. I said I had a headache and refused a nightcap. Anyway, Harvey wants to leave early and eat breakfast on the way home."

"You guys be careful driving home," I implored.

"Don't worry. One of the other guys will do the driving. Darling, you have a good night's sleep and I'll call you next week," she stated, kissed the receiver, and hung up.

Sunday found me raking leaves and basking in the comfort of familiar surroundings. My neighbor to the east was also hard at it. Evidently, on Saturday, we had heavy winds, coming from the west, and most of my leaves were blown into his yard. He reluctantly returned my friendly wave.

Personally, I seem to have become more tolerant. My rambunctious children were less irksome. Could they have grown up over the past week? I doubt it. There's something else. Could it be having Irene in my life? Only time will validate her.

Monday morning, on my way to the office, I stopped at Cliff's Restaurant for eggs and toast. Besides good food, Cliffs' is a morning meeting place for the town's most lively functionaries—an eclectic group of professionals and managers. The regulars included a veterinarian, lawyer, accountant, and principal of the local high school. They're not exclusive. Anyone with a good story to tell is openly invited. Just push another table alongside. Did I mention, you also must have thick skin? Anything you say is subject to ridicule by the best taunters and hecklers in the business. No one is excluded or protected. Although, a charter member, I usually keep my mouth concentrating on chewing and try to keep out of the current conversation. Anything else requires a suit of armor.

Walking in the office, I noticed a young man sitting in a chair by Jane's desk. It was Miguel Ángel Reyes, one of my Latino employees.

Jane said, "Mr. Baker, Miguel received his driver's license over the weekend. That makes everybody legal."

"Congratulations Miguel," I said, while taking the steps to my office. The Immigration Reform and Control Act (IRCA) are now being considered by Congress and will surely pass. President Reagan will sign it into law next year.

It requires employers to attest to their employee's immigration status. It will be illegal to knowingly hire illegal immigrants and subject to heavy financial fines for each employee in violation. First offense fines could be in the thousands of dollars.

Before leaving for the convention, I asked Jane to review the personnel records to make sure we are in compliance. Apparently, she found Miguel lacked one of the three pieces necessary—in his case, a driver's license.

I have three other Hispanic employees, actually two. Andres Alvaréz abruptly quit when he learned of the new law. Juan José Cruz and Carlos Gutierrez fully qualified. The men from south of the border are excellent workers and seldom carp about their pay or conditions. It took a while for them to fit in, but, eventually, they were well received by everybody.

My being gone for a week created a big stack of mail. Thumbing thru it, I found several forms from Uncle Sam—more government paperwork. Jane will fill out most of the questionnaires, especially, those concerning active personnel, ages, and marital status.

Two letters were from principals requesting to become dealers. Reading each one twice, I set them aside to discuss with Russell Webster. The others were either sent to file thirteen or coded for my personal records and placed in the out box. I buzzed Jane.

"Yes, Mister Baker," she replied.

"Jane, will you please locate Mister Webster and have him come see me?"

"I believe he went home, sir."

"Is everything all right?"

"Mrs. Webster called to tell him she was out of cigarettes," Jane answered.

I could hear the other girls snickering.

In a small company, the job of marketing manager requires many days away from home. Sometimes for weeks at a time while driving from state to state calling on customers and visiting dealers. Russell would rather drive than fly. A couple years ago, he and I flew from Chicago to Philadelphia and were scheduled to take a puddle jumper to Trenton, New Jersey. After I was boarded, they wouldn't let Russell on the plane. He had to rent a car and drive to the hotel—Russell is a very heavy man.

"When he comes back, tell him I have potential business to talk about," I said, and replaced the receiver. I guess I was the only person in the building who appreciates Russell. The girls view him as a malingerer, and, leaving to bring his wife cigarettes, doesn't do anything to change their opinion.

The familiar sound of a factory in operation tended to calm my nerves and relax me. I shut my eyes for a moment and was back at the convention and smelling bath salts. It was as though I were in Irene's room, sitting with a drink in my hand, and viewing her naked image in the bathroom mirror. I find it strange how I've exorcised any guilt resulting from my actions. My reverie burst like a soap bubble when I heard a knock on the door.

"Come in," said I.

It was Warren Brantley bringing me the mid-month financials. Warren always looked as though he was just caught shoplifting—not a good look for someone controlling the money. I thought the new company would discharge him. You always want your own financial man. Much to my surprise, they thought highly of him and retained his services.

"You look like you had a rough night," I commented.

"What do you mean?"

"Your eyes are all bloodshot."

"It's probably from doing up-close work. Concentrating on numbers all day can be an eye strain," he contended. "I think you'll like these numbers. We're on our way to a record month."

Warren was right. The numbers, thus far, were excellent and all the receipts were deposited in the interest bearing account. I leaned back in my chair, clasped my hands behind my head, and admired the oil painting on the wall facing the desk. It was an excellent copy of one of Maurice Utrillo's original street scenes, circa 1920. The artist who created the forgery lived in New Orleans and painted, in the style of Utrillo, at my request.

Being a frustrated artist myself, I took an interest in Maurice Utrillo. Like many talented artists, he led a life plagued by mental illness and alcohol.

A French painter of cityscapes, Utrillo was the son of Suzanne Valadon, also an accomplished artist. She was eighteen at the time and never revealed who the father was. Perhaps, she didn't know. Speculation existed that he was the offspring of another equally young amateur painter; although, she posed for many famous artists and became mistress to some. Any of which could have been the father.

Posing for Morisot, Renoir, and Henri de Toulouse-Lautrec provided her the opportunity to study their techniques and teach herself to paint.

Meanwhile, Suzanne Valadon was left to raise young Maurice, who was an incorrigible youth, showing signs of mental illness. At the age of 21, he was encouraged to paint and soon showed real talent, even though he had no training beyond what his mother taught him.

Maurice was acclaimed internationally; yet, throughout his life he was interned in mental asylums repeatedly.

At the age of 52, he married Lucie Valore and moved to just outside of Paris. Too ill to work outdoors, he painted landscapes viewed from windows, postcards, and memory. Although, plagued by alcoholism, he lived into his seventies.

Regarding his paternity, there is a dubious account told by Diego Rivera and related in unpublished memoirs of one of his American collectors: Ruth Bakwin.

"After Maurice was born to Suzanne Valadon, she went to Renoir, for whom she had modeled nine months previously. Renoir looked at the baby and said, "He can't be mine, the color is terrible!" Next, she went to Degas, for whom she had also modeled. He said, "He can't be mine, the form is terrible!" At a café, Valadon saw an artist she knew named Miguel Utrillo, to whom she spilled her woes. The man told her to name him Utrillo. "I would be glad to put my name to the work of either Renoir or Degas!"

The rest of my day was filled with work. Meetings with Bailey Marshall and Arnold Pratt lasted the entire morning. In fact, I had lunch brought in so we could continue without interruption. Both men usually brought theirs and ate in the lunchroom. There never is a complaint when I have it catered. They just picked at whatever was in their brown bags during the last break in the day. I liked to jest about them eating like birds—Arnold a sparrow and Bailey an ostrich.

The local café makes the best damn Italian beef sandwiches. Naturally, the pace of our meeting slowed down, like a train moving uphill. We had to keep at it since Arnold and his wife plan to spend next week in Minnesota visiting their daughter. We finished at three o'clock. By then, Jane had a stack of phone messages and two pieces of correspondence needing my signature. She also made a point to tell me that Mister Webster called and said he will be here in the morning. He didn't come back.

Chapter Four

CHECHNYA IS LOCATED IN THE North Caucasus, situated in the southernmost part of Eastern Europe. Archeologists believe prehistoric people, living in the area, resided in mountain cave settlements, used tools, mastered fire, and adapted animal skins for warmth. Traces of human settlement date back to 40,000 BC. Cave paintings and artifacts give evidence that there has been continuous habitation for some 8,000 years.

Going back to the 1700s, Chechens have always been a martial society and known as great and ferocious fighters. To even hear you have Chechens around, strikes fear into the hearts of many.

Since childhood, they grew up handling horses and were proficient shooting rifles from horseback. Culturally, they fostered the idea of the blood feud and take a dim view of outsiders. Their national symbol is the wolf, chosen because it's the only animal that, even when injured, will not whine or cry out. It will turn and face you, looking straight in your eyes.

Chechnya was flooded with many Ukrainians during the 1930s food famine, known as the Holodomor—extermination by hunger. Joseph Stalin rejected outside aid, confiscated all household foodstuffs, and restricted population movement in what appeared to be an effort to eradicate the rise of Ukrainian nationalism. Those successfully migrating into Chechnya were mostly Sunni Muslims which was composed of four different schools of legal thought.

In 1939, during the Second World War, Chechens established a guerrilla base in the mountains preparing for an armed insurrection against the Soviets. Their effectiveness drew the attention of the Germans, who, at the time, were at war with Russia. Several German agents were sent to recruit Chechens to join their war effort. Whether or not Chechens allied with the Germans is questionable since they have profound ideological differences.

At the end of the war, Stalin exerted appalling retribution against the Chechens and those who had immigrated into the Caucasus. He forcibly resettled them into Siberia and Central Asia. Many died during deportation due to the extremely harsh environment of Siberia. Others were massacred on the spot.

Many of those remaining in the North Caucasus had been Muslim for centuries, but, under Soviet rule, were forced underground. There are several different kinds of Islam. Chechens worship saints and visit their graves. They also revere the graves of their ancestors. For radical Islam, that is a strict no-no. Nevertheless, hardcore radicals fought for Shariah Law, had money, and were fierce fighters. They were readily accepted.

Zorva Yamadayev and Dokka Zakayev are cousins. Three years ago, they came to the United States on a student's visa from Chechnya, and soon disappeared into the general population. By necessity they maintain a low profile, although, Zorva spends an inordinate amount of time at the local gymnasium. He loves to work out, lift weights, and punch the heavy bag. Scars above each eye denote his fondness for boxing. No one at the gym will step into the ring with him. He is a vicious competitor with untamed aggression.

Dokka is the most cerebral of the pair, often found in the company of girls riding in his 1984 white Cadillac Eldorado convertible. He has no visible means of employment and tells people he receives an allowance from a rich uncle. When he and Zorva stand alongside each other, you can see the family resemblance. Dokka, however, is less athletic and could be considered handsome, in an Eastern European fashion.

They share an apartment on Chicago's far southwest side. Living quarters are over an empty warehouse. The property is protected with chain link fencing and two German shepherd watch dogs. While the warehouse looks shoddy from the street, the upstairs suite is equal to the Hyatt Regency.

"I have never liked this set up," Zorva said, while carefully pouring Stolichnaya in his glass. He is a moderate drinker with less than a quart a day.

"Bashir Shishani prefers it this way. It keeps us at arm's length from the operation," Dokka replied.

"Yes, but a sniveling American accountant. Why couldn't he have selected a blood, instead of an infidel?"

"That's the point. A blood would be the same as being a money mule ourselves. The accountant has worked for a year and without a hitch. He delivers the package where we tell him and drops off the money at the destination of our choosing. It's all done over the cell phone. He doesn't know us but we know him. If he screws up, you will take care of him."

With that, Zorva gave a sadistic grin and said, "He does a little dealing on the side and snorts cocaine. A user can never be trusted."

"Bashir Shishani is aware of that. This will be the last job."

"Then I can take care of him?"

"No. He hasn't a clue as to who we are. He'll be told his services will no longer be needed and he never knows for whom he was working. The dumb son of a bitch will be left at sea."

"Bashir's going to drown him?"

"No. That was just a figure of speech. It means he doesn't know what happened," said Dokka.

CHAPTER FIVE

TRUE TO HIS WORD, RUSSELL Webster did arrive the following morning. He cheerfully greeted the office girls and before undertaking the challenge of the stairway, Jane informed him that I wished to see him. His rap on the door was more like a feeble scratch. Sounds from below permeate well through the air vents and I knew exactly who it was.

"Come in, Russell," I asked, while searching my desk for the letters requesting dealerships. "I trust everything is all right at home."

"Oh yes, everything's okay," he replied.

"Russ, here are a couple requests for handling our product. I need you to tell me if we're covered in the territories they desire."

Russ held up the letters and waved then saying, "These people are lift truck dealers and will demand a commission on any batteries sold in their territories. They'll need a lot of my personal attention."

His words kind of made me smile and I said, "Our New York team has a lift truck dealer for a customer and receives $500,000 annual sales. And, they manage three times that amount with sales of their own."

"New York is a totally different marketplace compared to where these guys are," he replied, still waving the letters.

"You get the numbers on what the present representation is delivering from Warren and we can meet again to study them. If we decide to take new people on, we'll travel and have a look at their operation. I can tell a lot by just walking in their front door," I stated.

"I believe Mr. Brantley has gone to the bank."

"Well, ask Jane to total the numbers for us. She's pretty efficient and probably has them at her fingertips," I suggested. "Let's meet tomorrow at 10 o'clock."

For the past few weeks Russell hasn't been his jovial self. I know he's under pressure from the IRS for back taxes and that would trouble the best of us. Warren Brantley has suggested he negotiate a settlement and make payments on his debt. For the life of me I can't understand not pursuing such a solution. Russell complains they would demand so much that there wouldn't be enough left to maintain the family's lifestyle. I've never been one to worry about lifestyle. My first new automobile was purchased six month ago when the sale of the company was consummated. And that was a fuel efficient Ford Taurus. Russell always drove a Lincoln. When we travel to see the prospective dealers, I plan to have a serious heart to heart with him. At times, such subjects are best discussed away from the office. It makes it more personal.

"Mr. Baker, you have a call on line one," Jane announced, interrupting my concern over fiduciary duties.

"Hello, Steve Baker," I answered.

"Well, hello Steve Baker. How are you?" It was Irene Jones.

"I'm still recovering from the convention. How about you?"

"I can't say much now. Too many people around." There was a period of silence and I thought we were disconnected, but she continued, "I want to meet you somewhere. We need to talk."

"You kind of caught me off guard. I need a little time to figure out where we can meet," I honestly said.

"Don't trouble that handsome head of yours, I've already figured that out. Let's make it Friday night at the Ramada Inn in Danville. I'll get the room."

My heart was pounding like a jackhammer. I felt as though everybody in the building was listening to us. I agreed without further thought.

"Danville it is. I may be a little late due to some Friday meetings, but don't worry, I'll be there eventually. Let me give you a better phone number. It is directly to me without going through the switchboard. Best of all, no one can listen in."

"Do you miss me?" she asked.

"Of course. How about you?"

"I'm horny for you," she answered, and hung up.

Fully aware of sailing into uncharted waters, I chose to let the prevailing wind propel me through the shoals to an unknown destination. Irene was much more than a gentle wind. She was a full force storm. My sense of fundamental decency had been pushed to the back burner. A person's morality can be founded on a hard rock or soft sand. Up 'til now, I prided myself being anchored to stone, however, where Irene is concerned, I couldn't care less and ignored everything for the promise of an exciting moment in time.

In spite of it all, I dearly love my wife, Elaine. A professional psychiatrist would suggest my present moral indolence be connected to childhood. He might suggest group therapy. In my mind, sitting around a collection of people telling about sexual experiences only stimulates their problems—a porn flick can do the same thing.

After twenty-three years of marriage, depending on each other to travel through life's hedge of prickly thorns, an emotional bond hardens like cement. The thrill and passion of newness dwindles with the advent of children and daily grind of making a living. Long walks are a thing of the past. Initial love is broken into many pieces. Over time, fault finding works its way to the surface and criticism and blame overcome beauty, gracefulness, wit, and knowledge. The bed is mostly shared back to back. Life becomes routine. Nevertheless, the original bond, though often forgotten, lasts a lifetime.

When the choice apple hangs high up in the tree, out of reach, you either forget about it, settle for something less, or get a ladder. With Irene, the decision is already made. She is as cool as a cucumber on an October morning and dangles easily within reach, while standing. It's been said that with the first chilly fall day, life begins anew. For me, it portends to be intriguing, breathtaking, and stimulatingly dangerous.

I descended my steps and exchanged short glances with the office girls. My blameworthiness felt as though they heard every word.

"I'm going to the lunchroom for a soda. Can I get something for you guys?" Six sets of eyes flashed at each other and finally Paula Stevens spoke up, "I think a Coca Cola would go good right now." Jane and Beverly nodded their approval.

"Three cokes it is," I replied, opening the office door to the sounds of machinery in operation and the beeping of a lift truck, with a loaded skid, heading to a semi-trailer at the shipping dock.

The soft drink vending machines are set to only require 25 cents. The difference is made up out of my general fund. Warren Brantley was concerned the employees would come with a bag full of quarters and empty them by the case load. Granted, a few cans do make their way home every now and then, but Warren's fears never materialized.

Jane saw me coming as I juggled four cans of coke and opened the door for me. I took the chair by their desks and spent a few minutes at small talk. Ringing phone lines and a changing shift decided our break time was over. Being Thursday, Bailey Marshall had distributed paychecks during last break. Making Thursday payday is for the benefit of the third shift. It saves them a trip to the factory to pick up their checks. Managers' remuneration is placed in an envelope for privacy reasons; even so, I'm certain they know each other's salary.

By the time Friday rolled around, I had convinced myself that most men who claim a moral life have just the opposite buried somewhere beneath that fake façade. They thrill themselves by snatching peeks at young legs, rounded rears, and low cut necklines. Underneath it all, they're not much different than I am.

Addressing only perfunctory duties, my mind was able to conjure the essence of Irene and the last time we saw each other. Once her image came into tangible focus it burst like a toy balloon in contact with a lighted cigarette. This time the shouts from the office next door did the trick. There was a hotly contested argument going on. The minute I opened the door, you could hear a pin drop.

"Tone it down fellas. It's impossible to get any sleep with all the noise," I joshed. "What's all the fuss about?"

The argument was between Warren Brantley, Russell Webster, and Asher Horwitz, our insurance carrier. Asher had come to discuss next year's group health insurance rates and ended up quarreling over Israel and arms for Iran. Asher may not be over five-foot-three inches tall, but rises to become a bantam rooster if anything disparaging is said about Israel. The matter at hand dealt with rumors that Ronald Reagan's administration was selling arms to Iran using Israel as an intermediary.

Congress determined Iran to be a supporter of terrorism and forbid direct sales by the United States. On the surface, the transaction seems straightforward and illegal, but in actuality it is much more complicated. Events rarely arise in a vacuum. We need to go back in history for a more comprehensive understanding of world affairs and conditions at the time.

It was in 1979 when the Sandinista National Liberation Forces overthrew the dictatorial regime of Anastasio Somoza Debayle in Nicaragua—a regime which was acknowledged by the United States. In fact, U.S. assistance of military and financial support had continued since 1936.

Even though the Sandinistas did not attempt to create a communist government, they had close ties with Cuba and the Soviet Union. And, in keeping with the doctrine to oppose global influence of the Soviet Union, President Reagan chose to support the Nicaraguan Contras, a rebel group in opposition to the Sandinistas. Accordingly, the rebels received financial and military aid from the United States government.

During the war against the Sandinistas, it was reported the Contras carried out many human rights violations. Evidence suggested these were systematically committed as elements of their warfare strategy. The Reagan Administration tried to downplay these violations by insisting the Sandinistas carried out much more. Nevertheless, the U.S. legislature issued Amendments aimed at limiting assistance to the Contras. In December 1982, Congress attached an Amendment to the Defense Appropriations Act outlawing assistance to the Contras for the purpose of overthrowing the Nicaraguan government, while allowing aid for other purposes. The Reagan Administration circumvented the Amendment, without consent of Congress, in order to continue to supply arms to the Contras.

Elsewhere in the world, as reaction to the assassination attempt on Israel's ambassador to the United Kingdom, Israeli Defense Forces invaded southern Lebanon. Prime Minister Menachen Begin blamed the PLO for the incident and used it as pretext for the June 6, 1982 invasion. The incursion had several goals, by expelling the PLO, removing Syrian influence over Lebanon, and installing a pro-Israeli government.

One of the unintended consequences of the invasion was the creation of Hezbollah. Conceived by Muslim clerics, it was formed to offer resistance to Israel's occupation. Iran funded the group, and, with the permission of Syria, sent in 1,500 Revolutionary Guards to train them.

Israeli forces occupied southern Lebanon and surrounded the PLO and their Syrian allies. Subjected to heavy bombardment, the PLO negotiated passage from Lebanon with the aid of the United States and protection of international peacekeepers.

The occupation of Lebanon grew untenable. World opinion, as well as a fragile Lebanese military partner, forced a peace agreement. On May 17, 1983, Israeli forces were withdrawn with the establishment of a "security zone" in south Lebanon along the border. It was designed to prevent the Palestine Liberation Organization and others from infiltrating the border areas.

Now, to complicate the international discombobulating even further, Iraq invaded Iran on September 22, 1980. Attacking without warning, Saddam Hussein made limited progress into Iran and was quickly repelled. By June 1982, Iran was on the offensive.

President Reagan decided that the United States could not afford to allow Iraq to lose the war to Iran. Accordingly, his administration removed Iraq from the list of countries supporting terrorism and sold weapons via Jordan and Israel. France also sold helicopters, fighter planes, and missiles.

The Soviet Union, angry over Iran's elimination of their Iranian national communist party, sent large shipments of weapons to Iraq. With the help of the super powers, Saddam Hussein's army was soon replenished and invigorated. Iran lacked the same financial capability to purchase arms and faced a prolonged war.

Associates of Hezbollah were still holding several American hostages in Lebanon. It was determined, by some in the Reagan Administration, that by selling arms to Iran, their release would be secured. It was planned that Israel would ship weapons to Iran, and, then the United States, in turn, resupply Israel and receive the Israeli payment. A portion of the proceeds would be diverted to fund the anti-Communist Contra rebels. Should these rumors later become fact, it signaled serious problems for the 'Great Communicator' and the Republican Party.

Asher's ears were glowing red and he stuttered when he gave me the reason for his visit. No doubt there is a reminder from Jane buried in the papers on my desk. I've got to do a better job maintaining a more orderly surface.

"I brought next year's pricing from Prudential and thought you might want to go over it for budgeting purposes. If you're unhappy with them, I represent several other companies you might want to consider," Asher stated, as I opened the door to my office. He took the chair across from the desk and sat his briefcase on the floor. Obviously, he wanted a little face time before discussing business. Asher and I attended the same high school. He was a year ahead of me however his sister Shirley was in my class. Unlike her brother, Shirley was a lot more aggressive and active in school affairs. I guess Asher mainly concentrated on good grades and planned for a successful business career after he graduated. He attended the University of Chicago and shortly, thereafter, had his own insurance agency. The morning breakfast club at Cliff's claimed Asher had an agency in Colorado along with a winter home. The consensus of the daybreak diners is that Asher Horwitz is wealthy.

"I must confess, Warren Brantley has a way of getting under my skin. He actually said Israel is a partner with Iran," Asher complained. "If Iran had more power, they would annihilate the Jews."

"You mustn't let him get under your skin. I don't think Warren has felt well lately," I consoled. "By the way, Ash, are you Jewish?"

With that Asher heartily laughed and said, "No, I'm a Nuwaubian[1]." We both laughed until we needed to wipe our eyes. When composure finally took place, Ash said, "You're probably

---

1   Nuwaubianism originated as a Black Muslim group in New York in the 1970s and has gone through many changes since. They still exist and hold many controversial and weird beliefs.

right about Warren being under the weather. His eyes were awfully bloodshot."

There was a period of silence while I digested Ash's comment. I too had noticed Warren's eyes and made a mental note to have him see the company's doctor.

"With regards to my group insurance, which do you recommend?"

"I recommend staying with your present carrier. They seem to handle claims faster and I have more influence with them," said Asher, honestly. "Besides, their price increase is small, considering present inflation rates."

"So be it, my friend. Make sure you talk with Jane before you leave and I'll inform Warren. How's the family?" I asked, while he put on his coat.

"They're all doing fine. My son David plans to go in with me once he graduates from college."

"That's just like you Nuwaubians, keeping it all in the family."

"Yes, that way I don't have to pay him."

In the morning, while still at home, I had packed an overnight bag under the pretense of attending an open house conducted by our lift truck dealer in Danville. The supposed event takes place on Saturday and I planned to be back on Sunday in time to watch the Chicago Bears on television. Such events were commonplace in our business and my presence is always requested.

Our Friday meetings were concluded in a timely fashion. Seems as though everybody wanted an early start on the weekend. For my part, the inner excitement was masked by sangfroid, making sure no one was the wiser.

By six o'clock it was turning dark outside, telling me there was an hour and a half of night driving ahead. The shortest distance between two points is a straight line. Unfortunately, from the factory parking lot, the only line to Danville is a series of irregular turns before reaching Route 1 and the Ramada Inn. It requires retracing the morning steps to get to the factory, then crossing the bridge over the Kirksville River and on to Route 1. From that point, you pass several small towns before the illuminated area above Danville comes into view. Playing a Merle Haggard tape soothes my anxiety and assists in conceiving mental images of Irene. Various machinations of a libidinous tryst are mentally conjured up. Most of which will never happen. Nevertheless, it sure beats the next best thing, and keeps the mile markers clipping by.

I pulled into the Ramada parking lot about 7:45 p.m. and found a spot close to the front door. Apparently, Friday night isn't all that popular in this part of town, even though Interstate 74 runs right past the place. Entering the hotel, I was hit by the strong smell of ammonia and cleaners. The tiled floor had just been mopped and warning stands set about to caution guests of slippery footing.

Presumably, the owner of the mop and buffer is the fellow leaning against the front counter, giving his best effort to strike up a conversation with the young girl behind the front desk. He looked to be about 35 years old and was heavily tattooed. No doubt, underneath his multi-colored demeanor were layers of rejection by the women of his fancy.

Ironically, though she would never comply with his wishes, for some unexplainable reason no effort was given to discourage him. Not exactly a raving beauty, the girl still is attractive enough to not settle for a lifetime straddling a motorcycle. She was the kind of young woman who could make the right fellow want to go to work and carry a dinner-pail.

"Would you please ring Irene Jones' room and tell her a guest is waiting?"

After calling, the desk clerk handed me the phone saying, "She wants to speak to you."

"Hello," I said, after taking the handset.

"I'm in room 305. Take the elevator and come up," she replied.

After pushing the elevator button, I looked back to see the multicolored Romeo giving it another try.

Room 305 had a Do Not Disturb tag hanging from the door handle. A gentle tap prompted an immediate opening and the beautiful image of Irene made my heartbeat race. She quickly closed the door behind me and secured the locks.

"In case you were too tired to eat out, I stopped on my way over and picked up something, it's been a long day."

"I am kind of bushed. What time did you get here?"

"I left work early. Went home, packed a bag, drove to Wendy's, and got here around six o'clock."

"That reminds me. My travel bag is still in the car. I need to go down and retrieve it."

"The spare key is by the television. While you're fetching your suitcase, I'll take a bath," Irene chimed.

Stepping out of the elevator, I noticed the front desk had a changing of the guard. A man had replaced the young woman and the sound of the floor buffer signaled that the kaleidoscopic suitor had pulled a Casey and struck out.

Outside, the weather had turned colder and a misty rain began to fall. Comforted in the knowledge my fleece-lined jacket lay in the trunk, I grabbed the travel bag, locked the car, and quick stepped to the lobby. On the elevator ride up to the third floor, people were complaining about a freak winter storm ruining their weekend. The possibility of being cloistered with Irene for two days was far from spoiling my plans.

"It's turning nasty outside," I informed, as my travel bag found the suitcase table and rested beside the food sack from Wendy's. The aroma of fast food has a distinctive smell, which at the moment, has taken over the room.

"Well honey, that shouldn't bother us one little bit," Irene said, as she emerged from her bath, clad in the hotel terrycloth robe. At times, her Indiana dialect linguistically resembles that of the Deep South. That and knowing of what lies within the white robe's absorbing material, made me forget about food. The next hour was spent under the sheets.

The only light in the room came from the bathroom door, which was left ajar for that very purpose. As we lay on our backs reflecting on the intensity of what took place, Irene was the first to speak.

"I've moved out and have my own apartment," she stated.

"When did all this happen?"

"Earlier this week."

"You said there were no strings attached."

"That was before I fell in love with you. Don't worry dear. I don't want to put pressure on you."

I didn't actually feel pressure, but sensed the jaws of the vice moving a little.

"I've drawn a map, so you can find my new place."

"I'll sure need it. Outside of the Interstate highway, I'm lost in a big city."

"I know dear," she comforted. "Do you want to know another reason I moved out of the house? As things stand, if I got pregnant, I wouldn't know whose it was. Intimacy with him has been meaningless ever since we met."

"Don't you practice some sort of birth control?"

"No, should I?"

"Yes. Life's too complicated as it is. Bringing another baby into the world would make it worse."

"You wouldn't want my child?"

"That's not it, darling. I would love to give you a child, but not at this time. When things are more settled, we can start buying pink baby clothes."

"Pink baby clothes, you talk as if it will be a girl," she commented.

"You already have two boys."

"I'll get an IUD next week," she promised. "What about the rest of the weekend?"

"We'll just have to chance it," I answered, and rolled over to embrace her.

A half-hour later we were back on our backs.

By that time, the meals from Wendy's were at room temperature. Even so, it all tasted good.

With the wind slamming rain against the window and an occasional thunder clap we fell into the tender sleep of satisfaction. Waking once during the night I found Irene with her back to me and curled in a fetal position. I turned to her and cuddled, realizing what a perfect fit we made.

The next morning Irene immodestly paraded around the room unclothed. Even though I appreciated her unchaste effort, it wasn't until much later before I could get aroused. The rain continued for most of the day and the Wendy's sack contained nothing but wrappers. Irene stood in front of the mirror and said, "I look a little bloated.

Maybe I'm already pregnant," she mused, all the time flashing her gleaming white grin.

"That's not funny," I said, seriously.

"If I was, it would be all your fault."

"You've paraded around without clothes on so long, you have probably forgotten what it's like to wear them. Being clad will be a shock to your system."

"I'll just have to tough it out until I see you again. Then I can become au natural," she said, while moving to my chair and sitting on my lap.

I got aroused.

An hour later, both our stomachs were growling. In our present condition, going downtown to a restaurant seemed out of the question. The Ramada marquee advertised a live dance band on Saturdays and the dining room opened until midnight. If we were going to quiet the wolf in our bellies, the hotel's kitchen must do the job. That being said, we still had to get dressed. Irene suggested we shower together in order to save time. Under normal circumstances, that would result in another delay. However, not tonight. After all day in bed, I was unable to hold up my end of the bargain. A nice quiet meal will stem the hunger and a couple hours away from our room may correct the other problem.

We made it to the dining room by seven p.m. and, surprisingly, the bad weather hadn't frightened away the Saturday night dancers. The dining room also had a decent crowd and required a short wait at the reception stand before being directed to our table. We ordered a carafe of red wine and toasted the victory of making it to dinner under our own power. Considering the other activity, it was a major accomplishment.

Our waitress recommended prime rib and we wholeheartedly accepted her suggestion. After another carafe of wine, we made it to the dance floor for a couple of slow numbers. I felt as though every eye in the room was fixed on us and, unfortunately, recognized several people—it's a small world.

Safely back in our room, Irene had that look again.

"Darling, I'm too tired to respond," I confessed.

"That's okay, you just lay there and I'll take care of the rest." And she did.

We were both driving back by noon on Sunday. The map to Irene's new apartment was stashed safely in my wallet. There was hardly any traffic on the road and flashback episodes of Irene were recalled like a flickering movie. Despite spending the weekend in a living dream, I was anxious to return to Elaine and the protection of our home. As a result, trepidation floated on the surface of my emotions until I could sit safely in my recliner and watch the football game on television. That did not happen.

The minute I pushed the garage door opener, I saw Elaine standing inside.

"Have you heard about Warren Brantley?"

"No. What about him?"

"He was murdered last night. It's on television and headlines in the morning paper," Elaine reported. "Several people have called for you. I've got their numbers written down."

"Did I hear from Russell Webster?"

"Yes."

"I'll call him first."

For a better part of an hour I had the telephone handset against my ear. Little was learned beyond what was on TV and in the paper. Russell was the only one who asked regarding my whereabouts. I told him about Danville and the fictitious open house. He seemed upset not being invited. I made light of it, saying, the rain basically washed it out. The next open house will be all his.

The Chicago Bears won their game; however, I had to settle for the evening news replays. The remains of the day were spent in my home office making notes of things to do on Monday. Considering Warren's role with the company I needed to hire an auditor to go over the books. It would be a good idea to retain the accountant for a month, while seeking a replacement. Of course, the parent company must be notified.

At bedtime, my thoughts were consumed with concern over the possibility of missing something important. Irene, and the past two days, was temporarily forgotten.

On Monday, to avoid prying questions from the breakfast bunch, I drove directly to work. The factory, as well as the entire staff was abuzz over Brantley's murder. Jane was instructed not to write any checks until the certified public accountant finished the audit. While waiting for his arrival, I made a cursory inspection of Warren Brantley's desk. There was nothing unusual to be found, however, his notepad had the impression of a name and phone number faintly etched in the top sheet. For an unexplained reason I automatically tore it off and stuffed it in my shirt pocket. It was business as usual until the auditor arrived.

In the apartment on Chicago's southwest side, the Chechen cousins, Dokka Zakayev and Zorva Yamadayev, wore long faces. They, too, caught the news of Warren Brantley's untimely demise. Subsequently, they were instructed to sit tight until Khalid Umarov arrived. Even though they had no direct contact with the murder victim, Khalid Umarov was the most feared commander in the Chechen clique. He was known to behead rivals and never hesitate to shoot those opposed to his orders. To say the tenants of the southwest residence were nervous would be an immense understatement.

The sight of a dark limousine entering the property raised their anxiety to the roof. Standing away from the window allowed just enough of a view to see three men exit the car and enter the warehouse. Footsteps on the staircase were muffled by the sound of the young Chechens' heartbeats. They never knock. If the door is locked, they kick it open. The Chechen cousins were aware of the tactic and made certain their door was unlocked. They stood at attention until Khalid Umarov spoke.

"You boys can relax. I've talked to Bashir and was assured of your innocence. Do you know what has taken place?" he asked, with cold gray eyes searching their expression.

"We saw it on the television news and figured Bashir had put an end to his usefulness," Dokka answered.

"I wish that were true," Umarov replied. "Someone else iced him before he made the delivery. He had, in his possession, a package costing us $250,000. We could have turned it into a few million on the street. The local police did not make the connection and performed a half-assed investigation of his apartment. They consider his death a routine homicide, and, for the moment, an undetermined motive. I want you boys to search his car and apartment properly. I understand he was an accountant. Find out where he worked. See if he had an office. Report back to Bashir Shishani in two weeks."

Dokka knew there was no need to respond. On his level within the group, acceptance of an assignment is automatic. He also knew they should not offer further hospitality. The two henchmen would have readily accepted a drink of vodka, but could only speak when asked by Khalid. Without a further word the trio turned and descended the steps.

Once the limousine left the property, Zorva loudly exhaled and said, "We need a drink." After pouring two glasses of Stolichnaya, he continued, "Bashir should have had me take care of the accountant."

Dokka distorted his expression with a grimace and replied, "Let's just drink and think. I must devise a plan."

The Windy City is the heroin hub for the Midwest. Drug cartels often use stash houses in quiet residential neighborhoods. They don't want to have a heightened sense of police awareness. Therefore, they avoid areas where there are a lot of shootings and gang violence. While Chicago gangs make up a large part of their customer base, the anathema of shootings and murders are bad for business.

Some of the drugs, stored in stash houses, will end up heading north to Milwaukee or east to Detroit or south to Indianapolis. The rest will stay in Chicago.

Authorities believe the biggest drug syndicate in the Americas is being run out of Mexico. The powers that be are hidden within a well-guarded fortress somewhere south of the Rio Grande.

Chicago is their transportation hub ideally located within a day's drive of 70% of the U.S. population. Nearly 100,000 gang members are utilized to funnel cartel shipments into the streets. The Chechen combine buys in large quantities and is given a protected area. Only Khalid Umarov has met the Mexican kingpin. And, now that his $250,000 package has disappeared, Umarov must make another purchase quickly. A break in the delivery chain could open the door to competition. Honor in this business comes at a heavy price.

Meanwhile, at the Kirksville Police headquarters, the Investigations Commander, Ronald Homberg, was conducting a special meeting. Under normal circumstances, such meetings are held bi-monthly; however, a homicide calls for a gathering of the troops. A few years ago, homicides were rare—usually the result of bar fights or domestic violence. All of which had eyewitnesses. Lately, shooting deaths have increased, and most without apparent cause. Accordingly, a killing without obvious motives is very difficult to solve.

There are six investigators in the city's detective bureau, two of which were assigned to investigate Warren Brantley's death.

Detectives Michael 'Mike' Monahan and James 'Bubba' Watson were given the task. Although the work is sometimes tedious, both men enjoyed the extra freedom it affords—that, and a more liberal expense account, plus, a newer car to drive.

Mike Monahan had investigated two previous homicides, while this is the first for Bubba Watson. As a result, Monahan acted as lead detective. For the disgruntled, some believed the fact their desks faced each other was the deciding reason for assignment. Monahan was a ten-year veteran. Bubba Watson had been in the bureau less than a year. It's not unusual for the green-eyed monster to raise its head in the detective bureau. Some assignments are definitely better than others. In his own mind, Ron Homberg feels as though his assignments are equitable—an opinion not shared by many investigators.

Monahan has learned preparation is vital. Even though investigators are required to follow the manual, he likes to think outside the box. For the rest of the day, he and Bubba will brainstorm various scenarios, some of which nearly approach the inane. By day's end, they had compiled a 'to do list' well beyond the customary process.

CHAPTER SIX

WARREN BRANTLEY'S CAR HAD BEEN impounded by the police and now resides at the city's retention lot. A local garage, with towing service, has the contract for removal of abandoned vehicles as well as those impounded for drunk drivers and a variety of city ordinances. Clyde Martin, owner of the towing garage, is politically connected and reaps a sizable reward. All city vehicles fill their gas tanks at either of two stations, both of which he owns. The price of gasoline is a few cents more per gallon than charged by other stations. Owners of the impounded vehicles must pay an excessive price to retrieve their means of transportation. Clyde Martin is building an expensive new home in an exclusive neighborhood.

Detectives Monahan and Watson began their day eating breakfast at McDonalds. Usually they would buy it at the drive-thru and eat on the way to the police station. Today, they are officially on a case and sitting inside, at a table.

"After breakfast we will drive to the retention car lot and inspect Brantley's automobile. Excitement at the crime scene sometimes conceals useful clues. A thorough inspection may reveal something helpful," Mike stated, while washing down an Egg McMuffin with coffee. Bubba just nodded and continued concentrating on a sweet roll.

"You handle breakfast and I'll take care of lunch," Mike suggested. "Don't forget to get a receipt."

The impounded vehicle parking lot was conveniently located across from police headquarters. It's a rather unfriendly place protected by an opposing metal link fence with a chain and padlock, preventing unauthorized entry. Detective Watson bounced up the stations front steps and asked for someone to open the gate.

"Who the hell are you?" asked an officer sitting behind a desk.

"That's Monahan's partner on the Brantley murder," answered another.

"Where's Mike?" questioned the first.

"He's waiting outside by the gate," Bubba replied.

The floor squeaked from a sliding chair, as the first officer reluctantly stopped typing and led the young detective back down the front steps.

"You need to send your man with a note. We almost locked him up for truancy from grade school," said the first. "Why is he your partner on this case?"

"I don't make those decisions. I guess Homberg wants to give him some experience," Monahan replied. "Treat him nice. He's a graduate of the academy and might be your boss someday."

"Perish the thought," the officer said, as he unlocked the gate and swung it open. "Here's the key. It's the dark colored Buick at the end. Save me a trip and lock up when you're finished."

"Who is that officer?" Bubba asked.

"His name is Lee Rice. He comes from a family with a lengthy background in police work. His father, Fred, has his picture in the lobby."

"Those pictures are of officers killed in the line of duty," Bubba stated.

Mike was taciturn, and the only sound came from the crunch of leather on gravel as they walked to Brantley's automobile.

The dark blue Buick stood like a silent sentinel on the end of the first row. Monahan noticed the driver side window was rolled down. Obviously, left that way from the crime scene so as not to contaminate evidence. He made a mental note to roll it back up after their examination. The fact it was down gave a definite clue. The victim was probably talking to someone at the time he was shot. Odds are he knew the killer, although, it could have been a perfect stranger.

Nevertheless, we have to go with what fits the investigation—Brantley knew his assailant. Finding nothing hidden behind the hub coverings, the detectives searched the trunk with the same result.

"Not much here. Let's look inside. Pull the backseat out and check the ashtrays," Monahan instructed Bubba. "I'll check the front and the glove compartment."

"It just dawned on me, did our boys take fingerprints?" asked Bubba.

"Yeah, but the perpetrator would have to have a record for them to mean much. Dozens of people have touched this car. My guess is the killer didn't."

Bubba wrestled the backseat cushion off and found only bits of paper and gum wrappers. Mike Monahan had better luck. Two items were possible clues—a matchbook from the Vagabond Lounge and a trace of granular substance on the vehicle registration slip. If that turns out to be what he thinks it is, Warren Brantley had drugs in his car.

The first major snowstorm hit the area in early December. News of the Brantley murder had moved to the back page. The only question from Cliff's breakfast bunch was whether or not I had hired a new accountant. If not, they had several recommendations. Most of the names I knew and were out of my company's wage range. Besides, the certified public accountant indicated they had a young graduate from Business College, working as a temp, who would be a good fit for my company.

At the same time Cliff brought my breakfast, the front door opened and a blast of cold air got everybody's attention. Two snowplow drivers stood in the entryway stomping their boots and brushing away the snow from their coats. They took a table close to the door and Cliff was Johnny on the spot with the steaming coffee.

"How much snow have we got so far?" asked someone from our table.

I pulled off pieces of toast and dropped them on top the "easy over" eggs—a little trick allowing me to eat runny yokes with a fork.

"They say we got about five inches with a lot more to come. With the wind blowing like it is, the rural county roads are nearly closed," replied the older driver.

"Steve, you better stay in town until the roads get better," suggested Cliff.

"Hell, none of you guys are going to do anything today. You all might as well kick back and enjoy the camaraderie," said Bill Schneider, the Cadillac dealer's accountant and office manager.

"A couple hours are all I can take of present company. I'm already getting cabin fever," John Coffle, the veterinarian, stated.

That comment was like jabbing a Tasmanian devil with a stick. The entire table erupted with repartee and laughter. Deciding to brave the storm, we all paid our bills, leaving the money on the table, and donned coats and jackets.

The factory is located near a small community with schools. And, the county road commissioner lives there. If I can make it on the state highway, the other roads should be in better shape.

Driving west on Route 17 was directly facing the storm. Seeing several vehicles were off the road into the ditch, I continued behind a snowplow heading my way. It was slow going, however, a lot safer. Turning south on the county road, I encountered a few drifts; and since it was recently plowed, managed to reach the plant safe and sound. Our parking lot is east of the factory building and somewhat protected by its configuration. Bailey Marshall placed a 'Reserved for Plant Manager' sign by the front steps. Though I originally opposed it, today, am glad it was there.

It continued to snow until noon, after which, only tiny flurries. Just enough to keep us all inside for lunch. Jane had the speaker system tuned to the radio and playing Christmas music, making the atmosphere inside the factory walls seasonally festive.

I found Wayne Buckner, the CPA, at work in Warren Brantley's former office. He was engrossed in his work and jumped when I spoke.

"How are things coming along?"

"Not bad," he replied. "The account reconciliation checks out. The sum of entries equals the ending balance."

"Does that mean everything's okay?"

"Normally, yes, but, I'm going back a year looking for a consistent debit, possibly unrelated to your business. A clever accountant can systematically steal small amounts without anyone's knowledge. The total of which would surprise you."

"Have you found anything suspicious?"

"Too soon to tell. I'll know in a couple days."

"Wayne, you mentioned a certain temp working for your company. I'd be interested in interviewing him."

"It's a she. Her name is Callie Mellinger. She's a graduate of Kirksville Community College and majored in accounting," Wayne replied. "We think highly of her, but, unfortunately, unable to add a full time employee. I'd be willing to work with her for a week or two, if you decide to hire her."

"Have her drop by for an interview if you think she would fit in."

The girls downstairs heard every word spoken and were excited to have another woman in the office. She's very young and a lot depends on her interview.

Callie Mellinger called for an appointment the minute Wayne Buckner notified her of a possible full time job. On her resume, she omitted the fact of being a college cheerleader. Entering the workplace, Callie wanted to appear to be all business. She wore horn rimmed glasses instead of her contact lenses and walked into Steven Baker's office prim and proper. Fully aware of her inexperience and youth, she presented herself without the capriciousness of her age.

"You come highly recommended by your current employer," I commented. "Are you aware of the problem we have here?"

"Yes, your accountant was recently killed."

"Your present employer, Kirksville Public Accountants, is conducting an audit of our books and, thus far, everything appears to be okay. I will need to fill the position quickly. Wayne indicated he would stay two weeks to help train you about our routine practices."

"I'm confident it wouldn't take me long to handle the position," she said assuredly.

"Okay, do you know Jane O'Connor?"

"I believe so. Her office is directly below us."

"There are a few forms you'll need to fill out. Jane will set up an appointment with the company doctor. We manufacture lead acid batteries here and it's important to measure the amount of lead in the blood. Those working in the office must have it done once a year. Naturally, those exposed to lead dust are required to wear respirators and tested more frequently. Jane will explain the program. Do you have any questions?"

"Does this mean I'm hired?"

"Yes, each position has a salary range. You will start off at the lower end, but I will review it in six months. I've written the starting salary on this piece of paper. In as much as conversations are easily heard below, I try to keep salaries confidential. Jane is the only one who knows how much money we make."

Sliding the paper across the desk, Callie saw the numbers and couldn't restrain a gleaming grin.

"I would expect you to start Monday at eight a.m. and, it wouldn't hurt to be a little early. First shift in the factory begins at seven. Before you go downstairs you might walk over to the accountant's office and thank Wayne Buckner. His recommendation settled the deal."

With that, Steve Baker stood and welcomed Callie to the organization giving the customary handshake. In the office below, Jane O'Connor retrieved the employment papers to be ready when Callie Mellinger descended the steps.

CHAPTER SEVEN

WITH IRENE'S MAP IN MY shirt pocket, I drove south to spend the weekend in her new apartment. Christmas falls on the following Wednesday hence we will be able to exchange our gifts a couple days early and still share the holiday with our immediate families.

Interstate 65 was clean and clear after the snowstorm; and, while most of us were doing the speed limit, others had the hammer down and passed me like I was standing still. I goosed it up a little but still kept it less than 75 mph. A mile ahead the flashing lights on the side of the road signaled a state trooper had pulled over an unfortunate speeder. Tail lights of the cars in front of me were blinking red as drivers hit the brakes. I automatically reacted and tapped the brake pedal before putting it on cruise control at 65 mph and kept it there the rest of the way.

After two hours driving through December's darkness, the radiance of the illuminated skyline beckoned the city's welcome. Also, the closer I got to Indianapolis, the farther away societal morality and marital responsibility seemed.

The Lake View apartments were a newly constructed complex overlooking a spring-fed lake—a gated community made up of one to three bedroom units. By the age of some of the cars parked at the front doors, one could easily conclude the rent was modest. For a previous homeowner like Irene, this had to be a temporary fix. After a double check of the address on Irene's map, I got out of the car, grabbed my travel bag, locked the doors, and opened the front door to her apartment building. In doing so, I found myself standing in the foyer. The stairs to my left, obviously, led to the apartment above. The portal straight ahead had to be Irene's. Before I could knock, the door sprung open and Irene threw her arms around my neck and welcomed me with a passionate kiss.

"Aren't you concerned someone might see us?"

"Not with the goings on around here."

"Pretty wild, huh?"

"Come in. I'll tell you about it later," as she led me inside.

Once inside, the odor of fresh paint was strongly evident. Irene took me on a brief tour of the single bed apartment. In the kitchenette, lace curtains brightened the room, giving it a woman's touch; however, it was the sliding doors leading to the patio that mostly drew Irene's favor. The outside light revealed the patio's red brick flooring, a short yard, and the perfect view of the lake. Designed to catch rays of the morning sun, it was an excellent spot for safe tanning—not so much today with the outside temperature barely above freezing.

With the cook's tour completed, we sat at the kitchen table with a steaming cup of coffee warming our hands. Irene had her hair pulled back and wore a tight fitting pair of designer jeans. It was an image of her I witnessed for the first time. I liked it. I liked it very much.

The conversation between two lovers, for the first time in a strange setting, is always clumsy. Until love's physical initiation takes place, the subjects for discussion reside just beyond the prevailing tension. After which, lucidity has no bounds.

An hour later, we lay in bed, breathless and staring at the newly painted ceiling. No one spoke. It took a few minutes to come back to the reality of earth. Then Irene interrupted the golden silence with laughter.

"What's so funny?"

"The thing I've been waiting to tell you," she replied. "Directly above us is the upstairs apartment's bedroom. The tenants are two young girls, most likely office workers. Every weekend their boyfriends come over. It's never the same two guys. Well, their bedsprings squeak like hell and, coupled with loud moaning, it's nearly impossible to get a good night's sleep. I was planning on you getting a ringside seat, but, for some reason, they're quiet tonight. Maybe, better luck tomorrow."

"Darling, you're not exactly *Marcel Marceau* yourself," I stated.

"I know I can get loud. Don't you like it?"

"Irene, I love it."

The lovemaking image of Irene with her husband Ron became fixed in my mind. She was asleep for an hour before I finally dozed off.

CHAPTER EIGHT

A SUDDEN HEAVY SNOWSTORM PROVIDED GOOD cover for Zorva Yamadayev who had been observing Warren Brantley's apartment for most of the day. Both front and back doors still had yellow police tape stretched across and there were no fresh footprints in the snow. Zorva wasn't concerned about his own, because, at the rate snow was falling, they would be quickly covered over.

Ever since his divorce, Warren had lived in a two-family house. An elderly couple lived in the unit next door but rarely left the duplex. Tonight, with the present weather conditions, they would definitely hunker down. Zorva Yamadayev wasn't concerned about the older couple. They, obviously, were hard of hearing and played their television way too loud. Zorva could beat a bass drum and it wouldn't be heard. Standing in the rear of the house, he waited until a snowplow came by then dashed to the back door and was in before the plow's noise dissipated. Clearly this wasn't the Chechen's first breaking and entering. Calm as an overfed house cat, he stood in the kitchen gathering his thoughts—"*if Brantley still had the package, where would he hide it?*"

Wearing night vision goggles and dressed in Ninja black, Yamadayev moved first to the bedroom. Finding nothing under the bed, he quickly popped open his six-inch stiletto and opened the mattress—nothing there either. All wall hangings were raised looking for a hidden safe before pulling the drawers of Brantley's bureau—same result. At that point, Zorva withdrew his cell phone from a side pocket and dialed his cousin, Dokka Zakayev.

"Dokka, I'm inside okay and there's nothing in the bedroom. I'm about to remove the vent covers and look inside the shafts. I hope you're not too cold sitting in a warm car," he said sarcastically.

"Very funny. You just remember what Khalid Umarov said and keep looking. It will be best for all of us if you find the package," Dokka seriously responded. "This snow makes me think of the winters in the Caucasus Mountains. Do you ever get homesick?"

"Ha, but if I go back I might get hanged. I think I will stay here," Zorva replied.

A tool in the burly Chechen's black bag quickly allowed him to remove the screws in every air vent. Nothing was concealed. He inspected the floor for a loose tile or board and finally called his cousin again.

"There's no package here. I will be walking in the road."

Dokka's headlights revealed a dark figure on foot in the swirling snow. A brief stop and Zorva got in.

"We must execute the final plan. I will contact Bashir to keep him informed and request a different car," Dokka stated as they found the Interstate highway and sped north.

Lead detective Monahan and his rookie sidekick "Bubba" Watson were at their desks before 7 a.m. They wanted to read their messages before Chief Homberg arrived and started grilling them about progress on the murder case. Each had paper cups of steaming coffee leaving a circular sweat mark beneath their resting- place.

"Oh shit," Monahan blurted. "Give me a couple paper napkins from our sack. We don't want to leave evidence of our being here this early or Homberg and the rest of the gang will get suspicious and call for a meeting."

"Bubba" obliged and wiped away his own steam circle. Holding his cup higher he said, "They still are using Christmas cups even though the holiday has been over for more than a week."

"Saving nickels, saving dimes," replied Monahan, as he pulled the envelope from the medical examiner. "This is what we've been waiting for."

Detective Watson extended his letter opener but too late. Monahan tore the end off the envelope and blew into it, expanding the mailer enough to retrieve its contents. After reading the examiner's summary, he spun the analysis report for Watson to read and declared, "Just as we thought. Brantley had cocaine in his glove compartment and a lot more in his system."

"Do you believe there is a drug connection?" asked Watson.

"That's what we need to find out," answered Monahan.

The factory was back at full operation on Monday, January 6. Jane O'Connor and the other office girls were taking down Christmas decorations. They wanted to get started before Steve Baker arrived—a rarity when it came to being first in the office.

Steve Baker started the week off by stopping at Cliff's restaurant to kibitz with the breakfast bunch. With the weather improving, the main topic of the conversation returned to the Chicago Bears and the upcoming Super Bowl. After Miami spoiled the undefeated season all were pulling for a New England Patriot victory over the Dolphins in the AFC championship game on Sunday. The early morning Ad Hoc group still hasn't fully recovered from the surprising defeat at the hands of the boys from south Florida. Baker was tempted to stay longer but, since it was the first day back from the holiday break, he felt obligated to get to work early.

"It's always kind of sad when the Christmas decorations are taken down," Jane lamented. Paula Stevens and Beverly White gave the predictable agreement and continued boxing ornaments. After a few moments of thoughtful silence, Beverly stated, "There are a lot of people glad to see it over with. We women often suffer from the Christmas blues and sometimes they hang around until the tree is in the alley."

"I know what you mean," confirmed Paula. "When I see others all excited and happy, I get depressed for not experiencing the same emotion. Ever since my divorce, the holidays let me know how lonely I really am."

"I don't mean to make little about the way you feel but girl, you don't corner the market on loneliness," replied Beverly. "Nearly half the people in America are single and half of them live alone. Ever since my father died, my mother lives by herself and suffers terrible grief during Christmas time. She seems to handle it pretty well, until the decorations go up. Then it brings back memories of happier times with dad."

Adding to the discussion, Jane placed a box of ornaments on her desk and said, "Without a doubt we women get more depressed than men. We do all the planning, shopping, and cooking. We carry the greatest burden for family gatherings, trying to please every relative. And to top it off, do all these things without enough money to go around. We pinch pennies and stretch a dollar until it squeals. It's no wonder women get depressed."

"Speaking of stretching a dollar, look who just came in," Beverly announced, as the trio peered through the office glass windows.

"Don't say that about Mr. Baker. I can remember when he did without just to meet payroll," defended Jane.

"Maybe so, but he's doing pretty well now," returned Beverly.

"We all are doing pretty good now."

"I guess you're right," Beverly conceded.

When the office door opened, they chimed in chorus, "Good morning Mr. Baker."

"Good morning ladies, I trust you all had a good holiday. Jane, would you please join me in my office? There's an item I need your opinion on," while ascending the steps.

"Looks like you're in for it now," Paula mockingly commented. Beverly joined in by frinning a serious face.

"Innocent until proven guilty," Jane replied, and, at the same time, retrieving her note pad.

She waited a few minutes to give her boss enough time to remove his winter topcoat and occupy the leather chair behind his desk. When she was satisfied he was settled, she took the steps leading to the second floor.

"Come in Jane," I invited, sensing she was at the door. She has such a light step it's near impossible to hear her tread. One has to either perceive her presence or listen for her quiet tap.

"You won't need your notebook this time. I just wanted to discuss something with you. First, did you and your family have a happy holiday?"

"It was the best Christmas we've ever had, in spite of Pat having to work Christmas day," she replied.

"Obviously, his working is the result of seniority. How long has he been with the force?"

"Just under two years. The State troopers in our district are mostly veterans," Jane acknowledged.

"That, my dear, will surely be corrected with time."

"We understand and make the best of it. Speaking of the best of it, I want to thank you for the surprise bonus."

"As you know, we had a pretty good year and you were a valuable contributor. Let me put it differently—you've earned it. I've asked you up here this morning to get your opinion. How is Callie working out?"

"Oh Mr. Baker, she fits the job perfectly. She is sweet, smart, and self-sufficient," answered Jane. "I'm sure the other girls feel the same way."

"Well, Callie hasn't been with us long enough to qualify for holiday pay. How do you feel about making her an exception?"

"I'm all for it. She didn't make much working for KPA (Kirksville Public Accounting) and holiday pay would please her very much. She isn't expecting any," Jane stated.

"Then, I'd like you to quietly take care of it," I instructed, rising from my chair. "That's all I have at the moment."

Later that morning, a plain wrapped automobile pulled into a visitor parking spot. Detectives, Monahan and Watson got out and deeply inhaled the cold rural air before shutting their car doors. Steps to the entrance were located next to one of two shipping doors. A semi-trailer was backed against the first dock and being loaded with a factory lift-truck. Once inside the building, the detectives stood for a minute observing the shipping process. Impressed by the size and weight of the pallets, their eyes were drawn to the loading routine. Several skids of shrink-wrapped batteries were lined in rows and marked for loading.

"Those pallets look pretty heavy," Bubba Watson remarked to the shipping foreman.

"Yeah, the ones we're loading now nearly weigh a ton each," the foreman stated. "They need to be that heavy to act as counter balance when the lift trucks pick up hefty loads. It keeps them from nosing over."

Bubba was totally enthralled and could have watched much longer but Michael Monahan reminded him of the reason for being there and led the way to the office door. Reluctantly, like a small boy being taken away from his friends, Bubba kept looking back at the activity on the factory floor.

Jane O'Connor rose from her desk and greeted the visitors. She immediately recognized Michael Monahan as a fellow parishioner of St. Teresa Church and invited them in. After bidding them welcome, she asked, "What is the nature of your visit this morning?"

"We are investigating the murder of Warren Brantley. There are a few questions that need to be answered about his employment with your company." Turning to Bubba Watson, he introduced, "This is Detective James Watson. He is my partner in the investigation."

"I'm happy to make your acquaintance. Mike and I attend the same church. We've known each other for years. Mr. Baker is upstairs in his office. I'll let him know you gentlemen are here."

Jane returned to her desk and pressed the intercom button saying, "Mr. Baker, there are two gentlemen from the police department here to speak about Mr. Brantley."

"Send them right up," came the reply.

When the visitors reached the top landing, I met them outside my office door.

"Come in gentlemen. You can either hang your coats behind the door or place them on the sofa," I instructed and motioned to the small couch against the wall. After offering them chairs, I asked, "Now what can I do for you?"

"We're investigating the murder of one of your employees, Warren Brantley," Monahan said. "Detective Watson and I wish to question those having close contact with the deceased."

"Warren was our controller or accountant. His position rather dictates the manner in which he socializes with his coworkers. Outside of my secretary, Jane O'Connor, and me, the only other person he would have contact with is Russell Webster, our marketing manager. Russell's office is next to Warren's and they would pass each other several times during the day, whenever Russell is in town and not on the road. Miss Callie Mellinger, our new controller, occupies Warren's old office. She was hired shortly after our books were audited by KPA. The auditors found no discrepancies or unusual unauthorized activity."

"With your permission we'll start with Mr. Webster; then, perhaps, just take a look at his old office," Monahan said, as he checked his watch. "This shouldn't take too long and, before we leave, we can ask you a few questions and be out of your hair before lunch."

"Take your time gentlemen. This is the first day back from the holiday break. I plan to take lunch here in the factory."

At that moment, I recalled removing that tiny sheet of paper from Brantley's note pad. It was done impulsively and at the spur of the moment. Having the books audited was at the top of my concerns. My unconscious act was probably intended to tidy up the desktop for the auditors. It's likely still in my other suit coat and no doubt, insignificant—unworthy of mentioning.

The interviews took less than an hour. Monahan questioned Russell Webster and spent the remainder chatting with Jane O'Connor. Watson found it necessary to talk with Callie Mellinger. Though she was only recently employed, he managed to write down her address and phone number.

Finally, the pair knocked to regain entrance in my office.

"I believe we've concluded questioning for the present time," detective Monahan said. "Oh, yes, Mr. Webster told us you were out of town the night of the murder. Might I ask the reason you were away?"

"I was in Danville visiting Hyster Corporate headquarters. Hyster is a major lift truck manufacturer. This year's national contract is open for bidding," I replied.

"Then there should be no problem confirming who you were with and where you stayed," added Bubba Watson, in a suspicious tone.

"Yes, I can certainly prove I was there," I hesitantly said. Gentlemen, let's move this interview down the hall to our conference room. Every word said in my office travels downstairs. I need to give a more exact explanation about the Hyster visit."

On the way to the meeting room, I noticed Russell Webster had left for lunch and Callie had gone either downstairs to be with the other girls or was in the lunchroom. We took chairs around the conference table and I continued, "I was in Danville that night, but, not with people from Hyster. I was with someone whose companionship would be very embarrassing should it become common knowledge."

"You were with another woman," Monahan stated.

"Yes, she was registered at the Ramada Inn. On the night in question we were dining in the hotel's main room with a hundred other people. Two managers from Hyster corporate were having dinner with their families at the time and acknowledged my presence."

"When did you return to Kirksville?" asked detective Watson.

"Sunday morning. I found out from my wife that Warren Brantley had been killed. I hope you will use discretion when verifying my statement. Making my whereabouts public serves no purpose."

"Under what name were you registered?" asked Monahan.

"Jones, Irene Jones. She arrived before I did."

When Kirksville's finest left the building, I felt as though a great weight was off my shoulders. Some time ago I had learned, at the morning breakfast gathering, that detective Michael Monahan had a girlfriend—an affair that's gone on for a very long time. He often manages to spend time with her—for a weekend, a day, or an hour. Public knowledge of my liaison will not be revealed by him. That much I'm sure of. Throughout the remainder of the day I was hagridden by the slip of paper torn from Warren Brantley's note pad, and the name engraved into its surface. Could that have anything to do with his murder? Tonight, I plan to retrieve it and try to make heads or tails of the name on the original inscription.

The attitude of employees returning from the holiday break was a mixed bag. Being paid for the workdays missed could only serve to help improve their demeanor. For those working during the holiday and being paid double time was cheerful, earning enough to pay for a better Christmas. The manufacturing of lead-acid batteries does not permit a complete factory shut down. Individual cells, the component of a battery, must be on continuous electrical charge in order to form out or chemically develop internal plates—a process requiring close observation and maintenance.

Things went smoothly, considering the first day back, and the second shift was taking their first rest break when my phone line lit up. Apparently, Jane neglected to put the phones on speaker before she went home.

"Hello, Steve Baker," I answered, feeling as though I knew who was on the other end.

"How was your first day back?" the caller asked. "Did you miss me?"

"Of course, you're always on my mind," I replied.

"They want me to travel the rest of the week and call on some of the accounts. I was wondering if you could be in Louisville on Friday. I would arrange my calls so as to finish up there. We could have the weekend together," Irene suggested.

"I can work something out. Where would you be staying?"

"At the Ramada Inn, north of town, on Zorn Avenue. Just take 465 to 71 and get off at the second exit. I'll finish up early on Friday and check in about 3 or 4 o'clock. Darling, that's a long drive for you. It will take you five hours from Kirksville. You'll need to leave early so you won't have to drive at night."

"I'll work it out."

"I've got some news for you. I'm buying Ronald's half of the house and will have my home back. He's been out of work for a few weeks and hard up for money. We won't need to keep meeting in motels. I'll tell you all about it Friday," she stated, blowing a kiss in the receiver before hanging up.

There are times, when Irene and I aren't together, I use the left side of my brain. After replacing the receiver I kind of regretted agreeing to drive to Louisville for the weekend. But then, the right side takes over and I envision the enchanting temptress. Anticipation of being with her sends a thrill throughout my body, making the 5-hour trip imperative.

Friday will be here soon enough. Right now I must concentrate on retrieving the jotting from Warren Brantley's note pad.

Later that afternoon, I went directly home and slid the downstairs closet door open. Spreading coats and hangers, I found the suit coat in question and, feeling my side pocket, located the scrap of paper. Without my reading glasses, the image was a blur, along with being faint. Elaine was sitting at the dining table, playing solitaire, while waiting on the oven ringer to signal the roast was done.

"Can you make out the name on this piece of paper? My glasses are downstairs in the family room," I asked.

Turning it various ways and holding it to the chandelier light she said, "Best I can make out the last name is Lezotte. The first name is too pale for me to read. What's so important about it?"

"It's probably not that important. I found it on Warren Brantley's desk before the books were audited. For some reason it piqued my curiosity," slipping it into my wallet.

"If you think it's significant you should turn it over to the police," Elaine suggested. The oven ringer started to ding. "Supper will be ready in 30 minutes."

Sitting at the dining room table, to a meal the envy of most people in the world, I was immersed in the power of belonging. With the overhead chandelier providing its subtle illumination, the scene was reminiscent of a Norman Rockwell painting. Only the three youngest children joined the evening meal. The older two apparently had previous commitments. Elaine carried in the meat tray and sat it before me, then took her place at the end of the table. She made an unsuccessful attempt to blow a couple itinerant strands of hair away from her forehead, soon afterward resorting to her fingers on her left hand.

"Your father will carve the roast," she announced.

"Where are Rosemary and David?" I asked, while empty plates were being passed for me to deposit slices of the roast.

"Rosemary is at the junior college taking a night course and David is with his friends at the girls' basketball game," Elaine replied.

The atmosphere was comfortable and relaxed, evoking a warm and agreeable sensation. I began to have serious thoughts about my behavior and motives. *Elaine has been a loyal and loving wife. I marvel at the way she tends to the house and children. A man couldn't ask for more. Yet, for me, it's as though we have become the positive pole of the same magnet and my negative pole lies 130 miles south in the Circle City. What brought this all about? Was I just bored and drowsy and fell down Lewis Carroll's rabbit hole? Or was it a self-perceived death of a thousand cuts—little annoying and hurtful events that stacked one atop the other until the accumulative weight broke through the ceiling of logical thought. Tonight, at this very moment, there's no place else I would rather be.*

That night, when Elaine and Steven retired to their bed, Steven had never been more passionate, loving, and tender. For one evening they were no longer two petals on the same flower.

CHAPTER NINE

T HE NEXT COUPLE DAYS PASSED without incident; however, on Thursday morning, an official looking car arrived at the factory. On the side of each door were letters that read: *Cook County Building Inspector.* The word *Cook* was painted over. It didn't require a trained eye to determine the amateurish effort to disguise its origin. What made it even more bizarre, it seemed to be working. Two men entered the factory claiming to be county building inspectors and received courtesy as representatives of such a position. The Chechen cousins met first with Jane O'Connor and explained the purpose of the visit. She, in turn, called Bailey Marshall who escorted the inspectors around the premises.

"You people were in here last November. I thought you only inspected once a year," Bailey commented.

"There were some things missing from the report. We need to have another look at the offices," Dokka informed. (He was chosen to be the spokesman due to lesser of a Chechen dialect and accent).

Since the main purpose of the inspection was the offices, Bailey led the two county representatives back to that department and Jane O'Connor.

"Mr. Baker, the county building inspectors wish to have a look at the offices. Should I send them up?" said Jane over the intercom. After

I answered to the affirmative, she motioned to the stairway and said, "His office is the first on the right."

I met them at the landing and questioned, "Is there something in particular about which you gentlemen are concerned?" They paused for a second, as if considering their response, and then the spokesman replied, "Yes, the placement of fire extinguishers."

"We have one just inside the door to your left and another in the conference room. I have a small one behind my office door. They are routinely checked by the fire department."

"There's one by the accountant's office?"

"Yes, it's positioned in the conference room next door."

Acting as though they didn't believe me, the inspectors walked to the conference room. They stopped at Callie's desk and questioned, "Is this young lady your accountant?"

"Yes, Ms. Mellinger has been with us for a short time. Our previous accountant suffered a horrible tragedy," I stated.

"I believe we saw that on television," Dokka replied, looking at Zorva for acknowledgement. "That had to be a great loss to your company. Did he have close friends working here?"

"Strangely, thinking back on it, I'd have to say no. He was a very private person."

"Did he have close family?"

"He was divorced several years ago. That was before coming to work for us. From what I understand, his wife and daughter moved to California. He was reluctant to discuss his private life," I answered, thinking the direction the conversation was going, somewhat unusual.

"Well, we're satisfied with the fire extinguishers and won't interrupt your day any longer," Dokka announced, as they shook hands and walked briskly to the landing and down the steps. I guided the pair to the outside exit and contemplated on the condition of their automobile. *You would think the county could cut loose of enough money to get them better official transportation.*

When returning to the office, Beverly White asked, "Were those guys foreigners or something? The tall one was kind of creepy."

"I wouldn't want to meet either one of them in a dark alley," Paula Stevens added.

"I suppose that depended on how long it had been since your last date," Beverly joked.

"Yeah, that would have a great deal to do about it," Paula responded, with a snappy comeback.

Friday's ride to Louisville was one in which a million thoughts crossed my mind. With each passing mile, I felt the trip was inessential to my relationship with Irene. In my mind, spending every other weekend and daily phone calls should satisfy the situation. Absence makes the heart grow fonder and frequency tends to burn out the flame—*pray love me little so you love me long.* By the time I reached the halfway point, the undertaking began to make more sense. And, when less than an hour away, I convinced myself it was a necessary act of good judgment. Now my thoughts were totally on Irene. Ruminations of her image obliterated all else and when the lights of the Ramada Inn came into view, I was flushed with a racing heart—it's pounding rhythm soon to be relieved.

CHAPTER TEN

DOKKA AND ZORVA SAT AT their table wearing long faces. Bashir Shishani accompanied them—all three dejected and looking as though their dog just died. A half-empty bottle of Stolichnaya rested midway between the reach of the cheerless trio. Dokka was the first to speak, "The package was no longer in the possession of the American contact. We thoroughly searched his car, his apartment, and the office where he once worked. An enemy faction must have stolen it."

"I don't believe so. We would have heard something about it by this time. They all fear Khalid Umarov and his ties with Mexico," said Shishani. "Whoever has it is a rank amateur and inexperienced. They probably don't even know what it is or what to do with it."

"Do we still have a mole in the Kirksville Police Station?" Dokka asked.

"Yes, and he will alert me if they learn more about the package," Bashir replied.

"What do you want Zorva and me to do now?" Dokka enquired.

"Sit tight until you hear from me."

Zorva suppressed a smile thinking, *now I can return to the gymnasium and practice boxing.* He also filled his glass with the remainder in the vodka bottle.

The days of February literally flew off the calendar. While the shortest month of the year offers no promises, we are encouraged by knowledge that, hidden beneath the ground and within the bare tree branches, the buds of spring are beginning to develop. February also provides an excuse for interaction when confirming the emotion of love. Evidence provided when many households display Valentine cards on the dining room table and anxious correspondents, with pen in hand, eagerly awaiting their endorsement. Card shops, florists, and candy stores see a welcome increase in sales, especially after the post-holiday slump. My contribution consisted of sending two dozen red roses. Red roses were Elaine's favorite flower and where Irene was concerned, she would be happy with any color except yellow—signifying friendship and the end of an affair.

The end of February seemed to have moved Russell Webster off the dime. He presented me with a proposed itinerary of travel and the argument for both of us to visit established dealers, plus, calling on new prospects.

Standing well over six feet tall, with a flowing mane of white hair, Russ presented an impressive figure. However, he was well known in our industry and viewed to over-promise, occasionally. Having me at his side assured any declaration would be rock solid. I've asked Russ to schedule the second week in March. I will be out of pocket for nearly two weeks but shall keep tabs on the operation with daily phone calls—one at 9:30 a.m. and the other at 2:30 p.m. Russ will no doubt be calling on his own. Naturally, we both are free to make personal phone calls at night from our rooms.

Regarding Warren Brantley's scratch paper and the name Lezotte, Beverly White recalls a girl, by that name, which died from a drug overdose. I managed to read about it at the Kirksville Library, viewing old copies of the local newspaper. Rilla Lezotte was only sixteen years old. She lived with her sister Sharon in a part of the town called White City. As yet, I've been unable to muster enough courage to actually visit the sister, although, I had driven by the address twice. The small house was not very inviting and had the curtains pulled each time I drove by. I guess I'm waiting for my biorhythms to reach peak ascension before ringing the doorbell. With traveling a couple weeks for business, I won't make any attempt until I return.

The month of March came in like a lamb. The pleasant harbinger received goodly praise as we headed south for St. Louis and our first appointment on Tuesday. Anheuser Busch was evaluating our batteries and comparing them with like models from their current supplier. Their biggest concern centered on battery weight. After two serious accidents in which a loaded forklift tipped forward, safety engineers could only recommend carrying less product. Since we use heavier gauge steel for battery trays and the fact our design is heavier, in the first place, we have a safety feature to add to the element for consideration. The perpetual argument, made by most large companies, of choosing quality over price, can find no better situation than the one here in the city boasting a 630-foot catenary arch.

Those in the congenial meeting included the national purchasing manager, operations manager, and local supervision. Surprisingly, the corporate managers were unaware of a battery-testing program and couldn't provide data on performance. Apparently, Russell Webster set up the program with someone at the local level. The local operations supervisor acknowledged the test, but also couldn't provide evaluation data. He did relate several lift truck drivers had chosen to use our batteries and recharge and water them on their own. Weighing more, they could move more product than those using other batteries which didn't finish the shift—sometimes ten-hour work days.

The so-called test program never took place. New batteries arrived, and, because they were new, taken by the most senior drivers, put in operation sans any testing routine.

Bottom line, Russ and the operations supervisor dropped the ball. I blame Russ for not following through with his program. As things stood, he cost our company in excess of $10,000, with no evaluation data in return.

The operations supervisor made an issue out of service. The competition had a dealer in town while our closest representative was in Peoria, IL, some 180 miles away—about 3 hours on I-55 S and an overnight trip.

Russ, embarrassed by his blunder, began to tap dance. He assured those at the table our service could be performed by their current dealer, who could bill us for any work under warranty.

I could tell the suggestion didn't set well and we finally got down to plain unvarnished truth—comparing prices.

"Your prices are about even with what we are now paying. Is this the best you can do?" asked one of the maintenance buyers.

"I can review costs and submit another quotation," Russell replied.

"You certainly will need to, since these prices are way out of line," he replied, as he slid Russell's initial proposal back across the table.

By now, I could sense they wanted us to go. So, I thanked them for their courtesies and stated we would be happy to resubmit another quote, while thinking, *they're asking us to sell a better product at a loss just to have their business. I also knew our competition sold at prices higher than those listed on the paper pushed back to Russell. On many occasions, no matter how much you offer, the final decision is ensconced with personal prejudice and motives that are not made public or confessed. Perhaps the buying authority would award the order to their son-in-law or next door neighbor as an act of friendship. Other forms of human nature often overshadow the claim of neutrality, in favor of value.*

Back on the road and I-55 S heading to Memphis, Tennessee. We plan to look for a gas station and a place to have lunch. The boys in St. Louis declined lunch claiming it was their new company policy. No doubt, with a little arm twisting, I could have persuaded them to have a sandwich offsite; but, considering the outcome of our meeting, I was inclined to accept their refusal.

"When we return to the factory I'll write up another proposal," Russell said, breaking the silence.

"You might hold up on it. I'm not so sure that would be a good idea. Better yet, send them a thank you letter, expressing our appreciation for their courtesies. We can take another try at it in six months or around the holidays."

"One thing for sure, Steve, you will really need to sharpen your pencil," Russell replied.

"Russ, I'm reminded of a story. You see, there was once this bachelor who finally wanted to get married. The problem was he had three girlfriends. So he put them to the test as to which one could do the most for him.

The first one cooked him a great supper, washed his car and his clothes, and cleaned his house. The second one cooked him a great meal, washed his car and his clothes, cleaned his house, and mowed his lawn. The third one, not to be outdone, cooked him a great meal, washed his car and his clothes, cleaned his house, mowed his lawn, and straightened his garage. Which one did he marry?"

Russell thought for a while and answered, "The third one."

"Wrong," I replied.

"Which one did he marry?" Russ asked.

"The one with the biggest tits."

Russell chuckled for a minute then said, "I understand what you're telling me. There's usually something hidden when a major purchase order is involved."

Our representative in Memphis had gradually grown his business over the past two years. Mostly brought about by his relationship with the local Clark lift truck dealer. Clark management was aggressive and, teaming with them, certainly helped our industrial battery sales. I've got to give Russ credit for orchestrating the relationship and said so during a pleasant dinner that night with all parties present. After St. Louis, he needed a pat on the back. We all liked to be stroked once in a while.

Due to the length of the previous day's dinner we had a late breakfast and tardy start. Land based for an extra amount of time gave me the opportunity to check back at the office. Outside of the expected comments about how much better the operation is when I'm not there, we were having a problem-free week and good order entry. All Russ' calls were returned, everything on the home front was copacetic, and Irene was okay with me out of pocket, having experience in that regard herself.

We spent the night in Chattanooga and were pretty tired after the 340-mile drive. A good night's rest will do wonders and our dealer, located in Rossville, GA, can be visited Friday morning.

The representatives in Rossville are former Naval Officers who served in the Submarine Service. Their shop is located just a skip and a jump from Interstate highway 75 and basically covers east Tennessee to Knoxville and Kimberly-Clark Corp.—112 miles away. Battery types used by Kimberly-Clark are consigned in Rossville and, only two hours for delivery, in case of emergency.

From the very first day our dealer impressed me. Their offices consume a small part of the building leaving a large area for consignment storage and workshop. Every inch of their office space is put to good use but hidden from obvious view. You can tell they served in the Silent Service, since, aboard a submarine, space is at a premium. It's all there but unseen.

In order to reach our dealer's facility we must pass through the Chickamauga National Military Park, named for the battle of Chickamauga, fought in 1863. It was the first major battle of the Civil War contended in Georgia and the most significant Union defeat in the Western Theater, resulting in the highest number of casualties, second only to the Battle of Gettysburg.

Union General William Rosecrans and the Army of the Cumberland forced Confederate General Braxton Bragg's Army of Tennessee out of Chattanooga and pushed it south. Bragg, determined to reoccupy Chattanooga, organized a counter offensive. With the aid of Spencer repeating rifles, the Union forces withstood and held their line.

Rosecrans, over-wrought about possible gaps in the Federal line, actually created one by unnecessary movements to bolster one of his apprehensive imaginations. In so doing, he opened a path for eight brigades of Confederate General James Longstreet's forces, which drove one-third of the Union army, plus Rosecrans, from the field. Men in blue uniforms rallied to unite the Union defenses. However, Rosecrans was tired and beaten. Urged to hold the position until General Burnside arrived, he decided otherwise and retired to

Chattanooga with the Confederates holding the surrounding heights. The Confederates used their position to block supply lines and lay siege on the city.

President Lincoln's confidence in his general continued to weaken and, when he was unable to break the siege, Rosecrans was relieved of his command.

Meanwhile, Bragg had problems of his own. He strongly believed his subordinate generals had failed him and suspended two of them. In early October 1863, some of his officers attempted mutiny. As a result, Maj. General D.H. Hill was relieved of his command and General Longstreet re-assigned to the Knoxville Campaign—action that seriously weakened Bragg's army at Chattanooga.

Relief forces commanded by Maj. Gen. Ulysses S. Grant broke Bragg's grip on the city and sent the Confederate Army in retreat, opening the gateway to the Deep South for Maj. Gen. William T. Sherman in 1864.

Many historians believe, considering the large concentration of Confederate troops at Chickamauga, there was an opportunity to destroy the Union Army of the Cumberland and break the Union initiative in late 1863. It would have cost Lincoln's re-election and should the Peace Democrat, George McClellan, become president, the Union effort to subdue the South might have ended.

After the Chickamauga Military Park, we entered the nearby town of Rossville, Georgia, another place of historic consequence. The town is named after Cherokee Indian Chief John Ross who lived there until being forced to relocate with his people to Oklahoma after President Andrew Jackson put his signature to the Indian Removal Act in 1830. The act was a policy of ethnic cleansing supported by the government to move Native American tribes, living east of the Mississippi River, to an area designated as Indian Territory. An estimated 4,000 Cherokees died on the forced march. It became known as The Trail of Tears.

It's a universal truth that dealers who make you money become favorites. The representatives in Rossville are classic examples. They are truly southern gentlemen of both acumen and courtesy. Their sales have grown substantially because of it. And, as a result, they help maintain the Chattanooga Area Regional Transportation Authority's electric shuttles servicing the downtown area. Unfortunately, the electric busses use a different type battery than what we manufacture. All the same, it's still a great advertisement for those who do.

At the close of day we were invited to supper at the senior partner's home. His wife had prepared a sumptuous meal of pan-fried chicken and all the trimmings. Russell had picked up a fine bottle of red wine fitting for the occasion and the evening turned out to be the most relaxing thus far.

The following day being Saturday allowed us to visit the Hamilton Place Mall, the largest mall in Tennessee. The enclosed, two-story emporium featured several anchor stores and more satellite shops a person couldn't visit in a single day. After a relaxing breakfast, we purchased a few gifts for the family and toured for an hour or so window-shopping. The ides of March gave us a very pleasant day, weather wise.

Our next appointment was with the dealer in Birmingham on Monday. We figured it would take about three hours of leisurely driving on I-59 S in order to check in at the hotel downtown around suppertime. Russ promised he knew of a great restaurant nearby. Since he had previously visited this dealer, I took him at his word.

Thus far, no business had transpired. I wanted to wait until I had a chance to personally meet with the principals. I did, however, do some vetting on my own. John Raspberry represented a German battery manufacturer who stocked a great deal of consignment. That proved to be his downfall. It became easy to sell without reporting and bank full price instead of only commissions due. Their district marketing manager became suspicious when consignment stock was reordered when the company's records indicated the exact items were still in consignment. We call that selling out of trust. The Germans pulled his dealership and demanded payment for what had been sold. Remaining consignment stock was loaded on a semi-trailer and returned to the factory in Ohio. Like they say, *if you bare your ass to a vengeful unicorn, the outcome is predictable.*

Birmingham is the largest city in Alabama, followed closely by Montgomery, the state capitol. It was founded in 1871 during the Civil War reconstruction period and grew from there. Once a mining and steel manufacturer, the Magic City has diversified into financial and corporate headquarters.

Jane had booked us into a new hotel near the airport and downtown. She also got us single suites with king-size beds for the two-day stay over. She must have scored a good bargain since she was well aware of my penny pinching when it came to travel lodging. After all, I'm only sleeping in the room, not living there. That's not to say you couldn't live in the suites we were given. There was an ample living area and efficient kitchenette, with all the electric comforts of home. A separate bedroom contained a berth the size of Utah. I had to roll over twice to reach the other side—only kidding. The minute I unpacked, the phone rang.

"Are the accommodations suitable, your majesty?" it was Russell.

"I need a compass to get off the bed."

"Let me know when you're ready for supper."

"See you downstairs in ten minutes."

The restaurant Russell suggested was everything he said it was. Men waiters and white linen tablecloths established the ambience and the menu, the cuisine. I love a meal served in orderly sequence with soup and salad for openers. Nobody ever stopped here for a quick bite. Two hours later we took a pass on dessert and charged the meal to my room. Russ asked our waiter if there was a lively nightspot nearby and was given directions to a local favorite. The more popular clubs were to be found downtown.

"What do you think boss, are you in favor of a nightcap and a little music," Russ asked. Since there was no need to rise early in the morning he would have made book on me accepting. With my belt a little tight from a splendid supper, it was safe to assume that I was in an accommodating mood.

"I could use an aperitif," I replied in my best French accent.

Our waiter's lively nightspot turned out to be a guitar-slinging, red neck, country club, packed to the brim. According to the waiter's directions we circled the block and entered an alley behind the club. A blue light above the door signaled the way to the recommended entrance. The minute we opened the door, I was struck by a turbulent storm of hoots and hollers, piercing sound of amplified and raucous electric guitars, and John Raspberry standing at the bar leading the mob. Our point of entry isn't known by strangers. Accordingly, anyone entering that portal is a friend and magnetizes every eyeball in the house. We were welcomed like family. John and his associates made room at the bar and before I could decide what to drink, two bottles of Corona Extra were set in front of us.

"Glad you got here on the weekend. You couldn't have picked a better time. The girls' softball teams are out larkin'." John's eyes were bleary.

"They seem to occupy every table in the house," I stated.

"That's 'cause we're southern gentlemen," one of John's buddies slurred.

Nodding in agreement, I shouted to John we were in Chattanooga this morning and arrived here in Birmingham a short time ago. We planned to sleep late tomorrow and visit him on Monday, according to plan. He confirmed the 10 a.m. appointment. The din was suddenly halted when the music stopped and the apparent band leader grabbed the microphone and yelled, "Let's all dance for a while."

It was then I noticed her sitting at a table with five girls in softball uniforms. She wore an unadorned cotton housedress pulled tight by her divine figure. Without trying, she was a temptress of pure sensuality. Every man in the room shared the same thoughts.

"See anyone you'd like to dance with? I'll introduce you. Hell, I know just about every woman in the place," John was trying to butter me up.

I mentioned the girl in a housedress and John grabbed my arm and said, "Follow me."

Her name was Coralee Smallwood. She extended her hand when asked if she'd like to dance. Inhaling her essence just as soon as she pressed against me, I held my breath to avoid her sensual intoxication. After playing a game of softball, her fundamental womanhood was enhanced. Any cologne at this point would ruin her bouquet. *How old is she? She must be in her late twenties. Bottom line, at least half my age.*

I knew full well her turned up face was watching me intently. Much to my embarrassment, the cotton brief dangler was also awakened. She gave no indication anything was wrong.

"You're out of uniform," I said softly.

"I tore the seat out of my uniform pants sliding into third base. This dress belongs to my friend. Does it look bad?"

"That dress has never looked better since the day it was made." She gave me an ambrosial smile and laid her head against my chest. The bandleader was doing his best to sound like Randy Travis singing 'On the Other Hand.'

Circe could turn men into the form of animals. *Odysseus* possessed an herb to protect against her spell. All I've had is four bottles of Corona Extra and it only worked on me.

"Do you believe in love?" she asked.

"We humans have needs. Maslow claimed food, water, shelter, warmth, companionship, and sex are necessary. I believe love is the emotion we feel when these human cravings are satisfied," murmuring quietly in her ear to be heard beneath the resonant sound of the band.

"It's not love unless another satisfies their own in return. When that happens a lasting love is created," she replied.

I thought, *my God, this girl also has a mind. Rare for someone with her physical attributes.* Did I ever tell you that I am a male chauvinist?

Every Adam needs an Eve and this girl is heaven sent. I've never been much of a beer drinker and whatever amount I've ingested has brought on that queasy feeling. In spite of the possible need to dash to the men's room, the swelling in my briefs assumed command, making me determined to stay the course. I remained on the floor through four numbers, three slow dances, and a fast song, where I just stood and kept time by snapping my fingers. Coralee bounced with moves never witnessed before, without being arrested.

"Have you ever considered killing yourself?"

My jaw must have dropped thinking, "*Oh shit, that was very dark. This girl is Goth.*" Most women are like icebergs. You only see what they want you to. The real person is below the water and hidden from the outside world.

"Not that I can remember. Have you?"

"Of course not. I just asked to keep the conversation going," she explained. "Aren't you feeling okay?"

"Now that you've asked, it's awful hot in here. I just need to get some fresh air."

We walked to the back door together. The cold air was somewhat reviving although an upchuck could happen at any moment. I could see Coralee was getting goose pimples. "Let me go back in and get your coat."

"Are you parked around here? I could get warm in the car," she suggested.

No sooner had I started the engine, this erogenous gift from the gods raised her bare leg over mine and, with her arms around my neck, imparted the most passionate kiss of my life. I took the opportunity to satisfy myself whether or not she wore underclothes. There were none to be found. Blood is rushing everywhere except where it's needed most. I'm fighting the battle between passion and nausea—three cheers for Corona Extra…viva Mexico!

"Do you have protection?" she whispered.

"No. This is very unusual for me. I'm totally unprepared for it."

Coralee looked at me like she would a new puppy and said, "I'll be right back."

It was too late to summon her retreat, as she exited the rental car and returned faster than you can say Jack Robinson. Flashing a gleaming grin, she was waving a small package above her head.

Besides being sick to my stomach, I now had a painful, swimming, headache. To further my disappointment the cotton brief Johnson was flaccid.

"I'm sorry about this. It happens to a lot of men when they drink too much alcohol," hopeful for her understanding.

"How long does it last?"

"I've never measured it. Obviously, until the alcohol wears off," I sighed, disheartened and dejected.

"Do you want to take me back to the hotel? I would spend the night with you." Coralee's got it bad and refuses to give up.

"There's nothing I'd like better but there's one problem. The man traveling with me is my marketing manager and there's nothing he'd like better than for me to spend the night with you. It would be a story he'd promise to never tell but find ways to hold it over me forever."

"I thought you men stuck together."

"I guess we do to some extent; however, when the politics come in the situation, all bets are off."

We talked for nearly two hours with an occasional kiss and a little snogging in hopes for the resurrection that never materialized. Coralee bared her soul. She was born in a little town in Alabama and deemed to be uppity by most of her friends. She wants something more than the hardscrabble life, and, as yet, hasn't found the right person to give it to her. On this starlit night, sitting in the car with her in my arms, I regretted not being that person.

Finally, the bar was closing and noisy patrons began to leave through the back door. When her softball team appeared under the blue light, she kissed me passionately and said, "I could spend my time piddlin' with you forever. Still and all, I better skedaddle, if I want a ride home. I have your business card. Would you mind if I called you sometime?"

"I'd mind if you didn't," I replied. With that Coralee got out of the car and signaled to the girls she was going to join them. As I sat behind the wheel crestfallen, Russell Webster exited under the blue light and walked to the car. I slid to the passenger's side indicating he was to drive.

"How was she?" were the first words out of his mouth.

"She's a very sweet lady."

Changing the subject, Russ chimed, "You're going to shit when you see the bar bill."

"How much was it?"

Looking straight ahead as he left the parking lot, Russ replied, "Counting tips for the three waitresses wearing cowboy hats, it came to just under $300. There was a slight lull in the conversation then he asked, "Did you use a rubber?"

"Why are you so interested?"

"I was just thinking it wouldn't go well with England if there was a paternity suit."

"Don't worry Russ. There won't be any paternity suit." I couldn't tell if he was happy about that or not. At this point, I still was sick to my stomach and looked forward to the bathroom stool. In spite of a spinning bed, a new member joined my troubled dream world. The daughter of *Aphrodite* moved in between Elaine and Irene.

When I woke up Sunday morning, I had to feel around the other side of the bed to see if Coralee was there—no such luck. The light shining under the door revealed the Sunday morning paper. With a series of groans, to help me get out of bed, I picked it up and laid it on the coffee table. My wristwatch was too blurred to read, however, the glow from the clock radio read 7:45 a.m. Realizing the only thing that can save my life is hot coffee, I showered, shaved, dressed in slacks and a T- shirt, and headed to the elevator for breakfast. With the paper under my arm, I walked to a sign reading 'Seat Yourself' and noticed Russell Webster at a table, reading the Birmingham News.

"Did you sleep well?"

"Not bad, considering the booze."

"I didn't notice you drinking the hard stuff."

"It was the beer. I never could drink much of it without getting sick. Must be a carryover from old college bashes."

As the waitress filled my coffee cup I told her she had just saved my life. Her smile faded when I refused the menu. I pulled the sports section out of the paper and flattened it on my side of the table. The headline read: *Susan Butcher Wins Iditarod.* After finishing second two out of the last three years, Susan Butcher was slated to be the first woman to win the grueling sled dog race in 1985. Then tragedy struck. She was forced to withdraw when a crazed moose killed two of her dogs. Despite Butcher's attempts to ward off the animal, another thirteen dogs were injured.

Ironically, Libby Riddles, a long shot, became the first woman to win the race. As expected, this year Susan Butcher became the second woman to win the Iditarod. Braving Arctic blizzard conditions across the Alaskan wilderness, a test of endurance of both mushers and dogs, she covered the 1,158-mile course in 11 days, 15 hours, and 6 minutes.

A lover of dogs and the wilderness, Susan Butcher is a veterinary technician and breeder of Huskies. She told the world she plans to win the Iditarod again next year and, as things stand, there aren't many doubters.

"Did you read the article about the Iditarod?" I asked Russell.

"Yeah. Quite an accomplishment," he replied. "A woman would have a weight advantage."

"I imagine the race has weight restrictions for the sled. If the sled was too light, they probably added weight similar to handicapping racehorses," said I, theorizing.

The unsmiling waitress returned with the coffeepot and poured us each a warm up. Being a user of cream, I trickled a little half-and-half into the umber-colored brew and stirred it with my teaspoon. The white swirl blended quickly into the steaming beverage. All the while I was drifting back to the memory of Coralee Smallwood. That girl is tough to forget.

"Any good games on TV today?" Russ asked.

I hate it when Russell does that. He never was athletic and always the onlooker and bystander. Bottom line, he couldn't care less about sports and only asked in condescension to me. I also hate patronization in all its forms. Responding to his question, suggested, "It's such a nice day, why don't we take a walk around the hotel and enjoy the morning air and sunshine?"

The look on his face said it all. Nevertheless, he had to join me in order to preserve one's dignity. Russ had all day to recuperate from my little bit of vengeful punishment. Hell, it might do him well, if it didn't kill him.

The hotel was constructed on a slight elevation, hardly noticeable from outside. No matter what direction we decided, the first part would prove easier than the return. Initially, everything went well—most likely due to the slight decline. Then, on the return, we both began to sweat. Half way up the incline Russ began to stagger like a rhinoceros shot by a tranquilizer gun. He had had it. He sat on a knee-high wall fanning himself.

"All we need is a little rest, and then we can make it back," I assured.

"You're going to have to send a cab for me," he joked.

Seeing him prostrate on the edge of the flowered wall gave me a feeling of contrition. "We will sit here for as long as it takes. Our meeting isn't until 10 o'clock tomorrow," I said, also a little out of wind. Then we both had a good laugh.

Finally, returning to the hotel, we both napped until later that afternoon. There's nothing like a hot shower when you're tired and sweaty—the second best inducement for sleep.

The next day's meeting with John Raspberry went as expected. He asked for some consignment stock in order to provide same day delivery. A request I denied out of hand. Instead, I offered him the option to purchase from storage in Rossville, Ga. He had to think that over. The only other possibility was for my company to ship and bill his customer. He would receive a commission check after we receive payment. Once again, he had to think that over. My second sense told me having Mr. Raspberry as a dealer was very improbable.

Russ took him aside and said he will keep in touch and try to come up with a program I would be willing to accept—fat chance of that.

During lunch, John told me he always wanted to open a daycare center for children of working mothers. His wife could run it and provide additional income. Selling batteries was all he'd ever done and he would continue until his bones wouldn't let him move around.

We parted company with Raspberry handing Russell an order for several popular batteries. It will be interesting to see if the end customers are credit worthy. The onus will fall in the bailiwick of Callie Mellinger.

Our travel agenda next calls for driving south to Mobile, about 260 miles and four hours away. We're booked at the Courtyard Inn off I-65S and after registering, plan to be the guest of Landry Davis for dinner. Mr. Davis is from an old established family in business and politics. He seems to have his fingers in everything from his own museum to sales at the shipyards. His family holds the title to the building in which he makes his office; however, from my view, most business is done at dinner and 'good old boy' policies.

Russ made the phone call and gave Landry the hotel in which we're staying. He was expecting the call and said he'd pick us up at seven, giving us a needed hour to shower, shave, and change clothes.

We were seated in the lobby when Landry opened the front door. He spotted us right away and, with a perpetual friendly smile, said, "My favorite Yankee friends welcome to the real South." His handshake certainly supported his statement.

"Would you boys care for a libation before we go or would you like to wait and have one at the restaurant?" Landry Davis had that prominent southern drawl—a slow and drawn out pronunciation of English all his own. The word hurry wasn't in his lexicon. We agreed to wait.

Dinner was at a Dauphin Island restaurant. The maître d' was over condescending and led us to Davis' reserved table—he obviously ate there often. Several patrons recognized him on sight and gave friendly greetings on the way to our table.

"I hope this table is satisfactory for you gentlemen," he slowly uttered.

"We're just country boys from Illinois. We're not accustomed to such elegant surroundings."

"I've heard about you from John Raspberry. Mr. Baker, you're far from a country boy. And, if I may say so, you handled Mr. Raspberry properly," he returned. "Now that's enough business until we finish supper. What are y'all going to have to drink?"

"I can handle one martini. The other day, I got kinda sick on Corona Extra beer."

"I believe that brand comes out of Mexico," Landry slowly droned. "How about you, Mr. Webster. A southern martini be okay?"

Our drinks were served in a very large tumbler. I soon became pleased with Landry's slow, unhurried manner. He drank his martini the same way. Conversation was more important than alcohol. Our discourse was interrupted only to order appetizers.

The antipasto, served on a large silver tray, contained samples of the most popular delicacies from the Gulf— an epicurean delight, consisting of oysters in the half-shell to sautéed shrimp, plus, miscellaneous sauces and dips.

"Try some of the crayfish pâté," Landry suggested. "Just spread it on a piece of toasted Cajun French bread. I could make a whole meal out of it. It has brandy in it."

Doing as he suggested, I tasted crayfish pâté for the first time. He wasn't just a'woofin'. *My God I'm beginning to talk like him?* Nevertheless, it was delicious. Making a motion across the tray, "What are some of these other sauces?"

Landry pointed out and explained in detail the tangy dips—cream cheese, spinach, remoulade, and, another favorite, catsup and horseradish.

The main course started with a bibb-lettuce salad and bleu cheese, with bacon vinaigrette on the side. Following the salad, came the roasted brisket with onion and green chili glaze, mashed sweet potatoes and steaming vegetables.

By the time the meal ended, this was the most delightful evening of our trip—with the exception of meeting Coralee Smallwood, of course.

Once the china was cleared away, Landry lit a cigar and ordered us his favorite after dinner cocktail. Thus far, he's hit the bull's eye and his after dinner nightcap was surprising, yet, on the money. It contained bourbon, amaretto, dark crème de cacao and half-and-half.

"Y'all know I furnish the shippers with fork truck batteries," he stated, and chuckled to himself. "The boys at the shipyard sometimes get a little careless and drive off the docks into the water. I've told them, when they do that, the batteries are ruined. Am I right?"

Before Russell could speak, I answered. "Salt water is deleterious in a lead-acid battery. To salvage it, all the cells need to be emptied and flushed. In order to do that, the lead intercell connectors need to be cut off and re-burned. The whole process is costly and depending on the age of the battery, unrealistic. I, personally, think you're right."

"That's good to hear. I wouldn't want folks to say I'd been lying to them," Landry said, as he reached in his suit coat pocket and withdrew a folded paper. "I have a list of battery types to order. Pricing is important but not the only consideration. The freight cost from Chicago to Alabama is very steep. I have a question for you. Can I haul your batteries or do you insist on the carrier?"

"Any licensed and insured carrier can transport lead-acid batteries, as long as the rig is heavy enough and is properly stickered."

"By stickered, do you mean the proper signs on the truck?"

"Yes, the DOT requires placards to let you know there is hazardous material on board, such as battery acid."

"Don't the freight carriers have these signs?"

"Not necessarily. If they usually haul non-hazardous material, they may not have the proper posters. In cases when they don't, the shipper is responsible and must furnish the signs."

"Here's why I'm asking. One of my cousins is in the freight business and delivers to Chicago. I was thinking of having him pick up the batteries for a back haul. He won't charge me very much."

"That works. As long as he's insured, I can provide the right placards."

"Now that that's settled, can I get a discount for cash in 10 days?"

"I'm willing to offer 2% discount for cash."

"Mr. Baker, you have a deal," Davis stated, and stood to shake hands while handing me the battery order. "Let's celebrate with one more night cap."

Agreeing to only one more drink, I placed his order in my coat pocket without reading it. From the expression on Landry Davis' face, he appreciated my demonstration of trust.

Back at the hotel, Russ and I sat for a while in the lobby mulling over the evening and Landry Davis. Russ scrutinized the requisition and determined it to be a full semi-load, then asked, "What kind of pricing do you think appropriate? He didn't ask about cost."

"After talking to John Raspberry, he knows our pricing structure. Figure these out at our biggest dealer discount and deduct 2% for cash. We will benefit in two ways, no freight cost and cash payment."

Russell Webster was chomping at the bit to call and enter the order. Much to his chagrin, I returned Landry Davis' list to my inside jacket pocket, where it will remain until we return. Russell is so obvious. I read him like a book. He wanted to call the office and take credit for the transaction. If he only knew the girls read him easier than me, it would break his heart. On second thought, no it wouldn't. Russell's ego floats above us all and is impervious to insult. Be that as it may, he will probably become unhappy company on the trip to Hammond, LA, and the Kmart distribution center.

Our product found its way to the Kmart distribution center via a marketing company based in Milwaukee, WI. They represented another industrial battery manufacturer and were boxed out of Kmart because of price. The Milwaukee marketing group was intrigued with our design after a presentation I made late last year. Their sales manager and Russ worked out a deal for us to design a battery to fit a somewhat unusual lift truck battery compartment. They, in turn, would quote our product. As time would have it, they won the order. In spite of a constant push by Milwaukee to rush assembly, the batteries met my internal completion plan. Each unit was given a measured and recorded discharge test. If the performance met my standards, they would be signed off for release. The extended time of manufacturing was one day.

The batteries have been performing for about three months. Against the wishes of Milwaukee, I wanted to see the Hammond operation first hand. They most likely fear me taking the business from them. To do so would be unethical and against my personal principals of business. In time they will realize my visit will only enhance their relationship with Kmart.

From the hotel in Mobile, AL, Hammond, LA is only a little over two hours away on I-10W and I-12W. We were on the road by 8:30 and arrived at the Kmart distribution center before 11:00. The operations manager, Carl MacKinnon, was kind enough to give us a tour of the facility. Thank heavens for an electric transport— the distribution center covers well over one-million square feet. At my request, he took us to the battery charging room. It was quite impressive, having over twenty units under charge and a similar amount fully charged, awaiting change out at the end of the shift.

"Who designed your battery room?"

"I believe it was the people who sold us the batteries," he replied. "This is the second layout. It's more efficient than the original design. I think they're based in Milwaukee."

"Marvin Levy has done an excellent job," Russell stated, as if he was personally aware the president of the Milwaukee Company influenced the battery room design.

"You know the Milwaukee Company?" asked Mackinnon.

"Oh yes. They represent us in the state of Wisconsin," Russell replied.

"Their sales representative has suggested we install automatic watering devices on the batteries. He explained it would be a significant time changer. In our business, time is money," the operation manager stated. "My concern was, since the devices aren't original equipment, a malfunction could void your warranty. He assured me, if they are installed properly, I needn't be concerned."

Before Russell Webster could respond, I said, "You're right about the warranty and they can malfunction as they get older. Sometimes the float gets gummy and sticks in the down position, resulting in over-watering the cell. To avoid this, you would need to install devices about once a year."

"That would nullify the cost savings from the reduction of watering time," he flatly stated. "The little devices are expensive and take time to replace."

My honesty will probably queer any chances Milwaukee may have installing an automatic watering system but it saved me the headache of future warranty settlements.

We took lunch with the operations manager in the cafeteria. It was a far cry from the night before; however, the smorgasbord buffet offered a wide variety on its menu.

"Thank you for the lunch. You have a wonderful facility here in Hammond. It's been a pleasure meeting you and taking the tour. I'd be pleased to answer any questions you may have at this time."

"Likewise, it's been a knowledgeable experience having you visit us," Carl replied. "Regarding questions, you've answered the only question I had concerning the watering caps and you have explained it to my satisfaction. Feel free to stop by whenever you are in Hammond. I suppose you get down here at least once each year."

"Unfortunately, I don't usually make sales trips; however, Russell calls on our product representatives in the area two or three times each year."

"Well, my offer is extended to Mr. Webster as well."

We concluded the Kmart visit around 2 o'clock. The schedule calls for a diversion at this point in order to spend the evening in

New Orleans. We're booked for one night at Hotel St. Marie in the French Quarter and it reposes only a little over an hour away. For those visiting the Gulf coast, The Big Easy is always in the back of their mind. That's no exception for either Russ or me and the opportunity has now arrived.

Regretfully, the formations of black clouds, tumbling from the west, threaten plans for exploring the entertainment and nightclubs. We can only hope it holds off raining, since Gulf coast drenchers are notorious.

Heavy drops began to fall the moment we handed the car keys to the hotel's valet. Once entering St. Marie's lobby, it turned into a gully washer. Quickly glancing back, I saw cars splashing water high into the air as they passed by. A reverberating clap of thunder made everybody in the lobby jump. Moans from the guests indicated their evening plans were ruined. At that point, the bell captain took command. He couldn't do much about the weather. Even so, he could begin demonstrating St. Marie's excellent service. And, that he did.

The moment our reservations were confirmed, our luggage was placed on a cart and, with the bell captain leading the way, guided to the elevator. After a swift ride, the doors opened to the third floor. The captain and his two assistants led us to our rooms.

Our accommodations were spacious and decorated in an 18th century French décor. The walls were a combination of light pastel-colored flowers and vines. Where the four-poster bed stood, however, the partitions were covered with dark wood panels. A double window led to a balcony overlooking the courtyard. It provided an excellent view of the fountain and distinctive display of tropical flowers flaunting their spring time glory—a beautiful sight were it not for the constant downpour. The outside swimming pool was, naturally, without participants. Hotel St. Marie is perfect for a romantic adventure. At the moment, the guests must settle for one of its two restaurants. The phone ringing interrupted my transfixture.

"This is Russell. How do you like your room?"

"I love the room. But, I can't say much for the weather."

"I talked to the bell captain about the nearest entertainment. He told me it begins about two blocks from here," Russ stated. "We could get a bite to eat and then take a cab over there."

Checking my watch, I suggested we meet downstairs in the main dining room in two hours. That gives us a little time to make phone calls and rest up for what lies ahead this evening. My first call was to Jane O'Connor to keep up with factory business and let her know our destination. Then Elaine, to make sure the family was okay. Lastly, a call to Irene's office. The usual work parade around her desk keeps her end of the conversation at a minimum. I was able to tell her news on my end without any questions. Most importantly, I could express my feelings for her using a secret number sequence known only by the two of us. After ringing off, her voice remained in my consciousness for a considerable length of time.

Russ was sitting at a table when I walked into the main dining room. He had already devoured something served on a hors d'oeuvre tray.

"Hope you don't mind me having a snack before you got here. I was famished. If you want an appetizer, I recommend the shrimp. It's delicious."

"I'm really not that hungry. Maybe a salad would taste good right now. I can always get something else later. You go on and order what you want." Looking around, I could see the place was full. Apparently, because of the rain, a good supper stands as a substitute for hitting the nightlife. Several tables had a complimentary bottle of champagne— gratis gift of Hotel St. Marie. We were awarded the same once Russell ordered from the menu. I doubt if my salad alone would have been worthy.

Champagne and the house dressing made a perfect combination for the chef's ensemble of greens. The position of our table gave me a part view of the lobby. No one entered without an umbrella. The relentless torrent continued. I began to question the wisdom in braving such conditions when the friendliness of warm surroundings bade me to stay. Russ assured being sheltered by either roof or umbrella protected us against the rain. If he's correct, at this stage of our trip, there's no reason to be a killjoy.

With the exception of shoes and the bottom six inches of pants legs, he was right. Our heads were covered during the junket to the nearest New Orleans jazz club. The above mentioned lower extremities were soaked and drenched. Once inside, I squished to the first vacant table and squeezed what water I could from my pants cuffs.

In spite of the weather, it was a festive room and the blaring music encouraged jazz aficionados to gratifying response. There's nothing like appreciation to further energize the musicians—the place was rocking. It didn't take long before realizing a little water meant nothing compared to the polyrhythmic pleasure emanating from the bandstand. While immersed in musical stir, I was tormented by the thought of an early rise in the morning. A 350-mile drive lay ahead of us in order to reach Houston, Texas by early afternoon. It was now half past twelve and the crowd seemed larger and noisier than when we first arrived. A tough decision but we had to go. The rain seemed to have eased slightly, still, we hailed the first cab passing by.

Russ had already checked out and was sitting in the morning breakfast room at 8:30 when I carried my luggage to the front desk. Nothing stands in the way of a meal paid for by the company. He gave me the hi-sign and I nodded acknowledgement. I might as well join him and add breakfast to the hotel tab before settling the account. If we're on the road by 9:30, we should still have time to visit Grady Miller, our Houston representative, this afternoon—especially if Russell Webster drives. Russ has a string of speeding tickets to stand as proof of a heavy foot.

Shortly after we hit the highway and continued west, the rain lessened and finally stopped. Patchy skies broke apart and bright sunlight demanded shaded glasses. Traffic on I-10W raced along at 70 mph suggesting it will be no problem arriving early enough to meet with the dealer.

We pulled in the Marriott parking lot off Gulfstream Freeway at 3 o'clock. Fifteen minutes later we had registered and Russ made a call to Kelly Tractor. Grady Miller leases office space in their building. When Russ told him we had a flight out of William P. Hobby Airport in the morning, he invited us to come right over.

Having your office inside the complex of the area's major material handling business keeps you in touch of what's happening with their customers. One of which is the nation's largest independently owned food retailer—H.E. Butt Grocery Company. H.E. Butt services families all over Texas and Mexico with 275 grocery stores. The Houston facility is a cold storage distribution center using electric lift trucks. Grady Miller said they have about 200 industrial batteries in operation. Considering replacements and service on existing units, Grady Miller makes a pretty good living from only one customer.

After a brief tour of the Kelly facilities, we were offered to take part in their open house commencing at five o'clock. It was plain to see that Grady would rather be at the open house than go out to dinner. Much to our delight, Kelly really puts on the dog when it comes to open houses. Their sales manager also got a kick out of me when he offered hors d'oeuvres loaded with jalapeno peppers. Funny thing, after a while I got used to them and developed a taste for jalapeno. By nine o'clock, Texas hospitality was such that the morning flight to Chicago began to lose its importance. Thanks to Russell, a seemingly more devoted family man, I was encouraged to make our farewells and head back to the hotel. It was a good thing he did because a jalapeno fiesta was beginning to celebrate in my gurgling innards. I made it to my room in the nick of time.

The next morning we got up early, ate breakfast, and drove to Hobby Airport. Fortunately, at the entrance, a sign indicated the location of rental car services. We followed the arrows to National Car Rental and dropped off our automobile—arrangements to do so were made back in Kirksville. I've often wondered how National does that sort of thing but I won't rack my brain—I've got enough to worry about. I was currently concerned over my company car stationed in the long-term parking lot. Oh well, if it doesn't start, there's plenty of help at Midway Airport.

CHAPTER ELEVEN

I T FELT GOOD TO BE back at the post on Monday. The familiar chatter and activity works like a mystical therapeutic for whatever ails you. My return also resulted in a dramatic discontinuation of catcalls and playful insinuations when the girls from the office were on the factory floor—especially with Callie Mellinger, even though scuttlebutt had it that she is dating a policeman—James "Bubba" Watson. Counting Jane O'Connor's husband, we now have two officers of the law in our workplace family. Truth be known, the girls probably enjoyed it as much as the whistlers. Similar to home, there was a brief greeting, then, everything back to normal.

It took until late afternoon before I could see the bottom of my desktop. A list of phone calls, financial reports, confidential mail from England, and daily receivables for the two weeks buried the lustrous shine of dark oak. Those working the second shift unevenly entered the building and sauntered to the time clock. Each looking upward to my lighted window and acknowledging my return. At half past four, the girls in the office were still at their desks, obligating me to remind them it was past time to go home. There are occasions, which will require extra effort. This isn't one of them.

Soon after the office turned dark, my private line rang. The throatiness in her voice was indicative of seduction on the prowl. Little did she know it wasn't necessary for me. I'm still kicking myself for drinking too much Corona Extra. Ever since, I've been basking in the calming medicine of speculation. At least, in my imagination, we will see each other again.

"Steven, this is Coralee Smallwood," she breathed in a quiet voice.

"Darling, I would recognize your voice in the riot of a hurricane."

"I'm just calling to make sure you got back all right," she purred.

"Thanks for your concern. It was a long two weeks."

"Was it profitable?"

"Yes. I believe the trip was worthwhile; but, thank heavens, I only have to do it a couple times a year. I'm more of a stay at home type guy. Meeting you was the most exceptional part of the junket," I confessed.

"I love your honeyed words. Don't the Irish call that blarney" she inferred.

"It's not blarney if it's real. And, where you are concerned, it's the unvarnished truth," I assured.

"Will I ever see you again?"

"Yes." I answered without hesitation. "Give me a little time to figure it out."

"Then I'll keep myself for you. Please don't take too long," she stated, and then hung up.

I sat for a moment lost in my thoughts. My life is complicated enough without this sweet southern belle embrangling it further. Nevertheless, stoned on the glow of her memory, the dragon of my conscience demanded she stay. One thing for certain, the effectuation of Coralee's call made me relinquish a ring to Irene until tomorrow.

On my way home, while a smattering of daylight remained, I had an unexplained urge to drive by Sharon Lezotte's house. Much to my surprise, I saw what appeared to be an old woman removing mail from the box at the end of her driveway. Once she noticed me pull into her lane, she scurried to the house.

Considering her ringer may not be working, I rapped on the door. The first knock drew no response. I applied the knuckles with a little more emphasis. This time the entrance curtain was drawn and someone stared from behind it. The encouraging sound of the dead bolt release made me back away a step.

"What do you want?" came a voice from behind a two-inch opening.

"I'm here to talk about your sister, Rilla Lezotte." Actually, I had no idea why I was there other than an unspecific urge to learn more. Reluctantly, the door opened and the voice said, "Come in. I've been expecting you."

Sharon Lezotte looked as though she'd been living off the smell of a dishrag. Bones covered with ashen skin. Her appearance was the disguise of a formerly pretty woman. The first thought that came to my mind was Maria Ouspenskaya, the Russian stage actress famous in American films as Maleva, a Gypsy fortuneteller in horror movies. The ones I loved as a child. Even though the light was subdued, I could tell the face of the girl standing before me carried a tale of a bitter life. The corners of her mouth indicated no facial creases of happiness and, saturnine eyes dull, without even a memory of delight.

The room reflected neither companions, friends, nor spiritual connections. She definitely was someone who sang to an empty bench. There was an uncomfortable pause, during which I stumbled trying to think of something intelligent to open the conversation. Thankfully, she broke the ice.

"Are you with the police?" she timidly asked.

"Heavens no. My name is Steven Baker. I manage the battery factory west of town," breathing a sigh of relief.

"Please take a seat. Would you care for a beer or perhaps some water?"

"No thank you. On second thought, I would like a glass of water. What I'd like to talk about will take a little time," choosing an armchair near another, making it easier to maintain eye contact while we converse. The unforgettable sound of water running from a faucet made me smile to myself. *She's letting it run a while in order to make it colder.*

"The icemaker in the refrigerator is on the fritz. It costs a small fortune to have it repaired," she factually stated, while handing me a glass with droplets wiped from its outside surface. She retained one for herself having those dew shaped drops still clinging. I took a courteous swallow and exhaled appreciation while wondering why she thought I was from the police.

The tension in the room was thick enough to loosen the wallpaper. Sharon Lezotte sat twisting her handkerchief in fearful anticipation. My presence was definitely beyond normal convention. I don't recall a more awkward situation. I've usually found a humorous anecdote can break the ice but at this place and time it would be totally unacceptable. There was no other choice but to come right down to it and reveal my purpose no matter how senseless it might appear.

"Do you recall reading about the murder of Mr. Warren Brantley? It happened a few weeks ago. It was in all the papers and on TV," I inquired, at the same time trying to seem somewhat unattached and nonchalant in order to diminish its relativity.

If it's possible, Sharon Lezotte paled to a shade beyond her usual pallor.

"Are you sure you're not with the police?" she stammered suspiciously.

"Of course not. I told you before. I'm just an ordinary citizen. Warren Brantley was my accountant. What brought me to your door is curiosity, nothing more."

Seeing she still didn't believe me, I went on with my story. "After Warren Brantley was killed, I needed to have the company's books reviewed in case there was any malfeasance involved. Fortunately, the auditors found none. As I tidied up his office, preparing for the independent auditors, I noticed the name Rilla Lezotte etched on his notepad. Apparently, he had heard from her and jotted down the name. Don't ask me why, but I tore off the page and placed it in my coat pocket. Satisfied it had nothing to do with the case, it remained there until long after the police investigation. I found the name Rilla to be unusual and mentioned it to the girls in the office. It was then I learned she met with tragedy. I went to our public library and educated myself from the newspaper files. Would you have any idea why Warren Brantley had any contact with her?"

"Mr. Baker, my sister died a year ago from a drug overdose. Yes, I know Warren Brantley. He was a dark man in both mien and deed. How did she meet him? Most likely over the internet on one of the communal sites. It's an old story and I'm afraid it can only get worse. Innocent young girls begin by communicating with a phantom ally and over time meet them. They are introduced to drugs and the alternate afterlife. By the time I learned about it, Rilla was hooked.

Our father left when I was in eighth grade. Rilla was just a baby. It was a difficult time for all of us. My mother worked two jobs just to skim by and I shared motherhood for my little sister. We were a needy family but proud. The week after I graduated from high school, I found a job. The extra income made life much easier. We were able to purchase the occasional incidentals.

After Rilla started high school, our mother learned she had breast cancer. It had metastasized rapidly. Six months later, Rilla and I were alone. I did my best to earn a living, keep track of Rilla, and advise her against drugs.

She confessed her addiction and told me about Warren Brantley. The man was evil and used her as a sex slave. Can you imagine it? An innocent, sixteen year old, a sex slave to this monster.

I talked my baby sister into entering rehab at Lady of Angels. I told Warren Brantley to leave my sister alone. He laughed at me and denied everything. A month after Rilla left rehab she died of a drug overdose. The police found her in an alley. I'm certain he put her there."

I was in a state of shock and certainly unprepared to hear about the other side of a person I thought I knew. Thinking back, people may have sensed something antithetical regarding his workplace demeanor but it completely escaped me. I guess we never really know about other human beings. We just assume they are something like ourselves. When in fact, they aren't like us at all. Each of us is unique in our way and very much dissimilar to our neighbor. Warren Brantley was a competent accountant; however, at the end of the day, when he walked down the factory steps became Doctor Jekyll and Mister Hyde.

"You must believe me when I say I had no idea Warren Brantley was such a person. Had I known, I wouldn't have tolerated him for a second," I stated with conviction.

"I find it hard to believe he could fool you for so long a time but you seem like an honest man and I'll take you at your word," Sharon said tersely.

"It's getting dark outside and neither of us has had supper. Do you like Chinese food? I can order carry out."

"Thank you, Mr. Baker, but I've made other dinner plans," she lied.

"Then let me come back. I feel there's a lot more to be said and our conversations may help to ease the bitter memory of what transpired," I was hopeful she would agree.

"Please call me first so I can be more presentable."

"That's a promise and I'll bring Chinese food."

"I'd rather have a pizza," she replied with a smile.

Isolation, for whatever reason, is a prejudicial state of loneliness. It's a supine scrounger depriving you of value and self-esteem. I left the Lezotte residence harboring a feeling of unfulfillment and displeasure. Something told me there was a great deal more to be learned from Sharon Lezotte and the darkness surrounding Warren Brantley. The thought of further enlightenment excited me to the point of elevating my heart rate. It also stimulated my kidneys. Pushing down on the car's accelerator and heading home post-haste can only relieve that particular urge.

For the remainder of April and first part of May, world events laid claim to most of my interest. The boys at Cliff's breakfast club made it the topic of the day. Each morning we gave praises to the 'Great Communicator' and knew that some despot was getting the message, no pun intended. Currently, President Reagan was exchanging convictions with Muammar Gaddafi, the controversial leader of Libya, a sponsor of terrorism. Dislike for Gaddafi dated back to the beginning of Reagan's administration. He declared Gaddafi an international pariah and wrongly believed he led a puppet regime of the Soviets— most likely due to his commercial relationship and frequent visits to Moscow. Russians, on the other hand, viewed Gaddafi as an unpredictable extremist and acted accordingly.

As reciprocity for terrorist attacks on U.S. interests and the bombing of *La Belle* nightclub in West Berlin, President Reagan launched *El Dorado Canyon*—a coordinated air attack within mainland Libya. The targets were five terrorist training locations including the Tripoli airport. In twelve minutes the assault dropped

60 tons of munitions and so swift that Libyan anti-aircraft fire did not begin until American planes had passed over their targets.

Unfortunately, a Libyan surface-to-air-missile did strike a U.S. F-111 jet over the Gulf of Sidra and some bombs landed off target striking diplomatic and civilian sites in Tripoli narrowly missing the French Embassy. Being forewarned by an Italian Socialist Party representative, Gaddafi was able to escape.

Later, using the collateral damage against President Reagan, Gaddafi claimed Libya had won a spectacular military victory over the United States and labeled Reagan as a mad man and Israeli dog.

The raid itself demonstrated the tactical ability of U.S. forces. The United States was denied over flight rights by France, Spain, and Italy as well as other continental bases. American planes were forced to fly around France and Spain, adding an additional 1,300 miles each way, requiring multiple mid-airs refueling. That aspect went without a hitch and served as a lesson to our enemies they can be reached anywhere on the globe.

"Looks like old Dutch taught Gaddafi a lesson or two. He won't be messing around with our interests real soon," barked Bill Schneider.

"I'm not so sure about that," John Coffel countered. "There are a lot of terrorist dictators in north Africa with similar hatreds."

"Why do they feel as they do? The only reason we're in the Middle East is to help," Marshall Bloom rationalized.

"We call it help except they view it as intervention. Some of them think of America as imperialistic and forcing our beliefs on their culture," John Coffel answered.

"Specifically because they're still living back in the Stone Age," stated the Cadillac dealer's accountant. "I read somewhere their religion lets them stone women to death and behead unbelievers."

"Most of them act differently. I've got a Muslim neighbor, living in our subdivision, who has a fine family. Their kids attend the same high school as my son. She belongs to the PTA and he's a doctor," Coffel asserted. "What are your feelings on the matter, Steven?"

I hoped they wouldn't bring me in on the subject. Foreign affairs are not exactly my long suit. For fear of sounding foolish, I took a minute to organize my thoughts, as they were. Finishing the last bite of eggs over easy and swallowing the remains of the second cup of coffee, I finally expressed, "Ever since World War II our greatest concern has been the Soviet Union and the spread of Communism. Mikhail Gorbachev appears to be taking his country on a different path. He and President Reagan are working to end the Cold War and, if they are successful, it means a brighter future for us all. Other Middle East nations sort of take a back seat along with the way they actually feel about the United States. I believe we will need to restudy and shift out foreign policies toward the Islamic countries. We should listen to their concerns instead of blindly advancing our own. I love my country right or wrong but terrorism could become a serious issue if we remain complacent."

"Bullshit, we have the bomb. Terrorists like Gaddafi run the risk of being blown off the map," Bill Schneider blurted.

"Do you really think the United States would drop the atomic bomb again?" questioned John Coffel, wistfully.

Seeing where this was going, I waved my check aloft and called out to Cliff's waitress. It was a good time to head west to the factory.

CHAPTER TWELVE

O VER THE PAST FEW DAYS, I made several attempts to reach
Sharon Lezotte. Each time her answering machine took a
message. I was tempted to drive by her house only to learn
from Jane O'Connor she was now working as a cashier at Kroger's.
Later, on my way home, I stopped by the grocery and found the lady
in question operating the cash register. When I placed a loaf of bread
and a gallon of milk on the conveyor she looked up and greeted me
with a smile.

"I've been trying to reach you by phone," I stated.

"I know. I got your messages."

"Why didn't you return my calls?"

"I tried but, when Jane O'Connor answered, I hung up. I guess
I was just too frightened to ask for you. Embarrassed, she would
recognize my voice," Sharon explained.

"You're forgiven even though I had to eat three large pizzas all by
myself," I jested. "When can we have another talk?"

"Tomorrow is my day off. How about then? And you won't need to
bring anything. I'll fix supper," she asserted.

"Expect me at six o'clock," paying for my groceries and grabbing
the plastic bag.

The following day found me standing on her porch at the allotted
time. I took the liberty of picking up a bottle of red wine. The clerk at

the liquor store suggested a Grenache for the occasion. Being strictly a beer drinker, I needed all the help I could get. Yes, I call myself a beer drinker especially with a sandwich—and, as you already know, two bottles is my limit.

When the door opened, I was shocked again. Standing in front of me was a woman unlike the poor creature who greeted me a few weeks ago. Today, she glistened with loveliness. Lost for words, I stuttered, "I must be at the wrong address."

"You better not be after I worked my butt off making supper," she replied, with a fetching grin.

Walking into her front living room was like falling into the proverbial 'Rabbit Hole'. This surely wasn't Kansas anymore. Everything was fresh and lemony clean and her personal essence broadcast a hint of cologne, different from any I could recall, nevertheless quite intoxicating.

"I brought a bottle of wine. I'm not a connoisseur but the label says it is strawberry flavor."

"You needn't have. I purchased one myself. Looks like we may have a booze bash," she said mischievously. "Though, if we take our time, we probably can finish the hooch without getting into too much trouble."

Leading me to a comfortable chair she commented, "We'll just have to see about that," and retired to her kitchen. From there, with an elevated voice, told me the meal was being placed on the table and she will call me when it's time to come in. Shortly, the illumination in her kitchen began to dim.

"You can come in now," she called.

It was obvious Sharon had gone all out. The kitchen table was covered with a white cloth and two candles provided what light we would have during the meal.

"I hope you like meatloaf. It's a dish I'm most familiar with and Rilla's favorite," hopefully stated.

Taking the obligatory bite, I assured her it was delicious. Next, twisting the corkscrew into the stopper of my contribution, I managed to remove the plug with a Lawrence Welk pop, bringing a smile to my hostess' lips. The radiation from the candle flames gave a pleasant highlight to her image and I offered a toast to her efforts and the meal.

Only small talk passed between us without any serious discussion of Rilla and Warren Brantley. That will come later.

Dessert consisted of ramekins filled with vanilla pudding, which she removed from her refrigerator to serve. The cold custard soothed my throat going down, fitting for conclusion of a very agreeable dinner. Pouring the last of the wine, she retrieved her bottle saying, "Looks like we will need two bottles."

Her carafe had a screw on cap and easily opened with a twist. I offered to help with the dishes. She acquiesced only if we had another glass of wine to aid digestion. I was directed to remain seated while she stacked the dishes and returned to the table for another toast to her successful repast. The effects of the first bottle had stopped up my nose, making breathing require help from an open mouth. Prospects of a second bottle offered a dire outlook but, if she could do it, I'll give it my best shot. Thus far, the only influence on her is a flushed face and red tip of her nose, however, there's still another bottle to consume.

Holding the wine bottle by its neck she led me to her living room and placed it on the floor by the sofa. I sat. She flopped. The manner in which Sharon landed made her giggle. Reaching for the bottle she voiced, "Give me your glass so I can pour us another. I don't seem to be affected from the one you brought. It must not have high alcohol content." With our glasses filled to the brim, she lay back and closed her eyes.

"So you want to ruin a perfectly good dinner and talk about Warren Brantley," she lamented.

"If talking about Brantley disturbs you that much, we could wait for another time," wondering when she is going to open her eyes. As soon as they unlocked, she looked around for the wineglass and finding it in her hand, finished it off. Then, kicking loose her shoes, curled up on the couch and laid her head against my chest.

"Let's not talk about him tonight. I can't explain my emotions at the moment but perhaps you can. It's been two years since I've felt this way with a man. The wine has made me too dizzy to stand. You'll have to carry me to the bedroom," she suggestively whispered.

I awakened the next morning with Sharon resting her head on her hand and leaning on her elbow. "Did you sleep well last night?" she asked.

"I was out like a light. It must have been the wine."

"If you say so," she beamed.

"Well, naturally, that, as well. How about you?"

"Since I can't remember when," she confirmed. "Sleep as long as you want. I've got to be at work by eight," she declared, while rousing in her nakedness and reaching for a robe.

With the sound of water running in the bathtub I tried to gather my thoughts. What happened last night certainly changes my relationship with this woman. Glancing at my watch let me know it was seven a.m. and there's no way I can go anywhere smelling of lovemaking. "When you finish, would you please run a tub for me?"

A short time later she stood unclothed drying her hair with a bath towel. "Bath water is running. I put in some bubble crystals so you'll smell real good for the office girls," singing out on her way to the closet. "Steven, I don't want you to feel obligated because of what happened last night. It may never happen again but, if it does, there's no strings attached."

I was still amazed by the transformation from an old harridan to this beautiful seductive young woman. Her life, under different circumstances, would have known no bounds. Like so many before her, victims of fate and, in her case, the addition of Warren Brantley.

Arriving at the office with a day's growth of beard caught the attention of Jane O'Connor and the other girls. They seemed to believe my story of an all-night poker game at the country tavern located near the plant. Such things are routine when retired farmers get together. Whether or not Elaine buys it is somewhat doubtful but, that's my story and I'm sticking to it.

CHAPTER THIRTEEN

IT'S BEEN SAID, ALL THINGS seem possible in the month of May. Showers and flowers tend to support such a claim. Unfortunately, the news reported on May first by Tass, the Russian news agency, put a damper on the initial sweet spring morning. A mishap had occurred at their Chernobyl nuclear power plant in Ukraine. (It actually took place on April 26.) The accident turned out to be the worst nuclear power plant disaster in history. As a result of the explosion and fire, large quantities of radioactive particles were released into the atmosphere. The plume of radioactive fallout drifted over the western Soviet Union and Europe with Russia, Belarus, and Ukraine most severely contaminated. Directly attributed to the accident was the death of over thirty workers, which included staff and emergency personnel. The eventual death toll from exposure to cancer causing radiation varies by a wide margin among scientists. It will take years before accurate conclusions can be made. One thing is known. Millions of people will be facing increased levels of radiation and its cancer causing effects are real.

The tables at Cliff's have required rearranging to accommodate new attendees to the regular morning breakfast group. Harry Cook and John Coffel were awarded higher standing and distinction due to their medical background. Although a dentist and veterinarian, they are still assumed to have superior knowledge when it came to radioactive fallout. As such, they became the recipients of most questions concerning how much longer we all could expect to enjoy life. As expected, Bill Schneider was the most vocal and solicited the opinion of John Coffel, a veterinarian. John qualified his opinion by stating, "First of all, I know no more than the rest of you guys about the accident. The newspapers and television accounts are pretty sketchy. And, no doubt, the Russians will cover up the truth about this catastrophe. From what I understand, the real danger occurs nearest the source. Without question those at the nuclear generating station are seriously affected. They received the highest dose of radiation and from what we've read many have already died. The cities closest to the disaster area will, in all likelihood, need to be completely evacuated. Nevertheless, they face the continuing effects of exposure to radioactive contamination, as do billions worldwide, when airborne poisonous particles are carried by the winds."

"Yeah, but what about us here in America?" Schneider blurted.

"We will be affected," Coffel replied. "As in Europe, the effect will be lessened by the mountain ranges. The elevated peaks will filter a high percentage of poisonous clouds. Again, there will be increased radioactivity here in America, both north and south."

"How bad will it get?" several voices sounded in unison.

"From what we know right now, it won't be too bad. You do realize we all have been exposed to some radiation—such as medical treatment and x-rays, plus others which occur naturally. The amounts are small and its affects measured in years of continuous exposure. Scientists are projecting the increase caused by the Russian nuclear disaster will add two or three years of exposure at most and will cause no measurable harm; but, they will be monitoring cancer cases just to be sure."

"How long will that take?" Schneider queried.

"Meaningful results will come from monitoring children, taking 20 or 30 years. Old rascals like us won't live long enough to provide meaningful data," John snickered, as he sipped his coffee.

By this time Bill Schneider's embarrassment can be recognized by his crimson face. He apparently had conditioned himself for more dire news. Pausing for a minute or two he shouted, "You can't trust those Ruskies. What we ought to do is nuke them and get it over with."

"That would call for a recalculation of our own radiation numbers," Coffel chided. "Increased radiation associated with a nuclear war could very well mark the end of humanity."

With the majority, less one, in agreement, the breakfast meeting concluded and those newcomers, having arrived in deep concern, went on their way with a lighter step.

Later in the month another tragic accident commanded newspaper headlines. This time it was a maritime disaster in Bangladesh. A double deck river ferry, named *Shamia*, capsized during a storm with over 1,000 passengers aboard. The vessel was navigating the Meghna River, one of the most dangerous waterways in Bangladesh and cause of many deaths every year. Nearly 600 perished.

Whenever we think of maritime disasters, the *RMS Titanic* is brought to mind. With over 1,517 fatalities, it is the most famous shipwreck; however; considering loss of life, not the biggest. That record goes to the *Wilhelm Gustloff*, a German passenger ship, sunk by a Soviet submarine in World War II. It is estimated over 9,400 passengers were killed.

The rest of the summer months rolled by like a tuft of weeds in a shallow stream. Stopped at times, when hindered by a stone, then, breaking loose to pass at a quicker pace. You know the end of blissful nights is drawing to a close. Not so much as the cicadas singing their lullaby from the tree tops but from their molted shell left behind and clinging to its trunk. The hours of daylight are becoming noticeably shorter and summers conclusion confirmed by mail in a letter containing registration for the annual convention in October.

Maintaining my relationship with Irene Jones, Coralee Smallwood, Sharon Lezotte, and Elaine required exceptional juggling ability. Bobby May would have been proud of me. I must confess there are times when I need to make coded notes on my desk calendar. At the moment I feel land locked, unable to escape this situation of my own making. Things cannot remain as they are indefinitely. I've done some soul searching, regarding my state of affairs, and reached the conclusion that when it comes to virtue, some will agree with me. Put to the test they would react the same way. What is morality anyway? Immanuel Kant, the German philosopher, ascribes a theory that no person or group of persons determines what moral law requires of you. It's not religion or church but, human reason which chiefly determines ethical imperatives. The biblical commanding of trading eyes and teeth rarely guides us in real life. When it comes to sexual ethics, Kant expresses the view that humans should never be used merely as a means to an end.

That brings into focus the principles of conscience and imperatives as determined by the faculty of personal will and consent. I'm a firm believer in articulating a certain age for consent—those too young lack the wisdom to offer agreement. The women, currently in my life, have freely volunteered approval. Without knowledge of each other, our action causes no harm. Wasn't it Solomon who had 700 wives? Even Islam allows up to four wives and, in some cases, an unlimited amount. I guess what bothers me most, when taking time to think of it, is moral obligation derived from the concept of duty—both perfect and imperfect— and the claims reason places upon them.

I've made an inward diagnosis and determined my affair with Irene is an arrangement, Sharon a condition, and Coralee an aspiration. Though none of this is broached with Elaine, she knows without a word being spoken. No matter how confident a man is withholding his secrets, he's only fooling himself if he believes his wife doesn't know—especially true after several years of marriage. During reflective moments I'm sure Elaine both knows and endures. She too bides her time. She loves me as a woman loves her husband and suffers in silence. Ironically, becoming an accomplice— by guarding my secrets from the rest of the world in hopes I will 'mature' enough to overcome my 'moral' frailty. We play the game and share in the guilt.

CHAPTER FOURTEEN

THE ANNUAL BATTERY CONVENTION PRESENTED a justification to break the constant routine and spend a few days with colleagues and competitors. It also allowed Irene and me to be together in public. Still, not a time for complete relaxation since each night we secretly shared the same bed while over 500 members and convention goers roamed the halls. Nevertheless, Irene arranged for at least one private dinner—a time in which our future will be discussed. At the moment, not my favorite topic of conversation.

The restaurant of her choosing was a quaint romantic eatery and a fifteen-minute cab ride from the Drake hotel, this year's convention headquarters. When staying downtown, it would be considered out-of-the-way and, obviously, why it was selected. Irene wanted a direct and immediate commitment from me.

Inside, the restaurant had scant lighting and took time for my eyes to adjust. From what I could make out, mostly couples occupied tables. Indistinct, due to the lighting, they appeared to be young, a lot younger than us. When Irene announced, "Reservations for Jones," the hostess gave that look and condescending smile, grabbed two menus, and replied, "Follow me." She led us to the second level, protected by an ornate iron railing, and a lonely table at the end. Once we were seated, she made eye contact with me and said calmly, "Your waitress will be with you shortly." I felt like Jack the Ripper.

"How did you ever find this place?"

"Why, don't you like it?" Irene chimed. After a short uncomfortable pause, she continued, "Well, if you must know, I asked the girl at the front desk if she knew of a place away from prying eyes. She suggested this one."

"Did you ask her if they served good food?"

"To be honest, I didn't care that much," Irene replied. "I mainly wanted a place where we can have a serious discussion."

The prisoner received a temporary reprieve when our waitress mounted the steps and brought the water. "I apologize for taking so long. I didn't see you at first. Would you care for a before dinner drink?"

"Oh yes. Maybe more than one," I declared. "Make mine a double Scotch and water and a daiquiri for the lady."

Irene retained her smile long after the waitress descended the stairs. She sat with her elbow on the table and the back of her fingers against her chin and said, "My God, how I do love you."

"And I love you darling,"

"But not enough," she protested. "If you loved me half as much as I love you, we would be together by now."

"You need to be patient a little longer. My home life is coming together to the point in which I'll be able to leave."

Irene's resolve began to weaken. After hours of preparation for this very moment it all seems to be for naught. Her dreams and wishes will be fulfilled soon or at least in a few weeks. She reached across the table and took my hand. "Don't wait too long. I'm tired of being alone. Remember, if you let me go, you'll lose someone who loves you very much."

"Don't worry sweetheart, I'll never let you go," I said sincerely. "And, it won't be much longer." At that point the waitress returned with the drinks.

Irene appeared to be satisfied with my declaration, at least for the time being. Whether or not it pacifies her mother remains to be seen. Irene's widow mother, Thelma Jones, is a very devout churchgoer. Though she has accepted me, she hasn't accepted the situation with her daughter. Daily contact makes her the most influential dominator in Irene's daily life. Her affectionate persuasion is equal to mine and, if she ever completely holds sway, I'll be faced with a moment of truth. It would be prudent for me to bring Thelma a gift the next time I visit.

During the first part of November, President Reagan signed into law the Immigration Reform and Control Act, IRCA. The Act criminalizes employers. Outside of granting amnesty to four million illegal immigrants, living here before 1982, it placed the onus on employers to attest for employee's legal immigration status from that point forward. Once again our government has put the heat and cost on legitimate business. Most of which do not hire illegal aliens. Nevertheless, keeping with our government's insatiable appetite for paperwork, employers must maintain records indicating immigration status and complete the Federal Form 1-9 to ensure that all employees have proof of their eligibility for employment. Failure to comply means a levy of heavy fines per employee whose personnel records do not exhibit the completed form. Even if the employee is legally authorized to work in the United States, the Federal Form must be filled out and maintained in his or her personnel folder.

I met with all employees and explained the new law plus the requirement imposed on the company. After which, Jane O'Connor and the other office girls reviewed all personnel folders and arranged meetings with over 100 workers to fill out the 1-9 forms.

Outside of hardship on legitimate businesses, the IRCA Act will do little to stem illegal immigration. Most, but not all, illegal immigrants come from Mexico. Aliens from El Salvador, Cuba, and the Dominican Republic also seek the United States for jobs mainly requiring hard labor. Raised in a culture where *"If a man has two good hands, he can find work and provide for his family"* the United States with its porous borders offers such jobs.

Faced with stiff fines, amounting to thousands of dollars, I hesitated to hire anyone who looked foreign. Accordingly, for fear of discrimination lawsuits, hiring practices were changed. Because of the IRCA, hiring was conducted through the County Employment services. They supposedly screened potential candidates and complied with the new law. The result was a great many sub-par workers, no Hispanics, nevertheless, compliance with the IRCA.

Ironically, the Act allowed for less stringent requirements on subcontractors, especially in the building and agricultural industries, and, with higher paid employment boxed out, aliens were forced to take lesser paying jobs. To no one's surprise that is exactly what happened as illegal immigration continued, and, if that's possible, at an even higher rate.

The year ended with reports of President Reagan offering to assist Haitian president, Jean-Claude Duvalier's departure into exile. "Baby Doc" previously earned admiration because of a strong anticommunist stance, but, after years of squandering Haitian resources, the country was in turmoil and revolution. Reagan refused asylum here in the United States, however, used U.S. aircraft to fly him to France.

CHAPTER FIFTEEN

WITH THE HOLIDAYS OVER AND well into 1987 we witnessed a return to the daily routine of manufacturing lead-acid batteries. There were two significant changes to my personal animation. The intensity of the relationship with Irene has slackened somewhat. In fact, we haven't talked by phone for nearly three weeks. We're either testing the other's heart by absence, hoping it will grow fonder, or, without each other nurturing, letting it die of its own accord. The consequence of this current void has been taken up by Sharon Lezotte. Without the foggy screen of another woman, I've begun to see how beautiful she is in both makeup and manner. Albeit, when together, there are times I sense a mysterious notion about her. Not so with Irene. Irene is perfectly honest and holds nothing back. She lays it all out, thus, making herself unnecessarily fragile. Perhaps it's the main reason I'm drawn to her. Nevertheless, a woman's honesty can often be used against her. Maybe, subconsciously, I'm actually acting as her protector.

The February wind ignored my winter coat as I mounted Sharon's front steps. She opened the door encouraging me to hurry inside where it was warmer. Handing her my topcoat I asked, "Who shoveled your sidewalk?"

"Oh, a friend. Why do you ask?"

"I don't know, just jealous, I guess. You have every right to date and go out without concern over who you're with," answering while pulling off my scarf.

"Look. There are a lot of weirdoes out there. Since we met I've only dated a couple times. They can swing on my gate but not play in my back yard. You're the only one who can do that. Right now I'm perfectly satisfied the way things are."

Pleased with what she said, I halfheartedly stated, "Naturally, I'm flattered but don't you want someone more permanent?"

To that she didn't answer. Instead, taking my hand, Sharon led me directly to her kitchen. Dinner gave off a sweet-smelling aroma from the preset table, "Let's eat while it's still hot."

During the meal it appeared as though Sharon found it difficult to maintain eye contact. She was definitely troubled by something. My conversation centered on meaningless topics designed to relax her and induce a confession of whatever was being withheld. It failed.

The meal, as always, was excellent. This lady sure can cook. That said, I couldn't shake the fidgety feeling she dispensed. Assuming it will soon be revealed, I poured the remainder of our wine and settled in for the long haul.

Surprisingly, she allowed me to clear the table. I stacked the dishes and brought them to the sink. At that point, Sharon poured me a cup of hot coffee and said, "This won't take me long. Go into the front room and read the paper. I want to take a bath before we do anything friendly."

The Kirksville News rested unopened atop the recliner positioned near the reading lamp. A cursory glance was all I needed before searching for the page with a crossword puzzle. It turned out to be a poser, slowing my pace. Not being up on the latest movies, Sharon was standing before me when I filled in the last few spaces. She sat on the edge of the sofa and beckoned for me to come over. Before the cushions got warm, we were both in bed.

Several weeks of practice have educated us in the art of pleasuring each other. After which, we lay on our backs facing the shadows on the ceiling and me gently stroking the fine hair above her pudendum. Normally a tranquil moment, but, for Sharon, tonight, it is one of lingering tenseness. Gone was the mystic state of vacant listlessness.

"I need a drink," she stated and threw back the sheets, left the room, returning with two glasses and a bottle of vodka. The alcohol made her glib, "I want to talk about Warren Brantley."

At this point, once her mind is set, it would be like arguing with the east to detain the dawn. The psychological trauma caused by a shocking ordeal, such as, losing her sister to an excessive drug overdose, can leave a plethora of bad memories lurking in her subconscious. Warren Brantley, the apparent cause of Rilla's demise, evokes memories too difficult for Sharon to erase.

I've always believed improving your overall health can lessen bad memories. In this area Sharon has made immense progress from the first day we met. The ugly shell of depression has been gone for several weeks. Nevertheless, she seems to have fallen into troubled waters and my preaching for her to *look on the bright side* apparently won't help her tonight.

Splashing two glasses half full with the smooth alcoholic brew, Sharon took a healthy swallow and said, "I feel better already." Having no desire to keep apace, I sipped a small portion, and then noticed the dish of peeled cucumber spears resting on the bed between us. What is it about women, vodka, and cucumbers? I guess a sweet, crisp, cool cucumber spear makes it more of a cocktail than just plain hooch. Watching her pour herself another two fingers of vodka, I was conscious, if she continued drinking, I would soon have a very sick girl on my hands. When she gave me the nod of a tilted bottle, I refused and asked, "Why do you want to talk about Warren Brantley? He can never harm another innocent child. In a way, I sort of blame myself for not recognizing what a ghoul he was."

"Don't blame yourself. He fooled everybody. Steven, what would you have done if you learned he had seduced your daughter with drugs and used her as his sex slave?"

Without hesitation, I replied, "I would have shot him."

"Well, that's exactly what I did," she uttered frankly.

At first, I was too shocked for her comment to register. Outside of our heartbeats, there was silence. We lay starring at each other in inscrutable anticipation of the other's thoughts. Thereafter, my emotions scattered like a rabbit chased by hounds. I'm having a liaison with a confessed murderess—abetting a major crime. Needing time to think, I gulped the contents of my glass and extended an arm for a refill. Something my father once told me popped into my head—*you never get to really know somebody until there's just two inches left in a whiskey bottle. Then, you only learn his side of it.*

Sharon's cheeks glistened from her tears. She was bordering on a complete psychological breakdown. For the sanity of both of us, I needed her to keep talking, "Tell me the whole story. Where did you get the gun?"

"The gun belonged to my mother. She kept it in a box down in our basement. I have no idea how she came by it. It was a very long time ago."

"That might be a good thing. Being so old it likely didn't get registered," surmising, slightly above a whisper.

She continued, "My hatred drove me to avenge my little sister. He told me, in no uncertain terms, that Rilla was a junkie and if he didn't sell her drugs, she would have found someone else. I made contact with the monster's bloodshot eyes, drew the pistol, and fired twice. That was when I noticed his gym bag on the back seat. I can't explain why, but I grabbed it and hurried home."

"Where is the gym bag now?"

"I hid it in the basement along with the revolver."

"Did you look inside the satchel?"

"Yes. I think it contains drugs but it looks strange." After a short pause, she continued, "I'm at my wits end. Do you think I should confess to the police?"

"I'm not sure," I honestly replied. (To do so will ultimately involve our relationship and me. Bad publicity will put an end to my contract with England.) "Let's not go ape over this. We'll need time to figure things out. Keep in mind Warren Brantley deserves to be dead. You did the world a big favor by killing him. I'm the only other person who knows your secret. Let's keep it that way. Right now, show me where you put the satchel."

Sharon retrieved my glass and put it with hers and the bottle on a side table. Extending her hand she led me to the cellar steps.

The basement was illuminated by two bare light bulbs hanging from rafters. At the far end, the cement wall ended where the front porch began. From behind a stack of used lumber she withdrew the dusty gym bag, saying, "Let me wipe it off. It's been several weeks since I've looked inside."

Beneath the workout clothes lay the gun, and, under it, wrapped with brown paper, were several rectangular shaped parcels appearing to be compact. The content was white and rock solid. No doubt it is unadulterated cocaine. The complete cache weighed over 25 pounds. As pure as it appears, no middleman had previously cut it with a substance to make even more profit. A twenty thousand-dollar investment in Mexico or Columbia will bring $340,000 from the streets of Chicago—even more away from the city.

"Put the bag back for the time being, and let me figure how we can give it to the police without implicating either of us. The gun poses a different problem. It's got to be disposed of where it can never be found."

Returning from the somber cellar, Sharon had brightened appreciably. Sharing a deep dark secret can give relief. She wanted to tell Steven sooner but was unsure how he would react. Finally, when positive of his devotion and with the help of Smirnoff, she took the chance.

Back in the living room, Sharon refilled their goblets and offered a toast to better days. The manic change from deep depression to cheerful exuberance was astounding. Free from the confine of anguish and despair she suggested they return to the bedroom. Unsure if he was up to another bout of lovemaking, Steven still clasped her outreached hand and allowed himself to follow.

The only sounds in the room were from the clock on the wall. While its hands marked itself forward, the lovers exhausted their desire and now sat with backs touching pillows resting flat against the headboard. Neither spoke as their heart rhythm gradually slowed to normal. It would require a psychic spiritualist to read Sharon's thoughts; however, Steven had developed a concern about the uncorked bottle and the looseness of tongue thereafter. The problem they confronted must be resolved post haste.

The following day, I immersed myself in work in order to remove Sharon from the forethought of my mind. It didn't work. A greater portion of effort went to figure how best to give Warren Brantley's gym bag to the police anonymously. My life had become a cheap paperback detective thriller. I would never admit it, but it gave me a bit of a thrill. I guess you never get too old for a little undercover work, the intriguing part of being a plainclothes shamus.

A state park is positioned north of Kirksville. It's very popular with the community, especially the young. I make it a point to have a picnic, with the family, a couple times each year. It's well attended during the summer months but not so much in cold weather. Winding through a wooded area is a creek, strewn with rocks, and a few deep holes popular with fishermen. While I've never heard of any really large fish being caught, the shoreline is usually dotted with remains of campfires—left by those who spent the night. A two-lane bridge crosses over it at the edge of the grounds. The underside of the overpass could be a good place to stash Brantley's bag. With the temperature as cold as it is, the park should be deserted, especially at dawn. Sharon and I will give it a try tomorrow morning. I'll give her a call after she gets off work.

At five o'clock in the morning nothing was stirring. The eerie quiet was only disturbed by the sound from my tires pulling into Sharon's driveway. It was clear and crisp with objects only illuminated by naked moonlight. My vision of trust had her waiting in darkness by the front window. I flashed my headlights only once before recognizing her dark silhouette descending the front steps. She was holding Brantley's satchel.

The quiet drive to the State park only added to the machination. Consumed by the intrigue, neither of us spoke. A trickle of perspiration ran down my neck making me realize there was no further need for the car heater. Turning it down to low, while observing straight ahead, Sharon broke the ice saying, "Thank you."

"We needed it earlier but definitely not now."

This time of morning—no traffic on the road—took us under twenty minutes to reach the State forest grounds. Driving pass the main entrance, a chain conspicuously spanned the pathway. The park won't open until much later. My destination was the bridge, therefore,

I continued forward, whereupon it came into view. With my foot off the accelerator, the car coasted until finding an opening allowing me to pull over onto the roadside grass. Everything outside was still dead quiet—no headlights either up or down the main road. Grasping the handles of Brantley's gym bag, I stepped out of the car and navigated with only the aid of moonlight until reaching the bridge. Swift moving water made gurgling sounds as it cascaded around and over the rocks below. With a firm grip on the satchel, I swung a leg over the low hung wire fence—bent down by fishermen using that pathway to reach the water. My free hand held a flashlight, not to be turned on until safely under the bridge. Anytime sooner could draw too much attention should the stream be occupied.

My heart stopped when I noticed movement in the middle of the creek bed. Tree shadows further limited my vision. Scaling down the incline gave me a better angle and, to my surprise and relief, stood an antlered deer. The stag raised his regal head and whistled a high-pitched alarm, yet, didn't move. He brazenly held his ground. Its presence was a very good omen. He wouldn't be there if anyone were about.

I began slowly walking up stream to the bridge. Once under the overpass, I used the flashlight and immediately found a secure shelf near the point the bridge began its span over the water. After securing Brantley's gym bag, I shut off the flashlight and retraced my steps. The deer was gone. Ascending the grassy slope was more difficult than descending; nevertheless, after slipping twice to my knees, I found my way back to the car. Closing the door and giving out with a deep exhale, I stated, "Mission accomplished."

Having no idea as to how long it took, I was thankful to have it completed and with no automobile passing during the interim. The ride back was quite pleasant. Sharon curled next to me, put her head on my shoulder, and whispered, "Do you want to go back to bed?"

That was the furthest thing from my mind, "We better cool it for a while. I still have to figure how to let the police know where the bag is." Disappointed, she acquiesced.

"You can at least stop long enough for me to dry your pants. Your knees are sopping wet," she stated.

That I did.

CHAPTER SIXTEEN

"**M**R. BAKER, YOU HAVE A call on line two. She didn't give me her name but I believe it is Irene Jones from Spartan Chemicals."

It was odd hearing her company called by that name, even though I knew the sale was imminent. The owner wanted to retire in Arizona and cashed out by selling to his employees—and the bank. Placing the receiver to my ear I asked, "How have you been?"

Irene answered by saying, "It's good to hear your voice."

"I guess it's been a while."

"A while? That's putting it mildly," she replied. "If you think your absence will make me change my mind about us, you win. I won't pressure you anymore. I'll play it your way no matter how long it takes—if ever."

"Darling, that's not what's going on. I'm buried under tons of shit. I'm being hit from every different angle."

"When will I see you?" she asked emphatically.

I agreed to see her a week from this coming Saturday. More time was required to contemplate the way to enlighten the police of the location of Brantley's bag.

The minute I walked into the house, Irene's happiness was unquestionable. As for me, and, for the first time since meeting this exceptional beauty, I was counting the hours. A dark cloud of uneasiness seemed to blanket my thoughts, forcing me to live a lie while it skulked. There was no possible way Irene couldn't perceive it. I blamed it on England announcing a major change in direction and selling their battery manufacturing holdings around the world. Having just undergone a similar event—the sale of her own company—she empathized and understood.

In addition to sensual pleasure, another happening occurred during my visit. So simple I chided myself for not thinking of it sooner. While reading the *Indianapolis Star*, I took notice of the bold print heading each major story. I could cut and paste a letter together using newspaper print. I dismissed using the *Star* since it could be a possible clue. Instead, the *Chicago Tribune* will be substituted—with circulation in the millions, impossible to trace. Now, the only concern will be the postmark on the envelope. And then it dawned on me. I can address it using a computer in a South Side Chicago Library. Hell, for that matter, I could type the complete letter and envelope at a South Side Library—there are six million people in the surrounding area and nearly 80 libraries—it will be impossible to trace. No more of this cloak and dagger crap!

I drove back to Kirksville with an air of confidence. The French have a word for that—*sangfroid*—you don't say it like you spell it.

Kirksville police investigation commander Ronald Homberg dropped an opened envelope on Mike Monahan's desk. James "Bubba" Watson looked up, acknowledging his boss's presence and stood ready in case there was an assignment. Monahan wiped his hands with a paper napkin and blew the envelope open, retrieving its contents. After reading it, he turned the plain sachet over to check out the postmark. Doing so, he thought, *"Huh, Chicago postmark. Not much to go on there."* Replacing it in the envelope, he reached across the desk and handed it to his curious associate.

"Why don't you and detective Rice check this out," he said, as a recommendation rather than a question.

"Do you think it has merit?" asked Bubba.

"Who knows," Mike replied, shrugging his shoulders.

Under normal circumstances, Michael Monahan would have undertaken the task himself. However, his body was in a rest-and-digest mode. He previously had eaten a big breakfast. And, upon arriving at the station, was offered a jelly-filled sweet roll, his favorite. Enough blood sugar was created to release extra insulin increasing serotonin and melatonin to make him feel drowsy. He felt fortunate to be able to give the assignment to his juniors—James Watson and Lee Rice. (It makes one wonder about donuts, policemen, and a comfortable squad car.)

Bubba was elated. This type of duty, for the detective bureau, is seldom disliked especially when the weather is pleasant. It was one of those perfect spring days with cloudless skies and temperatures well in the seventies. An assignment involving the State Park was the frosting on the cake. He glided over to detective Rice's desk and said, "Come with me my man, we've been given a sweet assignment."

When the first opening occurred in the Investigation Department, Rice took the test. His grade swamped the other officers trying for the position. In a rare incident, intelligence trumped seniority and Rice was promoted.

They drove to the State Park with the windows down. The springtime air quickly cooled the car's interior, hot from sitting in the station's parking lot. Bubba had removed his suit coat before he got behind the wheel. Being the first time Rice was given assignment in the unmarked car, he deigned to follow Bubba's example and left his on. Now he wished he hadn't and lowered his window a little further.

"If we play this one right, we can take lunch on the taxpayers," Bubba stated, while looking straight ahead.

Concealing his frown, Lee remained silent. Bubba was quick to understand his partner's expression, thinking, *"After he spends a couple nights lying in a ditch half full of water, observing some criminals hideout, he'll think different about the taxpayer buying him a hamburger."*

"Are you still dating that girl working at the battery factory?" Lee asked, breaking the uncomfortable hush.

"You mean Callie Mellinger? As a matter of fact, I'm very serious about her—been checking out engagement rings."

"Wow, you are serious," Lee exclaimed. "Have you asked her yet?"

"No, not yet, but she's given me every indication she will say yes."

"I always thought a girl is hesitant to marry a policeman as opposed to a guy with a safer job," Lee said, seriously.

"Yeah, I've thought about that as well. But, I think Callie is okay with it. There's another woman working there as a secretary who is married to a state patrolman. She's very happy and a good example for Callie," Bubba stated with tepid confidence. "How long have you and Yvette been married?"

"We've been married two years. She still would rather me find a different kind of work," Lee confessed. "Yvette was born and raised in Chicago and the relationship with the police was confrontational. She grew up amidst some pretty tough incidents to make her feel this way."

"The only thing I know about the police in Chicago is what I read in the newspaper and watch on TV. Some of the big city neighborhoods can be very difficult to patrol. Many in the community view the police from a racial perspective, making it troubled all the way around," Bubba pondered.

"Yvette gets mad at me when I tell her all police are not racist. The majority is like brothers and depends on each other to protect our lives. There's less racism in a police department than anywhere else."

After a period of silence, Lee continued, "Yeah, it's different here in Kirksville. The population is more diverse. Where she lived before, it was nearly all black."

"Yvette always seems okay with me," Bubba stated.

"Like I say, she's a complicated woman. For some strange reason, she likes you," Lee joked.

"When you say there's less racism in a police department, you forget Haruki Fujimoto. He calls you a "fucking Jew bastard.""

"He calls everybody that."

"I guess you're right. It's probably the worse epithet he could think up. Personally, I think he suffers from the 'little man' complex."

"Don't tell him that or you'll have a five-foot tiger on your hands. One of these days he will be put to the test of having me ride with him—a black man and Japanese—we belong in California," Lee mused.

"You're black! I'm shocked. Nobody told me. How long have you been black? You people are so clever, working your way into the white community and not telling us."

"I must admit, I'm surprised you didn't know. I thought Fujimoto would have told you."

"No. He told me you were a "fucking Jew bastard" but never that you were black. I suppose Yvette is black as well."

"You're on to us."

"Does Commander Homberg know?"

"He might, being he's married to an African-American woman."

"That doesn't mean anything. He wouldn't know unless somebody told him."

"You mean eating chit'lins, fatback, and collards for breakfast the last ten years wouldn't give her away?"

"He wouldn't notice as long as she gave him lots of bananas," Bubba chortled.

Detective Rice had noticed the commander's appetite for bananas, religiously eating one for morning break and another at lunch. He found it amusing, but kept the attitude to himself.

"Any day now, I expect to see him swinging around the station from the rafters," stated Bubba.

Both detectives shared in the merriment with honest laughter until Bubba straightened himself behind the wheel and the State Park Bridge came into view. They drove past the main entrance and slowly proceeded to the bridge. Taking note of the bent wire fence, Bubba sensed it would be the easiest access to the bridge without raising too much curiosity. He backed the car a few feet and pulled off the road onto the opposite roadside grass, saying, "This appears to be a well-traveled path. Bring your flashlight and we'll have a look."

Bubba pushed down on the wire fence so Lee wouldn't catch and tear his trousers. Lee reciprocated once on the other side. They descended the embankment and, without knowing, found themselves at the exact spot Steven Baker stood a couple weeks earlier. Today, however, more traffic rumbled over the connection. Once beneath the overpass, Bubba reached for Lee's flashlight and shined its beam in the corner of the steel arch work.

"There's a bag or something pushed back of the ledge," Bubba said, as he reached and clasped its handle. Once retrieved, he read the ID tag, "It says, Warren Brantley."

"We gonna look inside?" Lee inquired.

"No, this is probably evidence and Homberg would be pissed if it was tampered with. Skip across those rocks and see if there's anything on the other side."

By now, a couple devoted fishermen took notice of their presence and strolled upstream. Bubba identified him and Lee and explained the mission, suggesting they not look under the bridge. And, at the same time began stretching yellow crime scene tape across the water entrance. Lee fastened the tape at his end before negotiating a rocky path leading to the primary side. With the gym bag safely in the trunk, Bubba said mockingly, "Those two guys will be under the bridge once we are out of sight."

A quick check of his watch indicated only forty-five minutes ahead of noon. Bubba eased up on the car's accelerator and began a leisurely return to town. The springtime sky was high overhead and only insignificant white puffs of clouds blocked the suns radiance. Satisfied with their expedition thus far, it was apparent the cities finest will take lunch before returning to the station. A community favorite was an eatery named Henry's Big Sandwich, known for tenderloin the size of an elephant's ear. Loaded with tomato, lettuce and onion, plus, a little mustard and ketchup, kept customers coming back—it was a meal by itself.

The entrance into town was guarded by rows of stately elm trees, planted by the WPA during the Great Depression. They now stood like silent sentinels watching over the safety of the road. And well they should since the main graveyard rests on the sharp curve entering town. Referred to as *cemetery curve*, it has recorded numerous serious accidents from either drivers unaware of its presence or those under the influence of alcohol—reflexes impaired by one-for-the-road at two-in-the-morning. The danger is well lighted and marked by traffic signs.

When the detectives pulled open Henry's door, they were greeted by those familiar smells of deep-fry and grill. Zigzagging past snatchers of conversation, rattling silverware, and dishes—they managed to find an empty table. It was yet to be cleared. Their waitress walked by, carrying an order and pausing long enough to say, "Just sit tight boys. I'll clean your table once I serve this." She managed to balance her tray on a hip and sweep the gratuity into her apron pocket with a free hand. Recognizing Bubba, Henry Santos, the owner, appeared from the kitchen, wiping his hands on his apron, and declared, "Jiggers the cops!" as he took the empty seat at their table.

"Homberg know you guys are footloose and unrestrained?" he quipped.

"No. We climbed out the back window," Bubba chirped with a smile. "Henry, I want you to meet Lee Rice. He's been a patrolman and now with the bureau."

Henry extended his hand and said, "I hope you realize that you're in bad company," nodding toward Bubba.

"I'm beginning to see that."

The detectives were sitting back, fingering the silverware, when the waitress delivered their sandwiches. Smiles of satisfaction sprouted on their faces as they moved the plates closer toward them to add the condiments.

"There's more meat outside the bun than under it. And, these are very large buns."

"Just wait 'til you taste it," replied Bubba, taking a big bite and squeezing a shot of mustard down the front of his suit coat. "Damn it. I just got my suit cleaned."

Rice was cutting his sandwich in half, making it easier to control. Corroborating the fact he had much better table manners— an oblique tribute to his upbringing and mother. Bubba's cleaning effort left small pieces of paper napkin on his lapels, appearing as snowflakes on a dark stain. Unfazed by the discoloration, his main concern was eating the delicious king-sized sandwich.

"I've changed my mind about eating lunch on the taxpayer," Rice grinned. "You'll have to show me how to expense it out."

"No problem partner. What we had today can be replenished out of the petty cash drawer—unless Homberg has already emptied it. He has a habit of doing that—probably to buy bananas."

The gym bag was laid on top of Monahan's desk, drawing the attention of everyone in the room. Bubba explained they only handled it by the handgrip and were careful not to open it. In order to conceal it from prying eyes, Monahan took hold of the handle and said, "Let's take this to the evidence room."

Placed upon the conference table, Monahan released the clasp and spread open Warren Brantley's satchel—it only contained hard blocks wrapped in brown paper. Although he had never personally seen such items, Monahan knew in an instant that it was nefarious and illegal. Further examination proved it to be cake cocaine.

In the subsequent meeting with Commander Homberg many questions were brought to bear. Why was it delivered to the police? Such an act would not have come about from any drug dealers. What is the connection of the bags original discoverer? Was he or they an enemy of Brantley? And, did he or they murder him?

"Mike, someone obviously wanted the drugs returned to the police. Now the FBI will be on the case but they will be up against a brick wall. We've made the only investigation without a true knowledge of any motive. You need to reopen your investigation and look for someone with a reason to murder him. Someone concealing a personal hatred, a girlfriend or jealous husband," Homberg directed. "I'm assigning Lee Rice to your team. He's a sharp fellow and trained at the academy." With that said the commander stood up and left the room. The remaining detectives were left silently pondering their re-assignment until Mike Monahan broke the ice, "We know Brantley was up to his neck in drugs. In all likelihood the killer shot him and took the satchel. Later, having second thoughts, decided to return it to the police. Which doesn't explain why he took it in the first place. Perhaps he thought there was incriminating evidence inside. After removing it, he felt safe in its return. Anybody got some suggestions?"

Detective Rice, hesitant in being the first to respond, waited until he was sure Bubba had nothing to offer and said, "It appears drugs are at the center of this crime. He either sold some bad stuff or failed to deliver. In either case, it was sufficient to make someone mad enough to murder him. Accordingly, it could have been a revenge killing. Let's say someone felt that Brantley was the cause of a loved one's death—a drug overdose initiated by him."

Rice's statement seemed to trigger Bubba Watson who replied, "That doesn't answer why the satchel was taken and returned, but, hold Lee's thought. Perhaps there's no reasonable answer. It could have been removed in the heat of confusion and the killer himself may not know why he took the gym bag. Later, finding it contained drugs, he returned it to the police."

Chief detective Monahan, realizing what the others said makes sense entered the conversation with a directive, "Let's run a background check for deaths by drug overdose and see if that turns up any motives."

"How far back should we go?" asked Bubba.

"Two years ought to be enough. Then match the deaths to the acquaintances of Brantley and see what materializes."

CHAPTER SEVENTEEN

A MORNING FOG HAD CLOAKED THE area leaving customary appearances in disguise from its provoking veil—a perfect characterization of the proverbial inability to see your hand before your eyes. As much as I wanted to join the breakfast bunch prudence begged perspicacity and I took my coffee alone at the dining room table. Gently stirring in powdered creamer, I watched the swirl slowly change the color from dark to light. After the first sip I became mindful of the peaceful hush of an unwakened household. Though brief, the quietude gave a short interlude for life's reflection. It would take a miracle to unravel the situation wholly created by my initiative. After meeting Irene Jones, my confidence has increased to the point of boldness resulting in Sharon Lezotte and Coralee Smallwood, a yet to be in Birmingham, Alabama. If there were an easy solution, I wouldn't take it. I want it all—my wife, my family, and definitely, the rest. Like most fools in similar situations, no thought is given to the ultimate downside.

While dropping a couple pieces of bread in the toaster, I heard Elaine beginning to stir. She entered the kitchen wearing her lace-chemise and matching robe. It was easy to see that she had been on a diet—a program recommended by her doctor. Sheer nightclothes and backlight accentuated the result.

"Is anything wrong?" she asked.

"Take a look outside. The fog's so thick you can't see to drive. I've made coffee. Pour yourself a cup."

While pouring her cup, the toast popped up, causing Elaine to ask, "Would you like a little jelly?"

"Yes, that will go good."

"How 'bout a couple eggs easy over?"

"Now you're talking my language. Add a little bacon and we have ourselves a breakfast."

Cars began to chance the road as seen through the Baker front picture window. Were it not so thick with fog, drivers would observe Elaine and Steve at the morning meal—a Norman Rockwell image. The pleasant aroma of fried bacon wafted upstairs and began to rouse the children.

"I think I'll give another try before the kids come down. Oh, by the way, you're beginning to look a lot better. Stay on that diet and I'll take you with me to the convention," Steven declared, missing a quick buss aimed for the cheek and headed to the garage.

The children found their mother in tears, with hands to her face.

The dense fog had broken into patches, at times making driving even more dangerous. Steven kept it less than thirty miles per hour and made the service station just before hitting the highway, his first stop. He pumped gas until the tank was full, and then went inside to pay and pick up a newspaper. The Kirksville daily won't be printed until eleven o'clock. The morning Chicago Tribune will have all the sport scores and financial stock market results. Steven never could get comfortable with the Wall Street Journal; however, he occasionally walked around with an edition under his arm just to look more important. If truth be known, others did the same thing, for the same reason.

The year had flown by faster than a peregrine falcon. It seemed like only yesterday when spring flowers came into bloom. Now, cornfields display their tan and golden foliage, biding time while waiting for the fall harvest.

Steven had no intention of taking Elaine to the annual manufacturer's convention. He only said it to make her feel good. He had to chuckle even at the thought. The convention belonged to Irene Jones and any free time will be spent with her. This will be the final year for his fiduciary duties. From that point forward he will join those who served before him as former president.

Ever since the news broke revealing the Kirksville police retrieved the cake cocaine, it was certain Bashir Shishani's days were numbered. He had recruited Warren Brantley to receive and deliver drugs. Transactions took place at the Vagabond Lounge in Chicago Heights, a strip club frequented by an unpleasant clientele. The club's main source of business occurs in back rooms and a sleazy motel nearby—an illicit operation protected by political payoff. Bashir must pay. Exactly how far down the ladder retribution goes is yet to be determined.

Weather conditions had quickly turned colder, accompanied by icy drizzle. The Chechen cousins sat solemnly sipping vodka. Their only hope was the ruthless avenging ended with Bashir Shishani. In the quiet darkness of their apartment the two men poured shots and stared at the street below while awaiting a fearful fate. At last it came. The headlights of the black mariah flashed on the entrance of the chain-link fence. The Chechens' hearts skipped a beat. Trembling hands made an accurate pour impossible. Zorva drank directly from the bottle, made slippery by sweat from his palms.

Footsteps grew louder as visitors neared the top flight. Dokka and Zorva held their breath. They had left the door unlocked anticipating Khalid Umarov's arrival. First to enter were the two Chechen bodyguards. Both hardwired against any emotional display. Like bookends they stood at either side of the entrance awaiting Khalid Umarov's appearance. He was not smiling when he entered the room.

"We are having organizational changes. Bashir Shishani is no longer your contact. He has been eliminated," Umarov stated without preliminaries.

The cousins realized that nothing in life calls on them to be more courageous than when facing the end. Dokka understood Bashir Shishani was a good man. For the fault of hiring the American accountant, he paid with his life. He also knew Umarov disliked his cousin Zorva.

"My cousin Zorva Yamadayev is loyal. He follows orders without reservation no matter what they are. You can ask Bashir Shishani," stopping short when he realized the former leader was dead.

"Was not your cousin supposed to find the killer of Warren Brantley?" asked Umarov. "Is it possible he learned certain information and kept it to himself for personal gain?"

"My cousin Zorva is simple-minded. He could never concoct such a scheme."

"You forget Dokka, he has you to devise the plan," Umarov's eyes narrowed. Turning to Zorva, Umarov said, "Before I count to ten you will tell me who killed the accountant."

Zorva was befuddled and quickly looked to Dokka for guidance and relief. Dokka averted his eyes and studied the floor. When Khalid started counting, the simple Chechen cousin began to grasp the severity of the situation and now breathing through his mouth called once again to Dokka. His supplication fell on deaf ears. The front of Zorva's trousers was wet to the floor emitting a pungent ammonia smell. Umarov was disgusted and provoked. When he reached the count of eight Zorva interrupted shouting, "Stop. Go back to five."

The stupidity of such a request caught Khalid Umarov off guard obligating him to stop counting. A spate of laughter emanated from the two guards standing at the doorway.

There is a fragile separation between humor and tragedy, especially when others are concerned. Mark Twain said, "Humor is tragedy plus time."

Unfortunately for Zorva time has run out. Umarov, infuriated by the comic scene, raised his PB (Pistolet Besshumnyy silent pistol) and fired two rounds into Zorva's chest. Even when the integral silencer is employed, a disturbing sound is obvious. However, an eerie silence now filled the room. Umarov turned to Dokka and commanded, "You will dispose of the body and await further instruction." The trio then descended the stairs, entered the black automobile, and slowly drove away.

The fact of very little blood indicted Zorva died immediately. His lifeless body gave Dokka compunction for leaving Chechnya—at the moment a foremost regret. It was Dokka who convinced Zorva to leave the Caucasus and go the United States. Living in the Chechen hills offered no opportunity for riches. In America good fortune was everywhere, or it seemed to be so. Up 'til now the cousins were living the dream. Today, however, it turned into a nightmare.

As if in a trance, Dokka stood over his cousin with an expression of remorse and said aloud, "I'm truly sorry my friend. You are the most innocent of all."

Aware he must act quickly, Dokka turned off the light at the entrance of the stairway, leaving the approach in pitch darkness. No one could see Zorva's body, wrapped in a blanket, being loaded into the trunk of the white Cadillac convertible. Battling a mental fog, he drove to the only place coming to mind—The Vagabond Lounge. A shot or two of vodka might clear his thoughts. He needed help in disposing the body.

It was always like entering another world when Dokka visited his cousin's favorite watering hole. The loud painful stomp of music and nude women gyrating to its beat seemed grotesque, especially today with Zorva's corpse residing in the trunk of his car. Seats encircling the bar gave a closer view of the stage located directly behind. Even this early in the night, all were occupied.

By treading a few carpeted steps to an elevated floor, Dokka found a small table guarded by an ornate iron railing—obviously intended to protect customers from falling off the landing in the darkness. A young waitress, winding her way around tables, approached Dokka's and lit the candle to signify his occupancy. After replacing the cut glass shade she asked, "What can I get you?"

"I'll have a double shot of vodka," he replied, at the time assessing the age of the young woman. Upon her return he inquired, "Please don't take this wrong, but you seem too young to be working here."

Making change for his twenty-dollar bill, she stated, "I am too young, however, my father is part owner of the lounge and allows me to help out."

"You obviously don't dance," Dokka expressed, leaving the interpretation either a question or statement.

"I get asked that a lot. My father would never allow me to be on the stage. I would be a lot better than half the girls he employs."

"I don't doubt it for a minute," Dokka agreed. At that moment, a dark figure bounded up the steps and came to Dokka's table. The

Chechen stood as the two embraced in a friendly hug. "Where is your brother tonight?" the visitor inquired.

"Zorva is not my brother, he is my cousin," replied Dokka. The young waitress moved on to service the other tables. "He has a date tonight."

"And left the Cadillac for you to drive?" the friend asked suspiciously.

"The girl picked him up in a limousine."

"Wow, Zorva is moving up in class."

"She apparently likes the rugged type," said Dokka.

"He's more animalistic than rugged. Sounds like a match made in heaven or, more accurately, in hell. Any bets how long it will last?"

"I wouldn't touch it," Dokka acknowledged. "By the way, I don't know what Zorva has told you but the Cadillac is mine, not his. I let him use it once in a while."

"I figured as much. Say, some of the gang is coming here later. Why don't you join us," asked the friend.

"Thanks, but I better get back in case Zorva ends up in jail," Dokka jested.

"From what I know of your cousin, that probably is a wise decision," declared the friend, hoisting a toast and skipping to the main floor.

The cold night air was invigorating. Dokka drove to the main highway and headed south. He had no idea how far or when he would stop. He reasoned that it wouldn't be soon as long as traffic remained heavy. After driving for what seemed like an hour, the sign denoting the exit to the state park came into view. Dokka slowed down and turned on the ramp finding him on a state road at the end of the loop. Another sign exhibited an arrow showing the way to the park. Underneath the arrow it indicted 5 miles. Like magic, the heavy traffic had disappeared. So much so an eerie feeling seized the moment and the Cadillac operated independent of his thoughts.

Large raindrops commenced to splatter against the windshield and Dokka automatically turned on his wipers and passed over the bridge before realizing he had reached the Kirksville State Park. It obliged him to travel nearly a quarter mile before finding an off road and turn around. With the car on the bridge, he raised the trunk lid and wrestled Zorva's body to the edge and reluctantly let it fall to the rushing water gurgling below. Certain he was unseen, Dokka accelerated the gas pedal. The Cadillac spun tires, and, directed northward, emitting billows of white exhaust smoke.

Emotionless, until seated at the apartment's kitchen table, the young Chechen sipped vodka until the first brightening of morning.

Stranded on foreign soil, Dokka longed for his homeland and the breathtaking elevation of the Caucasus.

While the Caucasus is mostly diverse, Chechnya has a uniform population, albeit a tribal society with each family or clan having a patriarch as the leader. Both proud and vengeful, the patriarch protects members and their culture. The clan's implacable nature regarding their women is reminiscent to the Cheyenne Indians of the American plains— each tribal society with strict rules in respect to courtship and marriage— two warrior groups, one disallowing non-Chechen and non-Muslim men, and the other, allowing only those proved worthy by ordeal.

Born a Muslim, Dokka now realized his destiny argued for his return home. No matter the consequences, it will be better than what happened to his cousin. He will face the music, take his medicine, and perhaps be able to sleep again.

CHAPTER EIGHTEEN

PREPARATIONS FOR THE ANNUAL CONVENTION occupied a hefty amount of my time. Order flow and receivables appeared to be in proper balance. As far as gross sales are concerned, 1987 looks to be the best since we opened the doors.

Efforts to pacify Irene seemed to be acceptable, although by now I know her too well. As my relationship with the manufacturer convention is coming to an end, so is the bond that ties us. I can't put her off any longer—*Soit lamerde ou descender le pot.* Unfortunately, I still have another week to think about it. This year's convention begins Tuesday, October 20, and ends Thursday. Most attendees, me included, will depart Friday morning. I'll have an hour drive facing me. Others will need O'Hare to return to homes around the world.

With preparations complete, I took a deep breath and planned to carry on with business as usual—also knowing full well the door is left open for mini crises to pop up at the most inconvenient moment. Like they say, "Don't put too many eggs in the pudding."

This time the major incident did not affect me directly. In fact, it didn't even occur here in the United States. At midmonth, England, France, and the Channel Islands were struck by severe hurricane like winds—a once-in-a-hundred-year storm. October in England is well known for rain. In fact, October is its rainiest month. It's also the month with the least fog. Temperatures vary between

55° and 60° Fahrenheit with rather calm winds from the southwest. On Sunday, October 11, the Farmer's forecast predicted bad weather on Thursday and Friday. By mid-week guidance from weather prediction models were somewhat inconclusive. Instead of the storm hitting a considerable part of the UK, the models suggested it would reach no farther north than the English Channel and coastal parts of Southern England. During early afternoon, winds were very light over most parts of the UK. The pressure gradient was slack, although a depression was drifting slowly northwards over the North Sea off Eastern Scotland. At the same time, a trough lay over England, Wales, and Ireland; however, across the Bay of Biscay a depression was developing.

On Thursday, the first gale warnings were issued for sea areas in the English Channel and four hours later, by warnings of severe gales.

By midnight, the depression was over the Western English Channel and, with a dramatic increase in temperature, the storm's warm front moved rapidly northeast. It is clear the warnings for sea areas were timely and adequate. On the other hand, forecasts for land areas left much to be desired, resulting in the mainland being unprepared. And then it struck.

On the night of October 15, a severe depression in the Bay of Biscay moved northeast resulting in winds with the force of a locomotive. With hurricane intensity, the tempest smashed across England, France, and the Channel Islands, causing death and crushing destruction. Wind gusts of 122 mph downed 15 million trees, many having historic classification.

With suchlike winds blowing continuously for three and four hours, trees were uprooted and fell on utility lines, snapping cables. Fallen trees blocked main roads and railways. Severed cables short-circuited and overheated the main system. Posing a possible damage to the national grid, it was decided to shut down most of South England, including London.

Frozen by fear of the storm, total darkness now added to the terror. Some of the older Londoners were reminded of the frightful and tragic nights of bombing which occurred during the Second World War. Naturally, this was definitely different from being bombed for 57 consecutive nights by the German Luftwaffe and resulting in 20,000 civilian deaths. All the same, a storm such as this resulted in 22 people being killed in England and France. In many places power wasn't restored for more than two weeks, leaving nearly two million French homes without electrical supply and water.

Total estimated cost of the damage ran in the billions—£2bn in England and ₣23bn in France. Generally speaking, the meteorological office was blamed for failure to forecast the storm correctly.

By the time the convention closed, no one was happier to see it at an end. Like the Christmas Holidays, anticipation followed by thankful gratitude once it was over. I can't be the only person who feels this way.

Irene left the hotel and her party drove away without a resolution to our personal situation. She said her goodbye with an air of indifference, a nonchalant and confusing farewell. Her composure contradicted the emotion she displayed last night after the light was out.

Nevertheless, I have the uneasy feeling of being appraised by an unspoken ultimatum. My wick is burning very close to the end. Oh well, she won't take dramatic steps until we see each other again, which will happen in a couple weeks. In the meantime, I have a company to run and a hundred employees to conciliate.

The farther south I drove the slower traffic appeared, indicating inclement weather. Tiny graupels of snow began to bounce against the hood and windshield. Visibility was still good so maybe I'm only confronting a brief snow flurry. All the same, it's a reminder of what lies ahead. Soon, Old Man Winter will be looking for a home, expecting to stay for three months. The battery factory is located in a rural area protected only by corn fields, which, after harvest, the remnants of stalk stubble leaves us subject to drifts and whiteouts.

When I arrived at the factory, my secretary informed me of an urgent message from England, I was to call back the minute I returned from the convention. Happy that I didn't stop for lunch or go home first, I checked my watch—11:00 a.m. here and 4:00 p.m. in London— and climbed the steps to my office. It's uncanny when you need a little privacy, people come out of the woodwork with a myriad of questions requesting my immediate attention. I apologized for a slight delay and closed the door.

"Jane, who called from England? Was it Mr. Mulchamp?" I inquired on our intercom.

"No. It was Miss Birdwhistle, his secretary," Jane responded. "She said it was very important you call right away."

More than likely this has to do with the sale of their worldwide battery businesses. Things must have moved along a lot faster than I was led to believe. By now my heart rate had slowed enough to punch the speed dial button to London. After a few dings and bells, the head office receptionist answered.

"Mr. Mulchamp please," I asked. While waiting, I pulled my legal pad in front of me and nervously tapped a pencil.

"You have reached Mr. Mulchamp's office. He is not available at the moment may I be of service?"

"Emily, this is Steve Baker from the US."

"Oh, Mr. Baker, it's so nice of you to call back. Mr. Mulchamp did want to speak with you but has been called to Queen Elizabeth Street. This place has been a madhouse. How have you been?"

"Very well, thank you. Did you receive the card I sent when your husband was in the hospital?"

"Yes, we did and thank you very much. Charlie is home now and ready to go back to work."

"I'm glad to hear it."

"Mr. Baker, Mr. Mulchamp won't be returning to his office today. I'll let him know you called and will call again first thing in the morning."

"What time does he usually get in?"

"I wouldn't wait any later than 9:00 a.m. GMT," she answered.

We rang off and I sat for a while and then wrote 4:00 a.m. on my yellow pad. Looks like an early start for me tomorrow.

That night I set my alarm for 3:00 a.m. I probably won't need it but it will serve as insurance against oversleeping. I was still deprived of shut-eye from the convention. Under the covers shortly after dinner, with the bedroom door closed, I planned to get as much rest as possible. Rest was all I got. Concern over calling England only allowed me to doze off and on between visions of the mind.

The parking lot was practically empty when I pulled into my assigned space. With main lights turned off it gave the work areas a colorless and eerie appearance. That all changes once the first shift supervisors arrive. At this time in the morning on a Friday, it looks like I'll be the only one here. I had to use my key to open the front door—lucky no one changed the lock.

Turning on the office lights I was stunned by how bright it made everything. When the whole building is illuminated it doesn't seem so bright. Taking the chair behind my desk, after laying my briefcase on a side table, I hit the speed dial.

Winnowing through the corporate particulars, Harold Mulchamp finally picked up.

"Steven, how nice of you to call. Sorry I wasn't available yesterday. There was an emergency meeting on Queen Elizabeth Street. It seems like the board of directors wants to speed up the changeover. To them, timing is everything. I'm not allowed to approve any capital expenditures; therefore, whatever you have going must be put on hold," he explained.

"How close are we in selling this operation?"

"I've been told we have a legitimate offer. Your contract gives you first right of refusal to repurchase the business; but, considering the fact we now have a firm offer, if I were you, I'd start shaking numbers—Mother England won't wait too long."

"How much is the asking price?"

"I believe it's a little over £4 million."

"That's roughly six million U.S. dollars and quite a bit more than the original purchase price."

"I know that. You have done a damn good job and increased the business value."

"Looks like it was too good. I might have worked myself out of contention."

"Well, we appreciate all you have done. If only others had done as well, we probably wouldn't be selling all the battery businesses. Take a look at it. You have a couple months. We both know that Mother England grinds the grain slowly, but, don't take too long."

I sat for a while staring at the wall. To buy the company back at half again as much as was originally paid would necessitate all the original profit plus a sizable loan. Being in unexplored territory, I will need outside assistance—someone to help with the banks. Right now, Arthur Anderson & Associates might be able to offer guidance. I'll call them when it's not so damn early. Meanwhile, I'd give anything for a hot cup of coffee.

Chapter Nineteen

THE KIRKSVILLE POLICE DETECTIVES WERE gathering in the station evidence room. Men with a firm finger grip in the handle of their coffee cup. As they took respective chairs, officer Fujimoto sounded out, "Is anybody bringing donuts or sweet rolls?"

"I'm having some delivered," Commander Homberg replied. "The bakery guy must be running late."

"What's in your brown bag?" Haruki Fujimoto fears no one.

"Bananas. After my last physical, the doctor said that I'm a little low on potassium. Apparently, potassium is crucial for life. It's needed to control high blood pressure and for the heart and kidneys to function properly. He wants me to eat healthier food. Bananas are high in potassium and my wife makes sure I snack on them. Would you like one?"

Fujimoto grimaced and said, "No thanks." Then, under his breath, *"Fucking Jew bastard will start growing a tail."*

Homberg either didn't hear him or just ignored the snide remark. Both Bubba Watson and Lee Rice heard him perfectly and sat with a frinking[2] expression on their faces.

---

2   An attempt to force a serious frown through a shit-eating grin and failing miserably.

The entrance of the bakery deliveryman saved the situation, and, for the moment, the scene was one of contentedness as the box was passed around the table. After a polite interval, Commander Homberg, expelling a muffled burp, formally opened the meeting.

"I believe you all know Miss Melody Harp, our station stenographer. I've asked Miss Harp to take the minutes of the meeting. The discovery of such a large amount of cake cocaine has brought the FBI back into the case. Accordingly, I felt it best to reopen the Warren Brantley murder as part of teamwork between the two agencies. Detective Chief Mike Monahan will administrate the investigation and report back to my office any significant leads or breakthrough. In that manner, summary notes of your meetings and assignments will keep me apprised of all progress. Miss Harp will be available to attend your meetings and document the permanent record. Try to avoid her presence during bullshit sessions. Her time is valuable and she has other duties."

"I bet she does. Kanojo wa okina ō shiri motte imasu. With a rear end that wide if she ever had to haul ass she'd need to make two trips," Fujimoto whispered.

Commander Homberg continued, "I'll provide all the help my authority allows but, remember, we are a small station and manpower is tight. I've added two patrolmen to your team and the use of a squad car."

With that, Homberg turned the meeting over to Mike Monahan and left the room.

"In case someone doesn't know the new members of the group, I'll make the introduction. Foot, bicycle, and motorcycle patrolmen don't spend much time in the station house. There was a time when we all were part of the foot patrol. That was usually the starting point for police work. Patrolmen looked forward to eventually being promoted to a desk. In most cases it took years since the inside desk job was a plum and nobody quit. Now, education rules. Officers attend college and take correspondence school to better prepare them for the next step up in duty and rank. Officers Robert Randall and Larry Buhrmeister are two such men. Accordingly, today we plan to indoctrinate them into the detective bureau."

After a few nods of recognition, Monahan continued, "Up 'til now we haven't been able to establish the true motive of the Warren Brantley murder. All we know for sure is somebody put a couple bullets into him. On the surface it looks like a drug deal gone badly."

Looking up from his prepared notes and glancing at Lee Rice, Monahan said, "Detective Rice suggested the motive may be one of revenge on a more personal nature rather than the typical drug related killing. Along those lines he agreed to research recent drug related deaths. I believe he has a few preliminary findings to report."

Lee Rice was a little nervous. For most of his adult life he had a fear of public speaking.[3] At the police academy Rice went to great length to avoid making presentations. Even during classroom discussions he avoided eye contact with other class members. It finally came down to accepting the fact he is anxious and work to overcome his speaking panic—face down his fear. Since fear robs you of the ability to think, he began by practicing at home, in front of his wife, during which he learned to breathe deeply from the diaphragm and make eye contact. If it weren't for the quivering subject notes, held in his hands, you might believe his speaking anxiety has been overcome.

"From all appearances, drugs are at the center of this crime. Let's assume that Brantley either sold some bad stuff or failed to deliver. If the latter is true, it's illogical it would eventually show up under the state park bridge. Drug dealers would have gone on with their normal distribution and we would never find it in cake form. Should Brantley's death be the result of someone holding a hatred or grudge, the killer, in this case, probably had no need to take ownership. Why he had it in the first case might have just been an unexplained impulse at the time of the murder and later returned where we could find it."

"You keep referring to the killer as he. Could the perpetrator just as likely be a she?" asked patrolman Buhrmeister.

"Definitely," Rice replied. "And what I turned up after perusing the Kirksville newspapers, makes it a possibility. Plausible, if I'm on the right track."

Rice began fumbling with his notes, looking for findings from the library. Having located what he was hunting, he read from the notation, "Over the past two years there have been seven deaths by

3   Fear of public speaking is the most common of all phobias.

drug overdose. These are deaths confirmed by the autopsy and coroner. Four were derelicts found in their sleeping room. It appeared they were destitute and without immediate family. Two of the remaining three, one man and one woman, were found in their bathtub and no indication of foul play. Finally, the last one was a high school girl named Rilla Lezotte. She was discovered in the alley behind a local gin mill. Miss Lezotte had a history of drug abuse. In fact, she recently returned from rehab at the Kirksville County Clinic."

"Is it possible that Brantley was the dope pusher?" asked Randall.

"For all the pieces to fit my puzzle, he has to be," affirmed detective Rice. "I've learned she has a sister—her only immediate family. Their mother is deceased and the two girls lived alone in the family residence. The older of the two, Sharon Lezotte, works as a checker at the Kroger grocery store."

Up to this point, Haruki Fujimoto had his eyes closed pretending sleep—a common occurrence for him during long, dull meetings. Fujimoto is a past master of feigning boredom. Whenever he is criticized for this ill-mannered behavior he invokes *Inemuri*[4]. Responding to Lee Rice's assertion, Fujimoto said, "We need to interview the sister."

"I've done just that, or rather, made initial contact."

"And, what happened?" asked Fujimoto.

"Nothing at this point. Modern interrogation isn't conducted like it used to be. Miss Lezotte was extremely ill at ease. When a subject is that nervous, it's nearly impossible to make valid assumptions." Rice explained.

Fujimoto's eyes darted round the table while he thought of something clever to say. He decided on declaring, "We need to bring her in."

"At this point, that would be a mistake. Nine chances out of ten she has very little to offer. In the event she does, however, I've told her, in all likelihood, I would be back with a few more questions."

"How did she respond?" asked Mike Monahan.

---

4   *Inemuri* is a Japanese word meaning sleeping while present. *Inemuri* is socially acceptable and a much respected practice in the Japanese workplace depicting ones dedication to work.

"I got the impression she didn't appreciate it very much. Nevertheless, I do need to talk to her again and try to establish a baseline."

Fujimoto snickered.

"I'll call her at home. That way she won't be embarrassed in the presence of co-workers."

Noting patrolman Randall wished to speak but hesitant in gesturing for the floor, detective Rice asked, "Larry, do you have something to add?"

"You spoke of establishing a baseline in the questioning. I'm not certain I understand what you mean. Could you explain exactly what that entails?"

Randall's request seemed to arouse more interest by the panel. To a man they became more attentive. Before having detective Rice explain the importance of establishing a baseline, Mike Monahan suggested a pee break, and the sound of scooting chairs filled the room.

"Look at that *Hakujin Josei*. I've never seen her move so fast," Fujimoto chided.

The bathroom break gave everyone a chance to stretch his or her legs, take care of business, and reorient for the remainder of the meeting. While the participants took longer than Chief Monahan desired, they slowly began to congregate around the meeting room door. We humans seem to be wired when it comes to returning to where we belong. It's like we are endowed with a magnetic compass intellect. Dissimilar to other animals and insects it's not an instinct. Instead, it's more of a cognitive skill. Over time, by accumulating proper social responses, we are automatically drawn to the assembly previously attended. Unless the reward is personal, there is usually the tendency to dawdle simply because we are human.

The time-out break was perhaps, most beneficial for detective Rice. He returned to the conference room in better control of his nervousness—it works that way sometimes. After the usual ado he began, "I believe we've all heard the old adage, the eyes are the windows to the soul. Knowledge of that has helped many a suitor win favor with the chosen other. It's a fact pupils dilate when we are interested in the person we are talking to or the object we are looking at. While this phenomenon presents a visible demeanor of the eyes, it's actually a response generated in the brain. To better understand this, familiarity with the eye itself and its relationship to the brain is essential."

Detective Rice was on a roll. No longer did he concern himself with stage fright, instead, he had become a teacher, a teacher with an engrossed gathering. Particular attention was being given as Rice fumbled with his file folder removing a drawing he personally sketched. Holding it before him, he lifted it up to eye level and said, "This is a drawing I made of the eye and its components. I'll pass it around so you can get a better idea of what I'm talking about."

Chief Mike Monahan interrupted and suggested, "Use the overhead projector. It will make the image bigger and we all can see it at the same time."

To the surprise of everyone at the table, Fujimoto quickly turned on the projector lamp and positioned the bright empty light image on the screen. Rice, at first, had placed the drawing upside down and then spun it around while glancing at Fujimoto, expecting his usual epithet. He wasn't disappointed. Grasping the extendable pointer, detective Rice began, "Expression of the eyes play an important role in forensic science. However, before we can interpret these expressions we must understand the function of the eyes and psychological history of the suspect. Other factors, rather than the question, may cause some curious expressions. These can be due to heredity, environment, and or injury. That's why it's important to establish a baseline with the suspect—visual expressions when they are relaxed and having no fear of other influence."

"A rubber hose is quicker," thought Fujimoto, with a self-predicating smile.

Pointing at his drawing, Rice explained, "Light passes through the cornea, the pupil, the lens, and strikes the rods and cones in the retina. Visual processing begins at the retina. The cells of the retina produce electrical activity and nerve fibers from these cells join at the back of the eye and form the optic nerve. Is everybody with me so far?"

The addled demeanor on the faces of Kirksville's finest answered without a vocal response.

"Hang in there with me. It all will make sense as we go on."

Even though their confidence was about as clear as dishwater, the group obviously will carry on and detective Rice continued, "By way of the optic nerve, electrical impulses are communicated to the visual cortex of the brain. The visual cortex of the brain interprets these electrical impulses and either stores them or sends a message to a motor area for action. Forensic psychologists find these motor actions useful when determining and evaluating personality traits. And, in turn, they help establish a baseline for suspicious individuals so we can better assess their reaction to our examination."

The human mind can only absorb what the rear end can endure. Chief Monahan was fully aware of this and called for a ten-minute break, prescribing they stand up and walk around.

While the room was still astir, Bubba Watson walked up to his partner, "I am very impressed. You never told me how smart you were. When they make you a captain, kindly remember your cohort."

"You forget. I'm not going anywhere. I work for the Kirksville Detective Bureau," Rice reported with a smile.

"Don't be too sure," Bubba replied, then, with the others, took his respective chair.

Detective Rice continued, "Before the break we were discussing motor action from the brain's visual cortex. These actions are most helpful during interrogation.

Suspects commonly cover or shield their eyes when they don't like what you're saying. They also tend to squint either because they don't like the examiner or the question.

Perhaps the most telling response relates to the pupils. Discounting variations of external light, which causes pupil response, we know our pupils dilate when we view something stimulating or pleasant. Conversely, our pupils tend to constrict to block out offensive imagery or thought."

Rice directed his pointer to the area designating the pupil. "The pupil itself is only a black vacant area in the center of the iris. It's the iris that controls the size of the pupil," Rice stated, while replacing the first drawing with one he made of the iris. "Besides creating eye color, the iris is the true cause of emotional pupil control. Components of the iris are not only intriguing but stand as the keystone of scientific forensic study. Each of us has a different structure of lines, dots, and colors in our irises and they are unique as fingerprints. The fundamental components consist of crypts or pits radiating from the pupil and contraction furrows or lines curving around the outer edge which serve to contract and dilate the pupil.

Scientists have found an extremely strong correlation between a person's iris and personality traits. For example, people with densely packed crypts tend to be warmhearted, tender and trusting. Those with more contracting furrows seem to be more neurotic, impulsive and likely to give way to anger. At this point I must remind you that correlation does not necessarily imply causation. Many other factors come into play, thus the need for establishing a baseline for interrogation. Are there any questions?"

Patrolman Randall raised his hand and was acknowledged by Detective Rice.

"I've read that eye color can determine personality traits. Is that true?"

"Yes, to a degree, but not to the point of exact causation," Rice replied. "I would think the correlation between the irises, rather than eye color, and certain personality traits, is more accurate. Although, studies have revealed women with lighter eye color experience less pain during childbirth when compared to women with darker eyes. And, it appears that those with lighter eye color can consume more alcohol without becoming intoxicated. That would explain why those with darker eyes are less likely to become alcoholics."

"I don't get that," Randall questioned.

"Since it takes less to get drunk, a lesser amount is consumed."

Randall nodded his understanding and detective Rice went to the blackboard and wrote the word Melanin.

"Melanin is the pigment that makes eyes darker. It also makes people more susceptible to alcohol. Melanin serves as an insulator for the electrical connection between brain cells. The more melanin in the brain, the more efficiently and faster the brain can work. Now, before we get off on a tangent, I'm not suggesting that people with dark eyes are more intelligent than their blue-eyed counterpart."

That was the next question Randall had in mind. With their bodies complaining of the long meeting, all were thankful no more questions were proffered. Attendants stood and stretched, making sure to congratulate Rice on his excellent and informative presentation while filing out the door.

Mike Monahan asked Rice and Watson to stop by his office before resuming their remaining schedule.

"The reason I've called you here is to first congratulate Lee on an outstanding presentation—I wish we had more on the force like him. Secondly, I want to know when you plan on talking to Sharon Lezotte again. I'm beginning to think there is more to be learned from her."

"My fiancée knows Sharon Lezotte. I may also be able to learn more about her," Bubba Watson interrupted.

"Your fiancée works at that battery factory, right?" asked Monahan.

"Yes. Callie has mentioned Ms. Lezotte before, but I can't remember the exact context of our conversation. It wasn't important at the time."

"I'll arrange a meeting with Lezotte next week," Lee Rice stated.

"And, I see Callie every day," reported Bubba.

When Harold Mulchamp said Mother England grids the grain slowly, he wasn't being facetious. Days, and weeks, for that matter, passed by in rapid fashion. Spring flowers were in full bloom without further word from across the Atlantic.

Arthur Anderson & Associates had performed a feasibility study and found our company worthy of becoming an ESOP (employee stock ownership plan). Such a plan provides the workforce with an ownership in the company at no upfront cost. Most of the employees are hourly and unable to purchase stock. The concept assumes ownership will increase productivity. Often, however, without skin in the game, attitudes slowly shift to previous perspectives. Nevertheless, the ESOP approach is workable only by utilizing all revenue earned from the original sale and a sizable bank loan. Even then, it leaves me without money to cover operating expenses, i.e., payroll and raw materials. Mother England would have to take back a note for $250,000—as if there isn't enough unsettledness in my life. Did I mention that Arthur Anderson charged $25,000 for their study?

It had been awhile since I stopped off at Cliffs for breakfast. An hour with the breakfast gang might lighten my load. Their brand of humor can relieve the burden of stress providing you are not the butt of their anecdotes.

Boisterous laughter could be heard even with the door closed. This much joviality means someone is receiving the brunt of a jokesters thorny humor. Three tables had been pushed together to accommodate the regular clique. Their breakfast orders were still being served. The waitress emptied her tray and asked, "Are you with this bunch?"

"He's with us," came a chorus of voices from the makeshift table.

"Put it down right here," Harry Cook said, as he slid a chair from the only empty table and scooted it at the vacant end of the one occupied by the group. The waitress took the order, flipped over an empty cup, and filled it with steaming brew without asking if he wanted regular or decaf. Long ago they came to the conclusion that the benefits of regular coffee outweighed the harm of caffeine. After all, regular coffee provides many health advantages over decaf. These include improved mental health, increased metabolic rate, and enhanced athletic performance. Their claim for improved athletic prowess is somewhat of a farce. Marshall Bloom plays golf an average of three times a year and Harry Cook only plays tennis with his daughter. She is ten years old. Nevertheless, they drink regular coffee with assurance that it is better for them.

"Steven, you haven't been around for a while, are you guys that busy?" Kenny Granger inquired.

"It's been rather hectic with the convention and sale of the company."

"Are you going to buy it back?"

"I don't know, England wants a lot more than what they paid for it." Steven truthfully replied. "It's a matter of corralling the money?"

Those at the table were quiet for the moment. The interlude allowed time to change the subject.

"I notice Bill Schneider isn't here today," averred Steven.

"He's in the hospital," Carl Landry blurted.

"What for?" asked Steven.

"Chest pains," Harry stated, while spreading jelly on his toast. "He's stabilized now and should be home soon. In fact, Schneider called Cliff's this morning to find out if he had gone back to using plastic water glasses."

Knowing smiles grew in all the faces.

"Breakfast just doesn't feel right without Bill Schneider," Steven confessed.

"I'm certain things will be back to normal next week." Harry Cook assured.

The remainder of the breakfast didn't pass without the usual humor but Kenny Granger took the most heat. Planting and harvest is performed by his young neighbor on a split the profit basis. The only time Kenny spends on a John Deere is when he mows the lawn. One topic that piqued the interest of everyone was the city of Chicago agreeing to allow lights at Wrigley Field and to be expected a contrast of separate opinions.

As usual, the most vocal was Bill Schneider. Today, however, he resides in Saint Mary's Hospital wearing an open-back gown a size too small. It's a wonder they couldn't hear him shouting for a nurse and demanding a release. This morning the group is safe but tomorrow may be a different matter. Bill Schneider couldn't care less about baseball. He enjoyed poker and gambling on horses at the racetrack. To his credit, Bill is a very good handicapper and after all is said and done wins more than he loses.

Everyone at the table is a Chicago Cub fan, save one. Steven Baker loves the White Sox. As a youngster, before television, he listened to "The Ol' Commander", Bob Elson's baseball broadcast on the radio. Bob Elson announced both Cubs and Sox games beginning in 1929 and White Sox exclusively from 1946 to 1970. The Chicago Cubs radio broadcast was turned over to Bert Wilson, who became noted for saying, "He didn't care who won as long as it's the Cubs."

Bob Elson's reporting style was characteristically unemotional, laid-back, and monotonous—more apparent on away games. Like many sportscasts of the day, away games were recreated in the studio using telegraph messages from the ball park. The sound of the ticker tape was prominent in the background along with recorded crowd noise that was amplified whenever there was excitement on the field.

Steven listened with a rapt ear and, as a youth, the seed was planted and it grew into a full-grown White Sox fan. He also liked night games at Comiskey Park. From Kirksville, he could reach the ball park in less than an hour with no inner-city traffic. The return home was even faster.

Being Cub fans, the majority at the table were torn regarding night baseball. Marshall Bloom had lived on the north side of Chicago. It deteriorated in the late 1960s, when residents moved to the suburbs. Gangs took over and the crime rate increased. Then, after young professionals began moving in, renovation occurred. Townhouses changed the community and the crime rate went down.

Upscale residents feared night baseball would encourage rowdy, drunken fans, littering and vandalizing the neighborhood. The friendly confines with its ivy covered outfield walls and a hand operated scoreboard recording runs and hits, had become near and dear to its loyal fans. However, the stance on lights and night baseball makes Wrigley Field antitheses to the major league. The Wrigley family no longer owns the ballpark, which was purchased by the Tribune Company. Any previous understanding about lights no longer exists. Major league baseball revenue benefits from night games. In time, a dark Wrigley Field will be punished financially. Eventually the opposition will have to say "uncle" and throw in the towel. Grudgingly, in 1988 they did just that and the lights went up.

That morning at Cliff's, after the dishes were cleared and fresh coffee around, the conversation turned to team records and best players. Ironically, the previous season, both Cubs and Sox had the same losing results—77 wins and 85 losses. Since hope springs eternal, the discussion evolved around managers and star pitchers. The Cub fans lauded Don Zimmer, Greg Maddux, and Rick Sutcliffe and I offered Jim Fregosi, Floyd Bannister, and Richard Dotson. The argument proved balanced until Harry Cook brought up the attendance. The White Sox drew 1,208,060 last year and the Cubs 2,035,130 with a much smaller ballpark. When it comes to loyalty, Cub fans are second to none. Win or lose they continue to fill their stands. White Sox fans are more perfidious. If the team loses, a great number of seats remain empty. It was time for Steven to cut and run.

"Don't leave now. We haven't talked about hitters," Harry sensed blood.

"I have to get back to the office. We've got the whole season to match hitters." Steven waived his guest check for the waitress and escaped while he could, with a semblance of dignity.

Any thoughts of a restful day were dashed the minute I walked in the door. Jane was standing with a look of uneasiness and a stack of pink phone messages in her hand. I knew it was something of importance when she followed me upstairs to keep it out of earshot of the other girls. Jane is the most excellent secretary I've ever had and obviously understands, if three people know classified information, everyone will soon know it.

"Mr. Mulchamp's secretary called this morning and asked for you to call England the minute you got in. She told me it was urgent and about the sale of the company. That was all she knew," Jane whispered, and handed me the other pink message slips. She returned to her desk under the petulant eyes of the other girls. Fortunately, the phones began to ring off the hook, busying all involved.

"Mr. Mulchamp's office," answered Emily Birdwhistle in her amiable voice. Her inflection reminded me of the cheerful song of a wren. On early summer mornings I often drank my coffee outside under the patio umbrella and, often as not, would be entertained by the variable trilling sound of a wren calling its mate. While other birds offered reply, the loudest yard music came from one so small and delicate. In actual face to face conversation Emily's tone-of-voice seems an octave lower. It's funny how the telephone changes our voices.

"Steven Baker calling from America," I announced.

"Mr. Baker thanks for returning our call so promptly. Mr. Mulchamp is on the other line. I'll let him know you are waiting."

"Thanks Emily. It sounds like it is something of rather urgent importance," I prompted.

"Everybody is all hush hush but I believe it has to do with the sale of the company. Mr. Mulchamp is off the line now so I'm plugging you in."

"Steven," came the familiar crisp British articulation. "Good to hear your voice."

"What's up," *Enough of this perfunctory bull shit. This call could only mean one thing.* "I'm returning your call."

"Yes, er…Let's get right down to it," Mulchamp stated. "The board of directors met last night and agreed to the sale of the battery company to a group out of India or Pakistan. I was left out of the decision. I was told, however, you are vital to the deal."

"What the hell does that mean?"

"That's all I was told. One would think it means they want you to stay on. They will have someone contact you regarding a meeting next week. Most likely with their attorneys and personnel based in the States," Mulchamp surmised. "They know about the arrangement England had with you and perhaps wish to continue the same way. Possibly you can buy in for a share."

"I'm willing to hear them out, but, I don't think I want to only own a share. You might recall I've been working on financing to buy the company back."*Actually, when considering the asking price and difficulty raising capital, I had given up on the idea. Though, at this stage, that's for only me to know.* "With the battery division gone are you becoming a director?"

"No son, I'm to be without a job. I guess I could go back making cars," Mulchamp sighed. "You might recall that I left British Rover to take the battery post. Such is life," he lamented.

It was apparent we rang off with both of our moods trending lower. The next few minutes found me, again, staring at the wall. I began formulating how best to explain the situation to the employees. I've got to put a good spin on it. *It will be total bull shit since I don't actually know, having never met the new owners.* Whatever I come up with mustn't demoralize the rank and file. Most of them will be required to continue floor operations.

The staff is another matter and I'll need to talk to each individual, personally. Jane will be first to know since she should be prepared for when their phone call comes in. Hell, they might walk in unannounced. I would.

Before the day ended I made certain to bring both Jane O'Connor and Callie Mellinger up to date with all the information I had. The rest will be updated tomorrow. By then my story will be properly devised. *Who am I kidding? With both Jane and Callie in the know, the scuttlebutt express will travel like wildfire.*

Astonishingly, the hourly employees took the news as a prelude to a wage increase and celebrated—so much for my concern over their morale. While I worried they might fear for their jobs, they took a different view. Was it the Rashomon effect? Probably not—they all seemed of the same opinion. Maslow's hierarchy of needs, belonging, esteem, and self-actualization, has little importance when you are living paycheck to paycheck.

Jane O'Connor was in a different frame of mind. She had told others that I was the best boss she ever had. Considering my own feelings, a little solace needed to be applied both ways. Paula Stevens and Beverly White seemed unconcerned and cool to new ownership. Russell Webster told me he had been thinking of making a move for several weeks. Accordingly, new ownership would not be devastating. His penchants for stretching the truth made me wonder. Nevertheless, everybody was brought on board and we all waited the meeting of the new owners.

I've always believed my best hopes and worst fears never materialize. It's always something in between. The new owners proved me right by arriving unannounced. Even though I would have done the same, it's still bush league.

All four doors of the rental sedan seemed to open at the same time. Those disengaging from the shiny new auto left no questions as to who they were. The new owners have arrived. Coming without notification was no doubt considered shrewd in their own minds; however, viewed by those expecting them, gauche and backwoods management.

Walking in, they found themselves caught up in the noisy increase of factory activity and stunned by the contrast between a peaceful outdoors and the dynamo of lift-truck warning horns loading and unloading freight, roar of machinery, and playful japes and shouting of those doing the activity. The office was taken up with semi-trailer drivers and employees seeking assignments and personnel help.

The visitors, in a bewildered state, stood outside the room. At that point John Anderson said, "Maybe we should have called them first." Their attorney, Bernard Ackerman, replied, "No. It's always best to catch them unawares." *Obviously, it was his idea.* The awkward situation lasted until those affiliated in the office thinned out. Once inside, their bumbling presence continued as they fumbled forward business cards and requested to see Steven Baker.

One of the drawbacks of having your office directly above the reception room is that sounds easily travel though the cold air duct. It takes a little getting used to in order to ignore the conversations downstairs. Eventually, it becomes part of the daily din. Today the girl's office was especially crowded and my visitors found themselves amidst those occupied with their own interests and unimpressed by strangers searching the floor for dropped business cards—the surprise visit, whatever the purpose, turned out to be a failure.

"Mr. Baker, you have visitors. I believe you have been expecting them," Jane announced over the intercom.

"Thank you, Jane. Please have them come right up."

While the quartet scaled the steps I arranged four chairs around my desk and opened the door to give a cheerful welcome. Once inside the room, I directed them to the awaiting furniture.

They say you never get a second chance to create a first impression. When asked how the battery company came about in the first place I took the opportunity to blow my horn.

"Much of what I'm about to tell you has probably been learned from your own investigation. Nevertheless, the complete story should fill in any gaps. I began my battery experience with American Battery, the largest battery manufacturer in the country by virtue of sales to the United States Navy and, domestically, the Atomic Energy Commission, for nuclear electric generating stations. I worked for American about ten years during which I received rising responsibility positions. I owe a great deal to American. They allowed me to work ten to twelve hours a day and any weekend I chose. In doing so, I learned the business of battery making from raw materials to engineering. Best of all, they didn't pay me enough to fear leaving. And that I did to start the company you gentlemen have purchased."

"How about sales?" asked John Anderson. "The marketplace is a tough challenge."

"Here, in the States, industrial batteries are sold in two ways, either by an in-house sales department and regional network or independent dealers. Right off the bat I knew we were too small for the former and, therefore, concentrated on the later. Even then I realized a one-man show could not grow the company at the desired rate. My sales manager, Russell Webster, came from the restaurant and fast food industry. After several planning sessions, he joined the team and we set about pursuing my marketing plan."

"I understand he is family related," Anderson stated.

"Yes, Russell is married to my wife's sister."

Up til now, John Anderson has been the only one to ask questions. Ramesh Patel had sat silently but exhibited clear and resentful facial expressions while I gave my background in the industry. His displeasure was so obvious it's a wonder there wasn't gnashing of teeth.

"Do you think you have a good design?" he questioned rather unsteadily.

"Yes. And because of it we have had a growing market share, year by year."

"Have you ever heard of Delta?" Patel inquired.

"Oh yes. They are a major competitor."

"Their research department has tested your product and said it is over engineered and will fail early in service," Patel was smiling.

"My product has been in service for about ten years and, in many cases, still performing. I'm sure you have already discovered that fact during due diligence.

The basic design features a heavy positive plate. One in which contains more active material. That alone gives longer service life and, additional battery weight is also a sales feature. Lift trucks need counterweight to balance the amount they can lift. In most cases, the competition forces forklift dealers to add steel plates to compensate and the costs are passed on to the end user. Bottom line, our product saves the customer money."

Patel resumed his previous demeanor. It was now John Anderson's turn again.

"I don't know if you're aware of this, but my experience is also with Delta—recently in top management." *I had learned from friends at Delta that Anderson held a second level position and was let go a couple years ago. He presented a good image but fell way short on accomplishment.* He continued, "The four major companies control the lion's share of the market, leaving very little for the little guy. How do you plan to compete against the big guys going forward?"

"Up til now my plan is to specialize. Cherry-pick dealers and persuade them to carry a second line. Give them sales assistance and protected territories. Grow the company without trying to compete directly with a large sales department. That said, we do compete when dealing face to face with the end user. At times, I personally make sales presentations. In some cases, we establish service with the best service group in the area or work out an arrangement with the competition. There is a large enough market to employ my tactic for the next few years," I stated.

"This is where I can help you. The market isn't that big and manufacturers have dwindled down to only six or so. We will need to go head to head against the big boys," said Anderson.

"To my recollection there are over 15 battery manufacturing companies still operating here in the United States. They all do enough business to stay alive. Some specialize in various industries such as railroad and mining."

"Trust me. There isn't anywhere near as many as you claim. I get my information from Delta marketing," said Anderson. "You are probably confused with the auto starting business."

"Not really. I know the auto starting business rather well, having served as president and chairman of the Independent Battery Manufacturing Association. We have 500 members worldwide," I proclaimed, smilingly.

John Anderson's eyes darted to his cohorts looking for help. Clearly a fact none of them had learned. While the collegiate-looking Hal Reed remained silent, with his legs crossed and penny loafers bouncing, the diminutive Pakistani rejoined the conversation.

"Do you believe your product design is good? I was manager of Delta's environmental compliance division and worked closely with the research laboratory. Research looked at your battery and slammed it. They said it was poorly designed, too expensive to make, and destined for failure. What do you think of that?"

It was becoming evident the new owners want to redesign the product and make it similar with everyone else. They believed by doing so the battery will weigh less and save money on lead. 'Joe College', with the dangling loafers, will perform time and motion studies and create job standards on each operation of the process. I spent years building the reputation of a battery that will last five years and they want to change it. At this point, I doubt if I can be a party to it. The niche market approach will be out the window and outside of yours truly. No one in this room has ever sold anything.

"Approximately 7% of my production is earmarked for private label," I replied. "Your former company is the principal customer. We make the Delta 90 and 110 ampere hour models and they are purchasing several Classic models. Classic is a tubular plate provided out of England (*actually manufactured in South Africa*). With England withdrawing from the industrial battery business we will need to wait and see how it all shakes out. I, personally, would not want to manufacture tubular here because of the environmental consequences. Ramesh, you understand where I'm coming from in that regard."

By the look on his face, he actually didn't know anything about the process. Nevertheless, he nodded, giving the impression for the benefit of the other three. Bernard Ackerman, their attorney, scooted his chair closer to my desk and put an elbow on a corner. His suit was ill fitting, looking as though he slept in it and the dark ring on the edge of his shirt collar gave evidence of several days between laundering. *He probably was chosen because he came cheap.* To make matters worse he had a punishing foul breath that forced me to hold mine until I could turn far enough away.

"I think we've had an opportunity to introduce ourselves this morning and we have a lot to discuss during the weeks ahead. My clients have a plane to catch at O'Hare airport," Ackerman stated. Turning to Patel he continued, "Ramesh and Hal will be back next week to explain the new management organization. I assure you Mr.

Patel will have a position to offer when he returns, so you can be comfortable in that knowledge. I know I can trust you to arrange for suitable offices. Ramesh is accustomed to fine furnishings. Perhaps this one will be suitable."

"When I started the company two empty crates and a wooden plank served as my desk. A fancy office does not make a company," I countered.

"I think you know what I mean," Ackerman replied.

Everyone rose to his feet and a round of handshakes sent the new owners on their way. The moment the rental car drove off, Russell Webster was in my office.

"Do we all still have a job?" were the first words out of his mouth.

"I'm afraid so," I replied. "But, nobody is going to be very happy and long range prospects are iffier. They don't understand squat about how this company defied the odds. As you are well aware, it took lots of personal contact in the field to tell our story and the power of persuasion to make buyers take a chance—how we worked with dealers in front of their customers, explaining the design that would last longer and save them money.

"Not one of them has ever had to meet a payroll. They existed under the aegis of a large corporation and, if they found themselves over budget, they merely cut the workforce. The result was losing solid, quality minded people and affecting the esprit de corps."

"Are you going to stay on?" Russell asked.

"That depends on how fixed they are with their faulty assumptions."

"What do you think?" followed Russell.

"I believe they're in over their heads. If I can't make them see the light, I'm gone. All seriousness aside, how do feel about this bunch?"

"Steve Baker is this company. It was built on a personal relationship between you and the dealers. They looked upon you for the improved design and help in explaining it to their customers. New ownership will undoubtedly cause fear the design will be changed and, in their minds, cheapened," Russell stated.

"Well, that is exactly what they plan to do, among other things."

Russell stood up, tugged his pants, scratched the top of his hair, and walked back to his office. A short time later his phone button lit up. No doubt he was calling home.

Later on I turned to look out the window facing the factory floor. The supervisors seemed to have an extra hop in their step. Fear of the unknown can do that sometimes. Assuming the worst, there will be an unhappy group at the dinner table tonight.

We all have had several jobs during our working career and, when disgusted for one reason or another, claimed we were going to quit. I've never quit a job without actually doing so. Today I'll keep my powder dry and see how things turn out. The whole morning seemed like an eldritch dream. Nevertheless, I managed to put on a happy face and took a late lunch in town.

CHAPTER TWENTY-ONE

T HE LAST THING SHARON LEZOTTE expected was a knock on the door and inspector Rice standing on her front porch. A multitude of thoughts ran through her mind as her heart rate sped upward. At first she decided to not answer pretending to be away. Then thinking he may have seen her go inside, decided to face the music. After all, Steve Baker had assured her there is no factual evidence linking her to a crime.

"Sorry to have kept you waiting. I was in the kitchen putting away groceries. The noise of my refrigerator makes it difficult to hear the door bell," she explained.

"I wasn't sure if the doorbell worked or not so I tapped on the door," Rice stated as he removed his hat and stepped inside.

"Please be seated inspector. Would you care for coffee or a glass of water?"

"No thank you. I'm here as a follow-up on the last discussion we had about the Warren Brantley killing. There are a couple questions requiring answers with more depth."

Inspector Rice averted his eyes acting as though he didn't notice the visible concerned expression on Sharon Lezotte's face. In an effort to compose herself she lost control of the timbre in her voice and claimed, "You must forgive me. The memory of my dear sister returns whenever I think of that monster Brantley."

It was Rice's turn to feel apologetic. Lezotte's tears were genuine and without question, his presence has caused them. Tear flooded irises masked the possibility of any deduction leaving little of importance in the interview. He said, "I only have two questions and I'll be on my way. How many times had you spoken to Mr. Brantley and when did they occur?"

Regaining her composure, Sharon stated, "I spoke to him only once. That was the day Rilla was released from the rehab hospital. I don't recall the exact date. It was two years ago."

"I can get the exact date from the hospital. How did you know Warren Brantley was the pusher?" Rice inquired, as he folded his tablet and returned it to his briefcase.

"My sister told me."

You don't need to be a member of Menses to see this interview isn't going the way detective Rice had anticipated. Thus far, the conversation isn't building on itself as he had hoped. His present situation was not in the nomenclature at the academy. Discretion, being the better part of valor, calls for a reassessment of his approach. Changing the playing field from the suspect's home to the police station might give the edge woefully needed. That of course, will require a court order, a long shot without evidence and probable cause. A subpoena, based on a hunch of the arresting officer, wouldn't move the friendliest of Kirksville judges. Lee Rice needs to wind this up and talk to Chief Monahan for advice.

Detective Rice paused for a few seconds looking directly at his subject as if he was composing the next statement. The room was so quiet you could hear the pensive breathing from the remote person of interest. It was obvious Sharon Lezotte was frightened. So much so she held her breath when the detective said, "Miss Lezotte, I'm going to be frank with you. Warren Brantley was a despicable person and the world is better without him in it, but, the manner of his demise makes it a criminal affair and must be investigated. The FBI is mainly concerned about the drugs; however, the Kirksville police have the responsibility of finding the person or persons connected with the murder. I believe you know more about this than you let on. Is there anything you would like to offer? Perhaps something you had overlooked or previously forgotten."

Sharon Lezotte made eye contact and said, "No. I've told you all I know."

Her contracting irises didn't escape the momentary glance of the young police officer.

"I'm going to return to the station and meet with my superiors. You may be subpoenaed to come to the office downtown. I believe it's time for you to contact a lawyer."

The moment Rice's car pulled away from her driveway, Sharon was dialing Steve Baker's private phone number.

When the button on Steve's private phone line began to flash, he had a premonition. He felt Irene was on the other end. He was wrong. The voice of Sharon Lezotte caused a momentary pause in his breathing.

"Sharon?" he asked, in a lesser tone.

"Yes. We need to talk," she answered.

"Are you home?"

"I'm home right now but I'm getting ready to head to the store. I'll be working until nine. It will be best we talk in public, the house is probably being watched," she informed.

"Yes or no, is this about the police detective?"

"Yes. He suggested I get a lawyer."

"I'll be at Kroger's in an hour," he assured.

After the longest fifteen minutes spent in his lofty upstairs office, he argued with himself and descended into the girls' dominion as though on a personal family mission.

"Will you be gone for the remainder of the day?" Jane asked. The ears of the other two women were focused and on alert. Their responsibilities won't change a microscopic iota; however, it seems more relaxed when the boss is not on the premises.

"Most likely," he replied. "My son has car trouble. He called me from Kroger's. If he didn't run out of gas, we will probably need a tow."

From the look on their faces, the girls were sympathetic, having experienced such problems themselves. They appeared to give permission, and Steven left the building without further questions.

The parking lot at Kroger's was full. This could be either good or bad but the problem was he was unsure. A crowded store gave the appearance of innocence, yet, increased the odds of being recognized. Elaine was the family's shopper. She routinely purchased the groceries, prepared the meals, maintained the house and cared for five children. Lately, a thankless activity considering how little Steven had become involved. His absence was claimed to be the result of business and he took full advantage of the falsehood. Guilt made him decide to do something nice for his wife—he'll figure out something later.

In an ineffective effort to remain unobserved, Steven grabbed a cart and, not seeing Sharon at the checkout registers, pushed it into the bakery department. Strange, he can summon her image in a daydream until now. Confronted by women wearing the company colors seemed to disguise their persona into a group likeness.

The cart had a wounded front wheel making it difficult to manage and creating the tendency to bear to the right—a universal frustration for any shopper. By the time he found Sharon, the cart exhibited three items: a loaf of bread, a gallon of whole milk and a rolled roast, bleeding profusely in the white paper tray designed to hold it. The butcher should have better drained the irksome package. It did give an opportunity to approach Sharon and ask for a towel. She had been helping out in the produce department and grabbed his hand to lead him to an employee's only door. While cleansing his hand she repeated, "The detective told me to get a lawyer."

"He was only bluffing. There isn't a shred of evidence to link you to any crime," he said consolingly.

"Why does he suspect me?" she appealed.

"I don't know but I can find out. Mike Monahan and I are friends from little league baseball. He might tell me what's going on. Right now, you just sit tight. It probably will take a day or two to arrange a meeting without raising suspicion. Above all, don't get a lawyer. To do so may confirm what the detective is thinking. By the way, what is his name?"

"Lee Rice. Do you know him?" she asked.

"No, he must be new. I'll learn more when I meet with Monahan. What time do you get off?"

"Not tonight Steve. I'm too nervous for that. Besides, you don't want to be seen with me with all this going on," she acknowledged.

"I guess so. I'll call you when I know more. Right now try not to worry about detective Rice. I'm sure he's only pulling a dodge."

Looking down at Steve's grocery cart Sharon asked, "Are you planning to check these out?"

"Not if I don't have to."

"You go on. I'll put the items back where they belong," Sharon said. The wounded cart now gave Sharon a rough time, fighting against her effort to keep a straight line. Steven exited with other shoppers heading for their automobiles.

CHAPTER TWENTY TWO

T HE OPPORTUNITY TO MEET WITH Chief Detective Monahan happened purely by chance. Over the past couple days Steven had pondered various strategies but was unable to agree on any one in particular.

Whenever up tight, or under pressure, he had always considered breakfast with the morning gang as a mental refresher. Often, the innocent remarks between verbal combatants sparked an idea helpful to determine a desired conclusion, independent of the subject being argued.

As they say, it was déjà vu all over again when Cliff's front entrance door pushed open. The entire crew was at their makeshift table and to top all, Chief Detective Monahan was perched on a stool at the counter. The sound of chairs scooting around the table to make room naturally caught the attention of those residing at the counter—especially, Chief Detective Monahan.

"Mike, come join us," Harry Cook called across the connected tables.

"Yeah, the more the merrier," chimed Carl Landry and Bill Schneider who stood so more chairs could be moved.

Kirksville is a small community. Nearly everyone either grew up with or attended the same institution from lower grades to high school. Doing so sometimes creates a bond lasting a lifetime. The breakfast meeting at Cliff's stands as a perfect example and Mike Monahan is a charter member of the club.

For the benefit of the waitress, Mike slid off his stool with coffee cup in hand and pointed to the group he intended to join. It didn't take long before he was holding his own when it came to cynical jests, which continued until toast was polishing clean the remnants of egg from their plates.

"I'll bet you'll be happy when the FBI wraps up their case and get out of your hair," stated Marshall Bloom. "Any idea when that's going to happen?"

Monahan, stirring creamer into a fresh cup of coffee replied, "It's difficult to run a department with them around. They always come first and you spend a lot of time just keeping them happy. They do a very thorough job and the federal bunch is the best in what they do but, thankfully, they plan to wrap things up this week."

Harry Cook was next speaking. With a serious expression he said, "Mike, one of my patients told me you are questioning Sharon Lezotte about the Brantley killing."

Chief Monahan grew an uncomfortable expression— obviously displeased. After an awkward pause he replied, "For the life of me I'm always amazed how confidential police business can leak out in the general public."

Steve Baker saw his opportunity and said, "That's easy in this case. Sharon Lezotte is a childhood friend of the girls in my office. They all share each other's thoughts and beliefs. It would be natural for them to talk about important events in their lives. There's an innate psychological difference between the sexes. Men may talk openly about their women but, hold fast to much of what involves them personally. Women talk about everything. I, myself, learned about Sharon Lezotte from my office girls."

Mike nodded in silent agreement then cautiously said, "That brings up another puzzle. Neighbors claim seeing your car in Ms. Lezotte's driveway on more than one occasion."

The waitress broke up any air of tension when she asked about another coffee refill. Steve had coffee coming out his ears, nevertheless, lifted his cup—others followed suit. After things settled down he continued, "When I learned about Sharon's sister dying of a drug overdose and Warren Brantley on my payroll, I felt a responsibility to apologize to her and see if we can be of any help. At first, she wouldn't come to the door. Then, when she finally did, she was a complete mess. It took several visits before she came out of deep depression and have confidence in what I was saying."

"When was the last time you saw her?" Monahan asked.

"A couple days ago at Kroger's," answered Steve.

"Did she mention the police or detective Rice?"

"No, I guess she only confided in the girls. Why is the department interested in interrogating her?"

"The department isn't. We have a hotshot detective who is an academy graduate. He senses something suspicious about the way Ms. Lezotte's eyes respond to his questions."

That brought a roar from the table and made a great subject for the jokesters and jape artists.

"Okay, okay, I tend to agree with you. Besides, it can't go further without a court order and I won't ask a judge for a subpoena based on my detective's hunch. I'm reassigning Rice to a desk job."

"You could have your guy check on Bill Schneider. He rides around in a brand new Cadillac with no appropriate means of support," suggested John Coffel.

"Oh yeah, what you guys don't know is I also work as a male escort in the evening," Schneider retorted.

"That's probably why you spent a week in the hospital monitoring your heart," Coffel countered along with more sounds of laughter.

"Let's get serious for a second," Coffel stated. Turning to Steve, he asked, "How's the new owners of Baker Battery Company getting along?"

"I wish I could say great. But, from what I see so far, there could be a problem. I'll know more after we meet again." Steve replied.

"I call this meeting to adjourn. Those in favor signify by saying aye," Bill Schneider announced. The ayes had it and they dispersed in deliberate order.

Lee Rice's investigation changed suddenly. He found himself at a desk immediately across from Haruki Fujimoto. Looking into the epicanthic eyes of the force's diminutive Asian gave Rice assurance he was a victim of a decision without explanation. Had Chief Monahan requested a warrant and been refused? If so, the reassignment, without telling him that fact, was unfair. To make matters worse, announcing the Brantley case officially closed seemed a personal affront. It was a slap in the face, leaving a sting that will linger long after the bruise fades away.

"Look on the bright side. You could have been put on the night desk," Fujimoto postulated, while withdrawing a lit cigarette from his desk drawer. More surprised than indignant, Rice responded, "There's no smoking in the station house."

"Who is enforcing it? Who is going to tell?" Fujimoto inferred in a threatening manner.

"Christ man, everybody can smell it. The first time Monahan walks in, your ass is grass." Rice stated confidently.

As luck would have it, Chief Monahan did just walk in, sniffed a couple times, and then approached Lee Rice's desk. After pausing a few seconds, asked, "Who is smoking?"

Without saying a word, Fujimoto nodded toward Rice. Monahan made a disgusted facial expression and announced, "You all know the rules. The next time I find someone smoking, it will result in either demotion of expulsion." You could hear the gulp from Fujimoto's swallow. "Further, officer Rice is a non-smoker. It doesn't take a genius to figure out who I'm referring to." The voiceless head bow of Fujimoto spoke volumes, drawing a smile from the distraught officer Rice.

Turning again to Lee Rice, Monahan said, "I took you off the case because you are doing a fine job. Let me explain, Commander Homberg wants to close the file. Whether the suspect knows more than she's telling is not relevant. The FBI has recommended we form an independent drug agency and I want you to head it up. We can talk more about it next week. In the meantime, give some thought as to who you want working for you."

As Monahan left the room he called back, "Open the damn windows and air it out in here."

I learned about detective Rice's 'promotion' through the cold-air vent on my office floor. Of course, the main concern of the office girls was their friend Sharon would no longer be harassed. Even though I had little to do with the outcome, Sharon naturally, would think otherwise. A quick trip to Kroger's should guarantee a copious sample of her appreciation. Just as sure as the weekend follows Friday, a bottle of wine and extricated tension proved me right.

Strange how strenuous amatory exercise can cure anxiety. After which, the ardor, that previously engulfed the psychic being, vanishes like the misty hint of smoke in an autumn breeze. Sharon lay supine beside me. Her face exhibited a cheerful glow with a quiet smile about her mouth. I, in turn, was confronted by the countenance of Irene Jones. I'd be kidding myself if I believed a romantic love existed with Sharon. It's more like a sexual friendship. We give each other satisfaction in that regard without the cloying annoyance of romance. While we both lay exhausted, Sharon will soon drift into the arms of Morpheus and I count the hours until I can leave. Even though my thoughts are tinctured with images of Irene Jones, I could not ascribe to lasting love.

What a blessing it would be if this all was just a dream and I could awaken to the safety of my bed, shackles gone and the present ghosts disappeared. Unfortunately, that's not a reality and staring at the ceiling, for the moment, must be my circumstance.

CHAPTER TWENTY-THREE

AFTER A FEW DAYS, THE battery factory operated as if the previous events hadn't occurred. When another week passed by, the new owners were yet to make an appearance. Finally, Ramesh Patel telephoned and alerted Jane O'Connor he would probably be away until after the holidays. Further, he asked her to tell me Hal Reed will be coming in to perform time study on the casting operation. Obviously, the little *ghatia insaan* didn't have balls enough to tell me direct.

In my opinion, time and motion studies are worthless when you are dealing with old temperamental refurbished machinery. Output is governed mostly by the skill of the operator. He learns the idiosyncrasies of the equipment and manages accordingly. Casting mold surface treatment and the speed, by which molten lead is fed, govern productivity. Experience and patience guides him as to when he performs this operation. Naturally, brand new equipment is more amenable to time-motion studies. Unfortunately, Baker Battery Company was unable to pay out a hundred thousand dollars for a new machine.

The only other grid caster is a stand up mold with molten lead added by hand ladle. The need for mold treatment also applies, and, the casting gate removal is performed using a metal saw, once again, by hand.

The pace, the new owners observed, no doubt underwhelmed them and ignorant to the need for it, immediately turned the old diagnosis with motivation and incentives as the prescription for cure. Coming from a much larger company, they were diametrically opposed to my concept of individual employees, working within themselves, produce the highest quality—of utmost importance when you guarantee the product will last five years in service.

Setting work standards based on volume usually sacrifices quality and establishes the 'good enough' attitude. When the casting operator is motivated by volume over quality, he might exceed the time study standard only to build a pallet load of castings (grids) unusable for the next operation (pasting). In such cases, the previous days output will require physical rework to make the product acceptable, and, depending on the severity of the defects, could end up back in the lead pot. Results of this action affect the total process—faulty inventory reports and delays caused by rescheduling.

Hal Reed called the following Monday afternoon. He had a serious problem and needed to talk to me. Jane alerted me to his problem before making the connection. After a moderate delay, I picked up, "Steve Baker, how may I help you?"

"Steve, this is Hal Reed. I'm at O'Hare airport and have a problem. Can you send somebody to pick me up?"

"Unfortunately, there's no car available. You need to rent one."

"That's my problem. The credit card Ramesh gave me wasn't accepted."

"Use your own and turn in an expense slip," I suggested.

"Mine is maxed out," Reed replied, sheepishly. "Have your secretary drive up and get me."

His tone gave me a slow burn and reminded me of how much I disliked him when we first met. "Oh, I wouldn't do that. O'Hare is seventy miles away and in the heart of dangerous Chicago traffic. You just need to figure something else out. Use cash. Didn't you receive a daily per diem in Philadelphia?"

"Yes, but that's for meals."

"You're just going to have to use it to rent a car. We probably can keep you from starving to death. In the meantime get a hold of Patel and explain the dilemma," I advised, and replaced the receiver.

Hesitating for a few seconds, I thought a hot cup of coffee would be the ticket. So, descending the steps and shuffling to the lunchroom, I felt better than I had for some time. While adding double creamer and sugar, I noticed Bailey Marshall taking a morning break and sat down at his table. After the usual pleasantries, I informed him of Hal Reed's arrival and making a time study of the casting operation. Bailey will need to be involved to assist him. The look in my plant manager's eyes was all that needed to be said. Bailey is a good man, we both think along the same line. During the walk back to the office, I wasn't quite as happy as before.

Presently, as I understand it, I'm still in charge of the operation, especially with Ramesh Patel out of the country. The panic call from Hal Reed drops him way down the organizational chart, if he fits on it at all. His assignment is an exercise in futility considering the age and condition of our casting equipment.

The philosophy of most large companies concerns itself with employee boredom and motivation, assuming incentive programs is the cure. Granted, repetitive operations create ennui and, in order to escape boredom, workers mentally remove themselves from the task at hand. Going through the motions, they envision themselves at more pleasing activities. Management often considers those comfortable with a repetitive job somehow unfit for more challenging positions or, at lease, at their highest levels of competence, vis-á-vie their Peter Principle. I believe those with more potential take such jobs because they are easy and offer opportunity for fantasy meditation. It's this type of operator we have working in the casting department.

I question whether Hal Reed will be able to establish any meaningful production standards employing our old equipment. He will probably work the week and offer something to Patel, but it will never be put in effect.

While things presently are up-in-the-air and Patel away until year's end, it affords the chance to get away for awhile. Russell Webster and I could take two weeks for visiting our dealers and quell any misinformation or discomfort with the sale of the company. Russell would love it and maybe I could clear my head. Bailey Marshall and Jane O'Connor will assure I have my finger on the pulse of business and it's Russell's habit to call in, several times a day.

Besides, the timing is also right because we should be back before the annual battery convention, in case I change my mind and decide to attend. The application and paperwork still rests on top of my desk, unopened. I would be flying blind without learning exactly what Ramesh Patel has in mind for the company. Oh well, I'll give it plenty of thought while we travel. At this point, I know one thing for certain, if Patel leaves me alone and lets me continue running the operation, I'll stay on. If he doesn't, I'll definitely move on.

It's a human frailty to consider personal problems superior to everything else, mine not excluded. Next door and around the world, hardship and woe is forever present. Many such tragedies occur to which mankind holds no responsibilities and is blameless. To wit, on September 9, a tropical storm formed on the coast of Africa. Moving west northwest, it passed over the Cape Verde Islands, strengthening in intensity. Its path took it across the warm waters of the Atlantic Ocean, which helped it grow into a category 5 hurricane. Because of its route, such storms are called Cape Verde Hurricanes.

On September 12, while causing minimal damage to Florida, it came ashore as a category 4 when it made landfall on the Carolinas— the full blunt of the dreaded tempest striking Isle of Palms, South Carolina, leaving devastation in its wake. Suffering the worst impact, South Carolina had thirty-five fatalities and totaled nearly six billion dollars in damage. Over 3,000 single-family homes were destroyed and 18,000 others, severely damaged. Several thousand mobile homes and 18,000 multi-family houses were either destroyed or damaged. Electrical power outages affected 227,000 residences and Marion County was without any electrical service[5]. The storm had downed over 8,800 square miles of timber in the Francis Marion National Forest. With the exception of newer growth, much of the mature pine trees were destroyed—enough to build over a half million homes. An

---

5   Data included for Hurricane Hugo was obtained from Wikipedia, the free encyclopedia.

immense salvage effort was quickly undertaken, to harvest downed pine for pulpwood, before they deteriorated to the point where they couldn't be saved.

Hurricane Hugo's heavy winds reached all the way to Charlotte, North Carolina—150 miles from shore—before weakening to a tropical storm.

Hurricane Hugo was the worst storm to ever hit South Carolina.

Later, at Cliff's breakfast powwow, the hottest subject was about what took place the day before. On Tuesday, October 17, the third game of the 1989 World Series between the Oakland Athletics and San Francisco Giants was finishing opening ceremonies when TV commentator Al Michaels could be heard saying, "I'll tell you what, we're having an earth...." The feed cut before he finished the word earthquake. When video and sound was restored, Michaels confirmed the tremor. By then, over 60,000 startled fans were exiting the stadium.

Northern California had been struck by the Loma Prieta earthquake. Registering a magnitude of 7.0, the shock was responsible for 63 deaths and 3,757 injuries. Heaviest damage was in Santa Cruz County and to the north into the San Francisco Bay area, on the peninsula and across the bay in Oakland.

The collapse of a section of the double-deck Nimitz Freeway, called the Cypress Street Viaduct, was the site of the single number of casualties. The upper tier collapsed on top of the lower tier and killed 42 people. Remarkably, it could have been worse. Rush hour traffic on the Bay area freeways was lighter than normal due to the 62,000 people attending the game at Candlestick Park in Oakland.

The World Series games were rescheduled for October 27 and 28 with Oakland winning in a four game sweep.

I asked Russell Webster to set the agenda for our sales trip, knowing full well he would exclude New York because of the need to fly. Although, I do recall a previous dealer tour included the Big Apple and he drove it by company car. It was arranged to give us the week end to ourselves and spend it at Saratoga racetrack—an experience I'll always remember. The Spa is still beautiful this late in the season. This time however, we will mostly cover the southern states. He asked me if I wanted to make a stop in Birmingham, Alabama. It was more like an allusion rather than an honest question. I didn't fall for the prompt and replied, "Maybe not this trip." Russell's face twisted in disappointment as he shuffled back to his office. Russell has no firsthand knowledge of any of my indiscretions, but, loaded with suspicions, which I'm sure he delightfully relates to his wife. I've often wondered why any man would do this other than deep felt begrudged envy—certainly not as a noble deed.

In spite of his shortcomings, I've always considered him my friend. Away from the influence of his wife, the man has a heart of gold—if not gold, perhaps silver, or at least, cardboard. Recently, with women dominating the friendship issue and no males that count, Russell fits the bill.

As expected, Hal Reed finished his assignment by Friday. He and Bailey Marshall managed a preliminary and definitely piece meal study of the casting operation. Hal also came up with suggested monetary rates for exceeding the standard. Bailey, not Hal, provided poignant information regarding their work. The little shit was too embarrassed to present evidence of his failure to yours truly. He simply told me he was done, thanked me for the hospitality, and made a dash for O'Hare. He lacked sangfroid to stand before me, the oppositionist of the project, and agree with my predetermined conclusion. There are certain aspects of my job somewhat satisfying.

The following Monday, Russell Webster laid the agenda of our sales trip on my desk. It identified stops in Peoria, Illinois; Saint Louis, Missouri; Indianapolis, Indiana; Louisville, Kentucky; Memphis, Tennessee; Atlanta, Georgia; then back to Columbus, Ohio, before heading home. I should point out he hadn't given up completely on Birmingham. He indicated in pencil, after Atlanta, if time permitted.

As things turned out, the trip was received well by the dealers. It's only natural when the principal supplier sells the company, consternation and unrest results. Would the new owner make changes to the product? Would the discounts and financial terms be changed? Without actually knowing the truthful answers, I had Russell respond and he lied like a champ. I must have consumed a carload of Tums.

On our return trip, Jane O'Connor informed me Ramesh Patel had called and wanted to hold a board of directors' meeting the first week in December. I assumed he meant all his people and me. Nevertheless, with the knowledge Patel and his gang won't be around for a few weeks tended to make the remainder of the journey quite pleasant. And, coupled with my decision to not visit Birmingham, gave me a touch of righteousness. But also a night of tossing, turning, and pillow flipping—a difficult decision for sure.

Basically, the return trip was uneventful. As far as I know, the battery convention was successful, even without my being there. According to Jane O'Connor, Irene called and left a message. She wanted to buy me dinner at Miller's Pub. Jane explained I was traveling for the company and probably wouldn't attend this year. Do I have regrets? Of course I do. When thinking about Miller's Pub, I'm reminded of the most thrilling time of my life.

It's been said distance never separates two hearts who really care, for their memories span the miles. That's probably true for soldiers separated from a loved one, sometimes for months or even years. But, in the case of Irene and me, the distance served as a safety factor preventing daily personal contact, which might lead to a dramatic life change. For the first few years the status quo satisfied us both. While I was perfectly happy, she became discontented. It's no surprise Irene eventually found it to be a cruel way to be in love and wanted more out of life. As the months flew by, phone calls became less frequent. I won't lie about it, hearing Irene called from the convention did fan the sparks a little, but, I'm not going to respond—there's safety in long distance partners.

Speaking of long distance partners, I've managed to maintain a telephone relationship with Coralee Smallwood, the little charmer in Birmingham, Alabama. She's still single and attends Samford University, a private coeducational Christian school located in Homewood, a suburb of Birmingham. Now in her second year of general studies, Coralee will soon have to select a major. She's thinking about nursing or pharmacy.

I was stunned when I first learned she attended Samford. The costs and tuition has to run over $30,000 annually, even with living at home. Apparently, grandma is sitting on a hefty nest egg. What's not surprising is her grandmother chose a Christian college for her to attend. Somehow that pleases me as well.

Each time Coralee and I conclude a phone conversation, I want to go to Birmingham and piss on all the trees around her grandmother's house. I'm not so self-centered to think I have a legitimate claim to her affections, after all, over the past couple years we've only communicated by phone—although, she does call on a regular basis.

Each time we hang up, I'm reminded of my stigma for drinking too much Corona Export and the opportunity lost in the midst of very favorable circumstances. It would be easier to catch a feather dancing in a windstorm than recreate a similar scene. Nevertheless, she still haunts my reverie. Can a beautiful body restrain the aggravation and annoyance of her soft southern twang? I sure would like to find out.

Once I walked through the front door of the factory, reality popped a hole in my fantasy balloon. I was beset by the duties of management—returning phone calls, writing letters, meeting with supervisors and the office staff.

Jane O'Connor took lunch in my office and brought me up to date with the shenanigans of our new owner and the upcoming board meeting. Just as we were about to finish, the phone rang. It was Ramesh Patel wanting to speak with me. Jane handed me the phone and I said, "Ramesh, it's been awhile."

"Yes, but you have an excellent secretary. She kept me abreast of your activities with the dealers. As you know, I have been doing a little traveling myself," he replied.

"I understand you have been out of the country."

"That is true. I have been to England and India meeting with people interested in investing in the company. One of the gentlemen came back with me and you will meet him the first week in December.

I've been wondering, do you know of a good place to hold our board meeting? Somewhere, off site, that might impress our visitor."

"The Gold Room at the Kirksville Hotel," I immediately answered. "I think it would be perfect and the hotel could also furnish lunch. If you really want to put on the dog I suggest you all stay there, rather than at a motel. If you provide your itinerary, Jane can make all the arrangements."

A short pause told me Ramesh was checking his calendar. When he returned he suggested, "We will fly out on the morning of December 4, have dinner in Chicago, and arrive in Kirksville in the afternoon. On Tuesday the 5th visit the factory and make a tour. The board meeting will be held on Wednesday the 6th and we will return to Philadelphia Thursday the 7th. I would appreciate your handling our lodging at the Kirksville Hotel, and reserve the board meeting room."

"How many people will be in your party?" I asked.

"There will be four, counting our guest."

"What is the guest's name?"

"Mr. Samar Manju, but, he does not speak much English. He and I will probably converse in Punjabi."

"To be safe, I'll put all the rooms in your name. Is Hal Reed going to make it to the meeting?"

"No, Hal isn't a board member. He is an employee."

That came as no surprise. Hal may have been an acceptable time study engineer but lacked the diplomacy and savoir-faire to work with a company recently sold. A great deal of suspicion and unrest lies just beneath the surface of the employees as well as supervision. It takes a certain amount of tact to be accepted. Hal came across as wanting. A deficiency of which he was either unaware or didn't care. Introspection would reveal my attitude wasn't helpful; nevertheless, the new owners were clueless and I took it out on him—the only one present at the time.

Thanks to Jane O'Connor's organization ability, everything came off like clockwork.

I wish I could say the same for the meeting, itself. Early on, I determined our visitor, Samar Manju, was only a financial backer. Obviously, this was his first visit to a battery factory since he constantly complained about the 'acid' smell. Those familiar with manufacturing lead acid batteries grow used to it. Of course, in the formation department, the cells on charge will gas and give off a small amount of weak acid in the atmosphere. Accordingly, the department is well ventilated. Confident his very existence was in peril Manju made certain the tour was short-lived.

"Should I get a stretcher for Mr. Manju?" I whispered to Ramesh. He thought I was serious and replied, "No, we'll just go back to the hotel and continue with the meeting." I pinched myself to make certain I wasn't dreaming.

The accoutrements at the Kirksville Hotel were excellent. The long mahogany conference table had comfortable high back chairs, well cushioned. Decanters of ice water were neatly spaced on the centerline of the table and each seat position was furnished with a heavy crystal drinking glass. I had to suppress my smugness as most of them acted surprised at such refinements here in little old Kirksville.

Ramesh Patel called the meeting to order. Samar Manju was still examining the crystal glassware. Feeling like telling him that it was for the water, I had second thoughts on the sarcasm.

My stomach hit the floor when Ramesh made the first announcement. He proudly stated he had purchased Atlas Manufacturing in Palo Alto, California. Their owners were asking five million and he bought it for three with $500,000 down and the balance in quarterly payments. I looked in the eyes of each member at the table and they revealed they knew about the transaction and supported it.

Ramesh continued, "One of your supplier friends had recommended the company to me."

I knew who it had to be and said, "He had recommended it to me about a year ago. I told him they couldn't give it to me. Their primary product was golf cart batteries and they bucked up against the largest producer in the country, also located in California—in San Jose. Sales were a pittance compared to the big competitor and mostly due to local glad-handing and payoff. Clearly, it wasn't enough to survive. Atlas has been bankrupt and out of business for the past seven years."

"Yes, but I personally examined their equipment and it is still in good shape. Besides golf cart batteries, Atlas had a contract with government for aircraft batteries."

"There was no contract," I expressed. "They only submitted some units for test which failed."

"Well, you will just have to resurrect the relationship," Ramesh countered. "From what I've been told you have a gift for persuasion."

"First of all, I know very little about aircraft and space age technology. Their batteries are quite different from lead acid."

Ramesh went on, "Times are changing. As far as it goes, you've done a good job with Baker Battery Company; but, today, in order to be successful, a new perspective is required. We must reorient our thinking to be in tune with what's happening now and in the future."

This guy has evidently been reading motivational literature.

"Because of gasoline shortages and higher fuel prices, there's a renewed interest in the electric car. The California factory is perfect for manufacturing the required batteries," Ramesh asserted.

"The electric car batteries will not be lead acid. Too much weight," I replied. "New types of fuel cells are needed. Cells with a very high amount of energy to weight ratio. I have a friend who has petitioned the U.S. Government for $300 million dollars to research and develop these maximum fuel cells."

"We're talking about entering an enterprise requiring millions of dollars. The financial burden creates a dangerous pond. Negotiating it by stepping on rocks to get across would be foolish. One slip means financial ruin. Even making batteries for power tools finds us far behind the curve. In my opinion, by purchasing Atlas, we now own a white elephant and have seriously injured our operating capital."

You could hear their guts gurgling on the street below. Samar Manju was white as a ghost. Obviously he was in a visible state of shock. Ramesh trembled with anger. His adrenaline level was off the chart. There's a German word describing my feelings......*Schadenfreude.* It means satisfaction or pleasure at someone else's misfortune.

Nevertheless, the handwriting was on the wall. There was no way I could remain with such a thick-witted top management. Besides, I'm certain once they are capable they will actively hunt for my replacement. The time has come for me to explore some of the offers made by my competitors.

Ironically, a few days later, I learned that Russell Webster, under the guise of giving assurances to our dealers, had traveled to Pennsylvania and visited with Ramesh and his wife for the weekend. Good ole Russell was attempting to ingratiate him, not surprising and definitely in character, but still, rather disappointing. I won't mention it to Russell since Ramesh Patel would unknowingly be aligning himself with the JV team.

There are two standing offers to be considered. One of them would not require me to relocate the family. As things stood and even though the offer by Liberty Battery paid less, the no-move proposal won out. With Ramesh and his cohorts back east, things were quiet for awhile. No doubt they weren't very placid in Pennsylvania. Whatever actions were being considered, my termination had to head the list.

To finalize the deal, I took a couple days off and drove to Cleveland, Ohio. The money aspect was less but, still pretty good, considering I'd only be required to be in the factory one week in the month. All travel expenses would be covered by the company—including mileage, should I choose to drive. They wanted a five-year contract. We settled on a two-year contract with an option.

On the return home, I was like the cat who got the bird. My family was suffering under a significant amount of tension due to a possible need for relocation. Before checking out of the hotel I called Elaine to relieve the family's anxiety. Like Walt Whitman's poem, "Afoot and light-hearted I take to the open road, healthy, free, the world before me." I think I smiled all the way back to Kirksville.

Considering the circumstances, I felt bound to give a thirty-day notice to Ramesh Patel even though, at this point, my value with the company is limited. Activity on the floor confirms a non sequitur. It appears the rank and file is in high spirits. My guess is Russell has been talking to them about the new management and promised higher wages. Is he really looking at the situation with new eyes? Or merely further ingratiating himself with Patel. Nevertheless, something definitely has gotten the employees pumped up.

Considering what was revealed at the board meeting, another recently purchased company will require being supported by Baker Battery's receivables. It has been a challenge to maintain and grow Baker Battery by itself. Adding another major expense will spell the demise of both. Venders aren't stupid. When the agreed upon operating terms are extended to 90 days or longer, they will get suspicious and cut off supply. That will end everything. I've a mind to have a heart to heart talk with Russell. His duplicity deserves a shock of reality.

The following day found me sitting at my desk tapping the eraser end of a pencil on the hard wood surface. Funny how the concerns of former importance lose their impact when your future lies elsewhere. Finally the bubble of my preoccupation was burst by Jane O'Connor's voice on the intercom.

"Mr. Baker, Mr. Patel is holding on the other line," Jane announced.

"Good morning Ramesh, how may I help you?"

"Well…..I would like to talk to you," he said after hesitation.

"If I'm not mistaken that's what we're doing now," I replied and felt immediately regretful after saying it.

Patel hesitated again then said, "Maybe we could have lunch or dinner at the restaurant you called the Little Frenchman or something. It would be more relaxing to talk away from the factory, less prying eyes and ears."

"I believe it's called the Little Corporal but don't recall it being exactly French, other than its name. When do you want to meet?"

"Tomorrow, say at noon or later. You pick the time. I'm flying out today," Patel offered.

"Lunch sounds good to me."

"Okay, I'll see you at the restaurant," Patel confirmed and then hung up, ending the conversation.

The more I thought about it, the less I wanted to meet with him. My decision to accept the Liberty Battery offer is cast in stone. There's no way for me to change my mind. But then, curiosity got the best of me and good old *schadenfreude* took over.

———◈———

Arriving about fifteen minutes early I took a table in the more illuminated section favored by the general public. Normally, I wouldn't sit facing the bright windows. Unfortunately, it was the only way for me to keep an eye on the entrance door. When the waitress brought water and asked my order, I told her there will be another guest and to please close the curtains which allowed sunlight to strike our table. Bless her. She selected the correct curtains on the first try.

A diminutive individual struggling with the entrance door signaled the appearance of Ramesh Patel—twenty minutes late. He looked as though he had slept in his suit. His necktie, tied in the Oriental style, pulled to one side, leaving the shirt collar outside the suit coat. Trying not to be conspicuous, I motioned to draw his attention. Ramesh found my table and sat down with a forced grin.

"Did you have a good flight?"

"Oh yes, air travel is quite comfortable now days." he replied.

The waitress, who had been waiting for my guest, hurried to the table. After a short pause Ramesh looked to me and said, "He can order first while I read the menu."

"I'm going to have your Chef Salad with Thousand Island dressing and a glass of iced tea," while Ramesh pondered the lunch menu. Finally, he ordered a toasted cheese sandwich with mayonnaise and a slice of tomato on top.

Confused, the waitress asked, "Do you want the tomato inside the sandwich?"

Yes, but on top," Ramesh counseled.

"Just make it the normal way but, when you bring it, make sure the sandwich is right side up," I instructed.

"It's always on top," she said to herself while walking away.

Ramesh had returned to his false grin and without eye contact said, "Well, I guess you are leaving?"

"You did get my message and letter of resignation? I tried to reach you several times."

"I was very busy when you called and away from Philadelphia for over a week," he replied.

I nodded as if I understood.

After an uncomfortable interlude, Ramesh continued, "I am in deep shit. Empire Capital summoned me to New York. They said I violated the terms of our agreement and cancelled it, plus, called my note."

"Was it because of the Atlas Battery deal?"

"They said so. You were against that from the beginning. I should have listened. Actually, I should have let you continue to run the company and remained a long distant owner. John Anderson suggested that but Bernard Ackerman felt I needed hands on management. I listened to the lawyer," Ramesh lamented.

"Losing a million dollar line of credit is a major impairment. How about Samar Manju, could he help with a loan?"

"Manju couldn't get back to India fast enough. He wanted no part of a battery factory," Ramesh admitted.

"Are your other investors willing to pony up more? Perhaps that attorney would help finance so you can keep the factory running, or at least until other sources are found."

"Most lawyers are not entrepreneurs. They just bill you for their time and make an occasional suggestion. Bernard Ackerman voted for the Atlas Battery purchase," Ramesh moaned, and continued. "John Anderson and his wife have already invested all their savings."

No one spoke for a while, and then Ramesh said, "I would like to ask you to stay on the full month of your resignation. It will give me time to travel back to India and meet with my family. Some of which are in banking, but, they are from the Pakistani side. Nevertheless, even though it will be embarrassing, I'll still beseech their help."

"I don't understand. Why would it be embarrassing?"

"I bragged too much about being an owner of a large battery business. Having similar investments in India, they resented that."

Considering his request, I agreed, but added, "I'll try to avoid personal questions from outside, however, I won't lie about them. That includes the employees."

"I must have shitty karma. Everything I've tried turned out bad," Ramesh lamented.

"You referred to karma. Isn't that part of your Indian religion?"

"Yes, we believe karma is a driving force," Ramesh replied.

"Your religion still holds for reincarnation?"

"They go hand in hand. It is difficult to define karma in exact terms because of the various views in the teaching of Hinduism. Those of my particular persuasion believe the present circumstances of an individual are related to actions in the past or in previous lives."

"If that's true, in the past life you must have been Jack the Ripper," I jested.

"By the way my luck has been running, that's a possibility," he replied.

Ramesh was the first to leave the restaurant. As I watched him exit the front door a feeling of compassion and regret came over me. Had he chosen a different approach, we could have definitely made a go of it. However, as the saying goes, if ifs and buts were cherries and nuts, everyday would be Christmas.

CHAPTER TWENTY-FOUR

THE NEXT TWO WEEKS DRAGGED by at a snail's pace. Both Jane O'Connor and Callie Mellinger had found other employment. After writing letters of recommendation, I encouraged them to accept and move on immediately. Apparently, the rank and file on the floor now had a new attitude—no whistles, hoots, laugh, or any other sounds of happiness. They now acted as robots with grim expressions.

Now, most of the phone calls were from suppliers. I placated their concerns by saying Patel was in India securing more money. At a time when we needed our agents to honor their credit terms, they chose not to remit, making matters worse. There seemed to be a pall over everything connected to Baker Battery.

Elsewhere, my life bounced along like the little ball in sing-a-long movies. Sharon Lezotte has found a steady boyfriend, although she will come through if I needed her. Thus far, I haven't pressed the issue. She deserves better. Each day Irene becomes a more distant memory. I'm happy keeping it that way.

The long awaited team up with Coralee Smallwood came to pass. She and a couple of her sorority sisters took a holiday weekend in Chicago. Coralee and I spent two nights in a motel twenty minutes from the city. The issue of her virginity is finally resolved. Our age differences were definitely reflected, however, she seemed perfectly satisfied, even though my lack of staying power was evident.

I nearly choked on my Mountain Dew soda when Coralee suggested we be together permanently once she graduates.

On my drive back to Kirksville the usual relief of flight was absent. Instead, a concern of responsibility for this sweet girl was foremost. Thankfully, she had another year in college and I will embark on a new avenue of employment. Both should keep us occupied before things explode.

The agreement with Ramesh Patel is about to expire and I still haven't heard from him. A woman, claiming to be the new controller, introduced herself and asked for my company credit card. She asserted she was acting at the behest of the new owner. When asked whether Mr. Patel had returned from his mission in India, she became uncommunicative. I thought, damn, I'll be glad to be removed from this place and all connected with it. Reaching for my hip pocket I extracted the company credit card—one of the more positive actions taken by Patel. He had issued a card for the accountant, marketing manager and me. While I personally wouldn't have done it, none the less, it was a show of confidence. This deed was long before the Atlas Battery brew-ha-ha. In addition to extracting my company credit card I removed a pair of scissors from the top desk drawer and snipped it in half, handing two pieces to her. The large unpleasant woman's face turned white as a sheet. Obviously, my card had a higher credit limit, something very important to Ramesh, especially at this time. Well, what's done is done. She only said, "You shouldn't have done that," and left the office. It was then I noticed her perceptible limp, something I will never ask about.

While loading the trunk of my car with a box of personal items my world was about to come crashing down. The vehicle churning the dust on its way to the factory turned out to be a state police car. It pulled along side of me and the officer methodically got out and approached.

"Mr. Baker, please come with me. Your wife has been in a serious traffic accident," he said without emotion.

"How serious is it? Is she okay?"

"Honestly sir, I cannot answer that. I was told to locate you and convey you to the hospital," replied the officer. Once on the main road, we were travelling at high speed with the siren ear-splitting.

After we arrived at the emergency entrance things became an intangible dream. Hospital staff, in blue scrubs, guided me down the halls, occasionally asking if I was all right. One of them wanted to know if I wanted orange juice. Orange juice!! I wanted to see my wife. Finally we entered a room with someone on a gurney. A white sheet covered the entire body concealing specific identity. The medic, in a white lab coat, pulled the sheet to her shoulders and asked, "Can you identify her?"

Caught in this surreal world, paralyzed to the point where I could hardly breathe, speak, or think, I at last uttered, "Yes, it's my wife, Elaine."

From that point a female in blue led me to a nearby office. Blue girl apparently had experience with his sort of tragedy since she was helpful in guiding me through the next few steps. Patterson Funeral Home would retrieve Elaine and I was to select a proper casket tomorrow morning. All I had to do now was go home and devastate the children.

For the first time I realized that my offspring are strangers. It was Elaine who was the selfless cornerstone of the family. She was the one who maintained the family unit, serving as the foundation for the developing youngsters. Not only mending their childhood hurts and illnesses but guiding their development toward adulthood. She was the rock they could both lean and rely on.

All the while, I spent countless hours building a business and whatever free time became available was squandered selfishly. In that, I'm no different than the average man. It's been stated that even the best of marriage life will eventually have a gap in it. The spark that initially brought you together over time fades into a monotonous routine. When living in that hollow space, most men try to do the right thing, even though that space might last for years.

Jumping into the gap, I went crazy thinking only of the moment, knowing full well it will never last. What does last, however, is the harm it does to others and especially you. If you're lucky, the life on the other end of the break can be revisited. An untimely traffic accident took that opportunity away from me. Now, the effect of my transgressions can be read in the faces of my children.

All were home with the exception of Rosemary and David, who I must notify by telephone. Rosemary graduated from junior college and received a bachelor's degree from the University of Illinois in Urbana-Champaign. She is now working on her master's degree in education. David enlisted in the air force and is stationed at Scott Air force base near Belleville, Illinois.

Michael is a sophomore in high school, Ashley's in eighth grade and Kristen is in sixth, all living at home.

I talked with the children, those at home, until wee hours of the morning. Trying to comfort them through the early stages of grief gave me the opportunity to become better acquainted and share their pain. Right now, they primarily suffer from shock and disbelief. Depression and deep sadness is yet to come.

The next day our neighbor lady, Mrs. Murphy, offered to watch the children while I visited Patterson's Funeral Home. I thought I was somewhat familiar with the exercise, however, learned a lot more about caskets than I wanted to. Young Patterson guided me through the experience and toward a metal coffin. I found choosing the right coffin could be rather complicated. Funerary boxes are usually made with metal, wood, or fiberglass. While none last forever, the metal boxes last the longest. I selected one made out of bronze. Also, they don't come one-size-fits-all. Elaine had changed from the slim young girl I married. Patterson suggested a slight increase of a half-inch in the width. Lastly, color and type cloth covering the interior was determined. It took nearly two hours before finishing the purchase.

All questions were answered and visitation was hopefully planned to begin the next day. Still operating in a mental fog, I seemed to have done things correctly. Patterson's will contact the newspaper and I will drop by the United Methodist Church and talk to its venerable Scottish minister, Doctor Morgan Williams, about his performing the services. The good reverend had married us, baptized the children, and now will lay Elaine to rest.

By the time I returned home, Mrs. Murphy had answered many telephone calls offering condolences. When asked about visitation hours, all Mary could tell them was check with the funeral home or call back later. As it turned out, visitation will be the next two days and burial on Saturday.

Rosemary and David arrived that evening. By the first day of visitation a steady stream of food had filled the refrigerator and dining room table. It was another kindness for which the whole family truly appreciated.

Radiant sunlight reflected through the east windows announcing the arrival of Thursday. Judging by the way I felt, it was doubtful all had a good night's sleep, especially Rosemary, the closest confidant of her mother.

Our plans called for the whole family to be at the funeral parlor early. Visitation was scheduled to begin at 2:00 p.m. Considering the sleepless night, I thought it best if we had brunch at a local diner. The idea was good but the light repast was silent.

Those wishing to pay respects began appearing at the scheduled time. Just a trickle at first, then by the numbers, which began to fill the oversize room. Rosemary was much better than I when it came to recognizing those offering condolences. I was beginning to feel like a 'third wheel' but, then, Cliff's breakfast club members showed up, followed by business acquaintances and folks from the factory. After a couple hours, young Patterson called me aside and mentioned an antechamber with comfortable chairs for the family members—it's going to be a long day. Just the thought of comfortable chairs gave me a shot of energy and allowed me to stand for another hour.

In the early afternoon, Mrs. Murphy arrived to offer condolences and view the deceased. She later volunteered to take the three youngest children home with her until we returned for the evening. So doing, a great deal of stress was relieved. Trying to control the vigor of adolescents, and their failed effort to maintain restraint, was beginning to test our patience.

Once alone, into the private anteroom, Rosemary broke down and wept. My daughter's bereavement brought about a father's natural sense of altruism. It also reminded me that, thus far, my eyes had remained dry—probably due to the awesome responsibilities of such an occasion. My time may come later. Formal observance of the loved one ended at 8:00 p.m. We were a wearied bunch when we finally returned home. Both tired and hungry for good reason. While depression and stress can interfere with normal bodily functions, making you feel hunger, even after a hearty meal, in our case, it's safe to say our craving is real. Our last meal was that silent episode this morning. Knowing the kitchen was full from the largess of friends, neighbors, and well-wishers, also stimulated the appetite.

That night, though dream-filled, served to rejuvenate the family. Rosemary and I managed to make a hearty breakfast and everyone ate better than the day before. More cognizant about how things work, we planned to go to the funeral parlor later than we did yesterday. As a result, we received several more consolers bearing gifts of food and sympathy here at home. I chose to attend the door and greet visitors. Between the ringing of the door chimes I tried to read last night's newspaper but found it too difficult to concentrate. I hadn't sat for long when the doorbell sounded again. I was shocked to see Sharon Lezotte standing before me. No words were spoken. Tears began to fill her eyes and I pulled her to me in a close embrace. For the first time since the accident I began to sob. At that moment, Sharon was my truest friend. There was no sex in these emotions, just honest compassion for pain and suffering.

Once I resumed composure she asserted, "I'm here to help."

"Come inside, I want you to meet my family."

Sharon entered with all five children curious to see the visitor—someone they didn't recognize. As I made customary introductions, only Rosemary was visibly reserved.

"Why are you here?" Rosemary asked judiciously.

"I was hoping to be of help in your time of need. I can cook. I can clean. I can baby-sit, if need be. The next few days will be the toughest of all. It will require thank you notes and letters to all those participating with gifts, flowers and condolences. Custom calls for serving a dinner after the burial ceremonies. I can help with the cooking and cleaning before and after," Sharon stated.

Relenting slightly, Rosemary admitted, "You can help me with dishes right now. I don't believe the boys have made their beds. (That brought a guilty acknowledgement by their heads bent downward and eyes studiously searching the floor.) I could use a little assistance in that regard and some house cleaning relief as well."

Apparently, Rosemary had prided herself with her effort thus far; however, the more she heard about the job, yet to come, her resolve began to weaken.

The two women were now standing side by side at the kitchen sink, one washing, and the other holding the drying towel. It didn't take long before Rosemary asseverated, "Are you one of my father's girlfriends?"

Taken aback, Sharon said, "If your connotation means what I think it means, my answer has to be no. Your father saved my life. At a time when I seriously contemplated suicide, he helped me overcome a terrible tragedy. And, over time, under his guidance, I came back to life. He was the only one who really cared. I owe him a debt of gratitude that can never be repaid."

Rosemary felt as though her question wasn't really answered and weighed it against the work facing her over the next few days. Reluctantly, she gave in.

The second day of the wake saw as many condolers expressing sympathy as the day before. I knew Elaine was active in several women's clubs as well as church groups but I had no idea she was recognized so highly. She never elaborated on her activities, apparently out of respect for my feelings. Once again, Rosemary appeared to know them all. Sadly I wondered, "Where have I been all these years?"

Those connected with business or my personal friendship was naturally beyond the purview of my oldest daughter. Therefore, I had to make introductions to the family. As time elapsed that would include, Asher Horwitz and his wife Shirley, Lucas Gardener and his wife Susan, and Ramesh Patel and his wife Maya. Asher and Lucas were both my high school classmates. We graduated together at Kirksville Senior High. Although, attending different colleges, miles apart, we three ended up back in Kirksville to ply our trade. Asher took up the insurance business and Lucas practices law.

Due to the magnitude of the procession, time spent with each sympathizer had to be greatly limited, much to my delight. In the main, a sentiment most likely shared with many. After several stressful hours standing on your feet, you begin to burn out. You hear the words of condolence but, being overwrought, they become phlegmatic. It's time for a breather in the anteroom.

After a short hiatus, I returned to the presumed role of head of the family. Just in time to receive the owner of Liberty Battery, Frank Turner and his wife Margaret. My new boss expressed his sympathy for our loss and encouraged me to take all the time necessary before showing up for work—appreciated, but, I'm not a person who sits around scratching his belly. I'll be there as agreed.

The next party disoriented my countenance. Since I'm no longer connected with Baker Battery and have accepted a position at Liberty, I had discounted any possibility of seeing vendors at Elaine's wake. The presence of Harvey Finefield and Irene Jones knocked me off-center. Harvey, a gregarious sort, obviously wanted to see for himself. Well liked in the industry, he frequently comes across as unpolished and often ignores decorum. Therefore, while whispering my current status to Harvey, the corner of my eye focused on Irene. When our eyes made contact, my heart skipped a beat. She was more beautiful than memory recalled. It was like my breath had frozen in my lungs—words were hard to bring forward. After what seemed like an eternity, I managed to muster, "Thank you for caring."

Speaking softly she said, "We won't be able to attend the burial. I'll call you in a couple weeks to see how you are doing."

"You'll have to call him at Liberty Battery. He's got a new job," Harvey interrupted.

"Then maybe I'll see you. Liberty is our customer, I'm there quite often."

Much to my relief, the press of the line forced them to move on. Now my concern was Rosemary. Thankfully, she appeared disinterested; a credit to Irene's acting ability. With Rosemary at the gate, there is no way I could bring another woman into our house.

Doctor Morgan Williams conducted services in the Patterson's funeral chapel, after which, a procession will continue to the gravesite for burial. The fact that the good doctor never lost his Scottish accent, tended to endear him even more with his congregation. With a hint of Scottish burr, he expressed, "God so loved the world that he gave us his only son. You all know Him. He's here with us today. Let us pray. Dear Heavenly Father, we come to you at this time of grief and sorrow asking that you give peace and comfort to all who mourn. Embrace the family and give them the healing consolation only you can give. Through Jesus' name we pray. Amen.

We are gathered here today not only to mourn over how different our lives will be without Elaine Baker but also to give thanks for how full life was with her. We are here to praise Elaine for a selfless life dedicated to helping others while actively serving her church, home, and family. Her life was rewarded by her love. She loved her women's clubs, she loved her church, she loved her friends, she loved her children, she loved her husband and she loved God. I might add a little levity here, she also loved country music."

That brought a smile to the teary eyed gathering. Then, three teenage girls, from the Methodist youth choir prepared to sing. Another youth softly played an electric keyboard. Their sweet celestial voices sounded like angels when they sang; In the Garden, Jesus Loves Me, and a third unfamiliar song—I guess it's a changing world.

While my family seemed engrossed, my mind began to wander. I drifted back to the time Elaine and I first met. She was tall, thin and beautiful. When we married, I became the luckiest man on earth. Back then, our lives were a struggle trying to finish college and the added pressure of meager, part-time income. Never once did Elaine complain. Her abiding faith in God lifted her up and carried her through the hardest of days. I know now, if it weren't for that steadfast faith, she would have left me long ago. Her faith in the Lord elevated her life as evidenced by so many here who are bereaved by her passing. My confidence is flagging when I contemplate the future without her.

Reverend Williams opened his King James Bible to a previously marked page, and then continued, "Being at Rome at the time, Saint Mark was the first to write a Gospel. A generation had passed since Jesus' crucifixion. The story of his life, death, and resurrection had up to this time circulated in oral form. By now, those who had been eyewitnesses of these things were dying off. It was of utmost importance the record be written down while living witnesses could corroborate it." A characteristic of the Scotsman sermons is a history lesson and, so doing, renders a tight hold on your attention.

"Reading from the Gospel of Mark, Chapter 12, verses 28 through 31, *'And one of the scribes came, and having heard them reasoning together, and perceiving that he had answered well, asked him, 'Which is the first commandment of all?'*

And Jesus answered him, 'The first of all the commandments is, Hear O Israel; the Lord our God is one Lord.

And thou shall love the Lord thy God with all thy heart, and with all thy soul, and with all thy mind, and with all thy strength: this is the first commandment.

And the second is like, namely this, Thou shalt love thy neighbor as thyself. There is none other commandment greater than these.'

The scribe mentioned here was likely a biblical scholar or theologian. The importance of Mark's Gospel is Jesus sanctioned the union of two commandments, love God and love thy neighbor. Jesus, whose life was a constant expression of this command, joined them not only in word but also in deed. As a result, these two commandments have become the focus of the Christian religion.

Elaine Baker led her life fixed on these commands. To some, knowing the devoted life she led, why did God let that accident happen? God does not ordain our future here on earth. God does not make our loved ones sick. Neither is He responsible for accidental deaths. The fact is, some things happen by chance, others are caused by someone else's sin, and occasionally because of our own acts of carelessness. We, here on earth, are free moral agents to act out our lives as we see fit. Eternal life depends on the choices we make. The Bible makes perfectly clear the righteous path to save our souls.

Let us pray, Heavenly Father, it is a time like this we suddenly realize the frailty of life and the brief portion permitted on the earth. Help us to be wise as suits thee Lord, knowing anytime you may choose to call us home. Lift into your arms of love and carry those of us who are suffering with grief. Amen."

Everyone remained at their positions while the pallbearers lifted the casket and carried it to an awaiting hearse. After which the immediate family and I were directed into a Patterson's limousine. My son David was one of the pallbearers and will travel with them.

Everything was performed with precision and soon we were on our way to the Kirksville cemetery.

Outside the chapel, the sun appeared to be radiating straight down and the cloudless sky revealed a deep azure-cyan color. It was as though heaven was anxious to receive its newly winged angel.

Memorial Gardens is the oldest cemetery in Kirksville, its headstones date back to a time before the city was officially founded. They sing a mystical song of generations past and quietly retain muted secrets of those families lying at rest. At dusk, when a misty fog sets in, the taller stones become the fata morgana of castles. Over the years the taller tombstones became a serious maintenance problem for the groundskeepers. Today, headstones must be flat.

At the burial site, two rows of temporary folding chairs were set up for the immediate family, relatives, and close friends. Remaining sympathizers stood behind, encircling the interment location.

The minister found his place near the casket and said, "I want to encourage you, as we gather this morning to lay our loved one to rest, to understand death is not the end. Yes, when she lived, Elaine Baker had touched all of us with her love, humor, and faith. Even though she has gone to a better place, her memory will be everlasting. It is we, who remain on earth, who are left with the pain of sorrow and grief. It is we who need the comfort given by the love and strength of God.

In the book of John, chapter 14, verses 1 through 6, Jesus said, *'let not your heart be troubled: ye believe in God, believe also in me.*

In my father's house are many mansions: if it were not so, I would have told you.

And if I go and prepare a place for you, I will come again, and receive you unto myself: that where I am, there ye may be also.

And whither I go ye know, and the way ye know.

Thomas saith unto him, Lord, we know not whither thou goest, and how can we know the way?

Jesus saith unto him, 'I am the way, the truth and the life: no man cometh unto the Father, but by me.'

In the book of Psalms 34, verses 17-19 it states, *'The righteous cry and the Lord heareth, and delivereth them out of all their troubles.*

The Lord is nigh unto them that are of a broken heart; saveth such as he of a contrite spirit.

Many are the afflictions of the righteous, but the Lord delivereth him out of them all.'"

Behind the minister stood a canvas screen placed there in order to hide the small tractor and backhoe. Much to my relief, digging the pit for receiving the casket will take place after we leave. Reverend Williams now led us all in reciting the Lord's Prayer. After which he gave the final benediction.

"In sure and certain hope of the resurrection to eternal life, through our Lord Jesus Christ, we commend to Almighty God our sister, wife, and mother, Elaine Baker. And, we commit her body to the ground, earth to earth, ashes to ashes, and dust to dust.

Now a word for those in this congregation. With his eye upon the sparrow, I know he watches thee. Shall we pray, may the lord bless you, and keep you, and make His face to shine upon you and give you peace. Amen."

The only advantage of standing at a burial service is you can be the first to head for your car once it's over. That was demonstrated perfectly today. The family must ride back to the funeral parlor in the limousine that brought them. At any rate, I had an envelope for Reverend Williams 'burning a hole' in my suit pocket. Even though conducting funeral services technically falls under his job description, it's customary to reward the minister for action above and beyond the call of duty. I guess the practice goes back to an earlier time when the preacher wasn't on salary. Another time honored tradition is the luncheon after the burial. I doubt if Dr Williams will accept the invitation, however, it's a lead pipe cinch he'll snatch that envelope while claiming it isn't necessary.

You can't always judge others by the way you feel. I would have avoided the luncheon like the plague. Surprisingly, the house was jam-packed. In fact, standing room only and people walking around with paper plates in their hands—another tribute to how much Elaine was loved.

Fortunately, Rosemary had isolated a chair at the dining room table for me. I've got to hand it to my daughter and Sharon Lezotte. If there is such a thing as success for this type of event, those two get the blue ribbon.

It was well into the afternoon before the last sympathizer walked out the front door. Finally, the two victorious women sat in recliners and kicked off their shoes. With a cup of hot coffee in their hands they lay back and silently listened to the tick of the clock on the fireplace mantle.

"Don't get too comfortable. We still have to clean up the mess," Sharon said, while their eyes remained unopened.

"Dishes and a quick pickup," Rosemary replied. "I'll be glad when it's all over."

"There will still be a lot left to do. You'll have nearly a hundred-fifty thank you cards and messages to write. But, you can wait a week before you need to do that. I can come over and help the Sunday after tomorrow," Sharon offered.

"Please do. I don't know where to begin." Rosemary confessed. "How do you know so much about this?"

"It's a long story," Sharon answered solemnly. "Maybe we can talk about it then."

"Good, I still have some questions about you and my father."

"You may not want to know the answers."

The next day, the Baker family didn't go to church. Instead, they used the day for guiltless recuperation. Rosemary's interest was piqued after Sharon told her she had to answer each one, plus, others who were instrumental to the funeral of her mother. Sliding the pile round with her hand she was able to distinguish between advertisements and those cards to be answered.

Among the pile of sympathy cards were two personal and confidential letters addressed to Steven Baker. By glancing at the return addresses she noted they were from Asher Horwitz, Insurance Brokerage and Lucas Gardener, Attorney at Law. Intuition told her these held utmost importance for her father and accordingly, she culled them from the group and placed them in front of her dad's breakfast plate. Debating whether to open them before or after breakfast, Steven compromised and poured syrup on his pancakes, then slit the letters open using a table knife. In each case, he was requested to visit their offices at the first convenient time. Without comment, he folded them neatly, laid one atop the other, and finished the morning meal. With the exception of Rosemary, the rest of the children, including David, showed no particular interest.

"When do you have to be back at the base?" Steven asked David.

"I can stick around for two or three more days but probably should leave next Thursday."

"How about you, Rosemary?" her father questioned.

"My time is more flexible than David's. I want to stay until arrangements are made for the family, when you need to be in Ohio."

Bidding approval, Steven uttered, "That's good news."

"Perhaps we could advertise for a housekeeper in the Kirksville News," suggested Rosemary.

"Maybe we won't have to," replied the father, "your mother has three sisters. I was flabbergasted when Virginia, her oldest, offered to look after the children the week I had to be away."

"Why did that come as such a surprise? It was a very nice thing to do."

Steven thought for a moment before saying, "Your mother's sisters, when in my presence, were saccharine sweet. That said, I'm positive they never really liked me. And, as far as I was concerned, that just made the pot right. Since one of the brothers-in-law was a true reprehensible miscreant, I was saved from being the black sheep.

I guess Virginia was a different story. Being divorced and alone gave her the freedom to make the proposal. Her ex-husband left her in meager circumstances; however, she's been able to carry on quite well with the monthly alimony directed by the court. Her own children, a boy and a girl, are both married and live out of state. Do you think I should give her a call and make her an offer?"

"Most definitely," Rosemary stated. "And make the pay enough to make it worthwhile for her. We children always felt Aunt Virginia was our favorite."

I had to smile at my daughter. It was obvious she sees Virginia as her savior who can release her to return to college more quickly. Considering how well she withstood this ordeal, I can't blame her one bit, and asked, "How much should I pay her?"

"Father, I have no idea, but I'll call the employment office and ask what the going rate for housekeeper runs and then you offer her half."

"Half the going rate for just one week's work?"

"Yes, and don't quibble about it, either," she finalized.

CHAPTER TWENTY-FIVE

V ISITING ASHER'S OFFICE, I WAS pretty sure what the nature of the discussion would be. Both Elaine and I had a term life insurance policy in the amount of $500,000. I assume it doubles in case of accidental death.

Looking up over his glasses, Asher commented, "I trust your family is back to daily living. Elaine's passing was a terrible loss for us all and I can't imagine the toll on all of you.

I've filed, on your behalf, an insurance claim for $1,000,000. Your policies have the accidental death clause. There are some requirements for your signature, so if you indulge me, I'll have my secretary bring in the necessary forms."

After signing the forms, the conversation turned more sociable. I enlightened Asher to the fact that Rosemary had returned to college, David was back on the base, and I have a nanny for the children when I'm out of town.

"Things appear to be getting back to normal," Asher surmised. "I'll contact you when the check arrives. It's a lot of money, but when you consider raising a family nowadays, with college in the future, the costs are very high."

My next appointment was with Lucas Gardener. Lucas's office wasn't as pristine as Asher's; however, with law books crowding the shelves, quite impressive. He welcomed me to his desk, and after social amenities, asked, "Have you heard from the Trucking Company?"

"I just found a card from them asking for a meeting. It was mixed in with all the sympathy cards."

"Then you haven't met with them. Good. If you wish, I can handle your case or suggest someone to represent your position, someone with more experience in this type situation. I've performed some preliminary work. The trucking company is very rich and their driver was both drunk and high on drugs. I've obtained a copy of the official police report."

"Lucas, I know you and trust you. I don't believe someone else can do better. I'd like you to take my case."

"I won't have any fee. They probably would offer $250,000 in settlement. Therefore, anything over that amount I will receive one-third. Do you think that's fair?"

"Yes."

"I'll contact their office right away. One other thing, I usually require a signed agreement, nothing personal but it makes everything legal," the attorney stipulated.

Steven left his lawyer friend's office humming the melody of 'London Bridge is falling down'. He owned a sense of self-satisfaction, having his ducks in a row, and now can begin new employment without immediate pressing concerns. Keep in mind, self-satisfaction has always been Steven's métier, whether warranted or not.

At that point, he missed having a secretary. It's times like this when the value of a so-called second in command comes to the forefront. Be that as it may, he will return home and make travel arrangements by himself—a task formerly delegated to Jane O'Connor.

While on the sidewalk, the misty cold began to annoy his cheeks, reminding him winter is just round the corner. Pleasant days will last about as long as the shelf life of a banana. Soon the air will be filled with white missiles tossed by teenagers in their annual jubilation. At the moment, wind gusts sent withered leaves scattering like mice in the company of a cat. It won't be long before such leaves will be joined by others, forcing neighbors to brush the cobwebs from their rakes.

Don't be fooled by his enlivened step, walking to his car. There are times, mostly at night, when the guttering candle of sleep begins to die out, his conscience, ground deep in his soul, reminds him of Elaine. It was remarkable how well her love continued to grow in the shade, even though his actions directed sunlight toward others whom he felt worthier. The flicker of nocturnal remorse continues to disturb his nighttime slumber. Hopefully, a new job, new surroundings, and new people, will be enough of a distraction to override a troubled conscience.

It was prearranged for Virginia to have Rosemary's bedroom the week she looked after the children. It had its own bathroom facilities including, toilet, sink, tub, and shower, which will give her appropriate privacy. And, since I was still debating whether I will arrive in Cleveland Sunday evening or Monday morning, she came over on Saturday, just in case. Either way, it will give Virginia a little more time to better acquaint herself with the house and household.

Not wanting to set a precedent, I decided to leave on Monday morning and get to Liberty Battery around lunchtime. Isn't it wonderful when you have financial independence? I refuse to quail. By doing so I may avoid the weary treadmill of typical or routine employment. I will set durable parameters—no more traveling on my own time. With Elaine gone, I'm drawing breath in a new life.

Liberty Battery must have established some form of surveillance, because, after I parked my rental car and walked the front pavement, a small management group was waiting to welcome me inside. Among the gathering stood Frank Turner, owner and president. He personally gave me a hearty welcome and then made introductions with each person occupying the entryway. Afterwards, he led me up the stairs to the managers' offices.

"I believe you already know most of them," while directing me into his headquarters and offering me a chair. As we sat across from each other Frank explained, "Liberty Battery has always manufactured auto starting and golf cart batteries. About two years ago we undertook the fabrication of the industrial types for electric lift trucks. Internally, I don't have anybody familiar with this type product. Wrongfully assuming all lead-acid batteries are the same, we ended up with steel cased product but not one to pass existing quality standards of initial capacity. We can only give 80% of the required rating. I guess there is a significant difference between SLI and industrial."

"Most definitely," I agreed. "This week will make me more familiar with your current processes, no pun intended, and evaluate design and raw materials. We've learned a great deal regarding oxide crystal morphology and curing techniques."

Frank Turner broke out with an authentic smile and stated firmly, "I believe you know exactly what I want. Right now, let's pick up some of my top management and luncheon at the country club."

By the time we got back from lunch, there was only two hours left for the morning shift. I did manage to walk through the factory to get a feel for the operation and meet some of the first shift supervisors. You can learn more from these gentlemen than any one upstairs.

Employees were leaving the building like there was a bomb scare. I satisfied myself by acknowledging the fact Liberty Battery was union. About that time, my name reverberated from the speaker system requesting me to pick up the phone. I didn't have a clue where the phones were so I light-footed upstairs. The place was dark and empty; however, just as I started for the steps leading to the front entrance, someone opened the women's restroom door.

"Oh, Mr. Baker, Mr. Turner wants you to have the office by the conference room. Your briefcase and a few other items are on your desk," she announced, while buttoning her coat and scurrying down the steps. Smiling at the humor of the situation, the first day on the job, and still the last to leave; however, it won't be hard for me to fall in line. This sure is a far cry from the previous role of ten-hour days.

The next morning I ate a sumptuous breakfast and arrived at the factory with the office staff hard at it—not a hint of resentment in the room. A quick glance at the clock displayed nearly nine o'clock. Feeling a tad sheepish, I decided to arrive tomorrow a little bit earlier. There still were smiles and greetings all the way around when I left my office and walked to the stairway leading to the manufacturing plant floor. Refreshed by the sound of a factory in operation, caused my circulation to pick up speed, reminding me how much I enjoyed it.

Having the freedom to walk through the factory, once workers were assured I posed no threat, allowed me to learn both union/management problems and those associated with the manufacturing process.

Perhaps the most outstanding flaw may be due to the type of oxide used for industrial battery applications. Like most automotive battery manufacturers, Liberty incorporates the ball mill technology to produce lead oxide. Traditionally, such lead oxide is utilized making auto starting battery plates but not the best choice when it comes to industrial lift truck batteries. Ball milled oxide contains about 15 to 30% metallic lead particles which are too large to properly hydroset when making battery plates. The tetragonal shaped lead crystals are less reactive with acid and limit the electrical capacity.

I may have solved Liberty Battery's problem the second day on the job. Correcting it, however, will require a significant capital outlay. There are still the other processes to be audited before formulating my review and recommendations.

On Wednesday morning, while sitting at my desk summarizing the previous day's notes, the phone rang. It was Frank Turner.

"Good morning Steve. Do you have plans for lunch today?"

"Only with the fellows from the oxide lab," I answered.

"Harvey Finefield, with Spartan Chemicals, is making a call and I would like you to join us. Your input will be appreciated," Frank confessed. "I don't know that much about lead chemistry and with you there, he won't be able to bull shit me."

"I see you know Harvey," I said. "He's a very nice guy but makes up for his lack of science too easily."

"That's him," Frank replied. "See you at noon."

After replacing the receiver, my mind began to meander and finally landed on what Irene Jones said at Elaine's funeral. There is nothing I can do about it at this point. Time will tell, so I checked my watch and descended the steps to the factory floor. The hour I had to spend before noon seemed to drag like the last drop of rain from the downspout. Nevertheless, while in the casting department I did examine the positive and negative plate castings. The positive plate grid appeared adequate to deliver rating if all else was equal. The casting machine operator was oblivious when it came to specifications, leaving me with the need to spend more time with the engineers, one of which controls blueprint and specs.

Often the pain in a soldier's leg, amputated long ago, still leaves throbbing episodes destined to last a lifetime. Similarly, having lunch with Harvey Finefield gives one the pain of déjà vu. In particular, Harvey's puffy face and eyes give credence to his habit of packing a bottle in his suitcase when traveling for the company. Remarkably, overlooking his trembling hands and fingers, he maintains the ability to function in conversations as one sober as a judge. Unsurprisingly, on this visit, he was accompanied by someone who directly influenced my behavior for several years—Irene Jones.

She acted as though she were a person who knew me only through business contact. You've got to hand it to her. Like the feathers on a duck, her manner was perfectly placed. Without question, she was fooling everybody seated at the table. And, one other thing, Irene, even at her mature age, never appeared more seductive and beautiful.

Most of the table talk was about my old company and Ramesh Patel. Without saying, their concern for Ramesh indicated a problem with his account. He was in arrears while I was still there and, as far as I know, things hadn't gotten any better. My response to their questions only pertained to what I personally knew while working with the new company. Ramesh had been aggressively seeking additional funding. Unsatisfied, Harvey changed the subject and asked Frank, "Are you bringing a large contingent to the convention this year?"

"Not too large of a group. Most likely the same as last year, my wife and the marketing manager, and plant manager," Frank replied.

"How about Steve? He's a past president," Irene added.

"That's entirely up to Steve. As far as I'm concerned, whatever he decides has my approval. Liberty will cover all expenses."

With her most fetching smile, Irene asked, "How 'bout it Steve? Are you going to be there?"

While my answer was forthcoming, Harvey interrupted, "No matter, your crew is invited to be Spartan's guest for dinner." Pausing, while he checked his pocket planner. "On Wednesday, October 24th."

"If the good Lord is willing and the creek don't rise, we'll be there," Frank replied, while chuckling to himself for his bit of levity.

At that point the servers began bringing the food, saving me from further questioning. I was spared from questioning, but not the piercing blue eyes of the lovely inamorata sitting across the table from me. If her stare were a laser beam, I'd be cut in half.

After dinner we had an aperitif and made our excuses. Having driven our own cars to the restaurant made it easier. Harvey usually ends the day at the bar. That said, Irene asked Frank Turner for a ride back to the motel. As things turned out, we were staying at the same lodge.

I was pulling on a shoestring when the phone began to ring. At first, I was concerned it might be Kirksville calling and quickly snatched the receiver.

"Hello," I answered, as my heartbeat lessened.

"Did I catch you between the sheets?" It was Irene Jones.

"No, I was just removing my shoes."

"We didn't have an opportunity to really talk to each other. How are you doing?"

"If you are referring to the loss of Elaine, the process is taking longer than previously anticipated. However, time does tend to heal," I confessed.

"I'm glad to hear it. You must know my feelings have never changed."

"Harvey told Frank Turner you were still single and had been dating."

"What did you expect me to do? I've had dinner dates but that's as far as it gets. Not many ask me out a second time and never a third."

A pause in the conversation lingered while I processed her confession.

"Please come to the convention. We don't have to join Harvey's dinner party. We could go alone to Miller's Pub."

Irene's suggestion of Miller's Pub awakened a pleasant memory. She's no fool and grasped for a chance to rekindle an old relationship. With just the thought, I'm reminded of salad days and the rebirth of my mid-life awakening. To decline outright would be unfair considering the favorable memories and current mood. I ended our conversation with, "Let's wait and see."

The next morning I grabbed a quick cup of coffee and drove directly to the factory. I did so primarily for two reasons. First, eliminate the chance of running into Irene again and second, with a full day on the project I should collect enough data to complete a summary and, on Friday, catch an early flight back to Chicago's Midway airport.

Frank Turner must have relayed to his management team how important it was to solve his motive power problem. Product drawings, material specifications, and factory procedures found their way to my desk before the parking lot grand prix took place. Amy Johnson, the secretary who told me about my office, kindly offered to loan her bookbag to carry all the paperwork. I planned to pack it into my hanging clothes bag and check it through. As promised, I'll return the bag to Amy Johnson Friday morning.

The next day, I found Frank Turner's office dark. He either was running late or taking a long weekend. Clad in traveling clothes signified to the office group my imminent return home. A final walk through the factory drew no apparent attention.

The return flight was without incident and the drive home felt shorter than usual.

According to Virginia Prouder, the week passed without any problems and the children were well behaved. I got the feeling she was a little too protective, so I gave her a wink, and said, "I've hired another housekeeper who is strong on discipline and she can keep it that way."

The children went ballistic. They insisted I tell her that the job was taken. Their Aunt Virginia makes them behave and they want to keep her. I reluctantly conceded.

"I'll stay until you get better situated, maybe another day or two," Virginia offered. "Supper is on the stove. It will be ready in an hour. I put a list of telephone messages on your desk."

The aroma emanating from the kitchen was bewitching. Did it always smell so good? For the life of me I can't remember. My eyes began to fill while walking to the desk. I wiped the blur away with the back of my hand and sat down. All but two phone calls found my wastebasket.

Oddly, I felt the gratification of coming home. Nothing here has actually changed, same town, same house, and same surroundings. I guess the only thing changed is me. Perhaps, it all is part of the healing process. While I don't exactly see myself as the Prodigal Son, I enjoy this sensation of warmth and closeness. It was entirely different when I returned from being with Irene. Looking back on those occasions, home became a harbor, a safe shelter from transgression. These ruminations were disrupted when Virginia called out, "Dinner is on the table."

By night the built up stress from the week at Liberty Battery finally began to taper off. So often, when anxiety lessens, weariness increases. I hit the sack early. The influence of fresh clean sheets worked like a tranquilizer and I was in the arms of Morpheus before I knew it. Ever faithful, my thoughts and dreams came with me. My nighttime mental illusions usually involved a work-related story line. Tonight, it was interrupted by the presence of Elaine. She was in a jovial mood and tending to the children. I called out to her but through the gossamer mist she didn't hear me. It was so real and she was so alive. When I awakened, it was a saddening situation realizing Elaine was still gone. The narcotic of clean sheets had worn off and the remainder of the night was spent reversing the pillow.

The next morning, while eager to get started with the project, the paperwork remained on the desk. My new life forbids me to work on the weekend. Instead, I plan to tackle the carpet of fallen leaves in the back yard. The day was winter crisp; and, even though I needed to wear a crew necked sweater now, it won't be long before I'll be in shirt sleeves. My targets were ankle-deep and crackled under foot while awaiting the rake. Tree leaves are certainly God's miracle. Like many things in His creation, human and otherwise, you need to die before rebirth—the resurrection and nature's new growth.

By noon, the neighborhood resembled the base of an active volcano with smoke plumes scattered across the edge of frontage streets. Living just beyond the city limits allows us to burn leaves. The backside of my property accommodates three mature maple trees. Trees of the species can grow 200,000 leaves each year and I have three of them. One thing for sure, when the sun goes down, I'll be suffering from muscle pain and since I don't do yoga, I'll rely on ibuprofen and bed rest.

Virginia, staying for a couple days longer, turned out to be a blessing. I had always garnished respect for her mental endowments. Sharing my home and children with her has opened my eyes to other things in addition to domestic assets. Virginia is a fine figure of womanhood. Her manner, complexion, fashionable dress, and figure bear this out. I better not concentrate too much on her figure. There is enough going on elsewhere to keep me on my toes. Our relationship must be purely platonic.

As expected, it was hard to get out of bed Sunday morning. Virginia found a heating pad and kept the ibuprofen going every four hours. She wanted me to exercise but I convinced her I didn't need it. You've got to hand it to her for practicing what she preaches. Yoga every morning before leaving the bedroom, runs three days a week on the nearby forest preserve jogging path, walks every day to the same preserve and back (unless it is raining). She seems to be in perpetual motion with cooking and housework. When waiting for the washing machine to cycle out her hands are in the mending basket patching and sewing up holes. She tells me that idle hands are the devil's workshop. I couldn't help thinking, *I'd like to give her some personal exercise, and she would never do Yoga again.*

In spite of my annoyance with her picayune and regimental attitude, under the present circumstances, I must confess, she fits in well. We're both too old to change. Virginia has lived alone way too long and I don't own a white flag.

On Monday, it didn't take long before I was receiving phone calls from Liberty Battery, mostly concerning the quality of negative grid castings. It appears the second shift operator had trouble filling the casting machine mold with lead. Consequently, the Quality Control inspector rejected a few skid loads. Losing a shifts output is always an anathema for production planning. It throws a monkey wrench into the materials aspect. Apparently, I now am the motive power guru as to how bad is bad. Considering the defect involves negative grids, I could offer latitude which would be impossible were they positive grids. I recommended any grid with three or more missing inner members go back into the lead pot. Others can be used under an engineering deviation, which must be documented in writing and signed by manufacturing and quality control. I will affix my signature on the next visit. Such decisions and records are to be kept on file by both parties. That tends to eliminate future finger pointing.

The euphony heard outside my office suggested the children were home from school. That, coupled with the stringent tones of Virginia, let me know their youthful exuberance was under control. A glimpse at my wristwatch divulged a great deal of time had passed quickly. Science claims the more knowledge one has about any particular subject matter or favorite activity, the perception of time passes faster. Conversely, the less we know of a new activity seems to slow things down. While I don't exactly agree, however, that might explain why a grade school day took forever.

The approaching convention is turning out to be a tenebrous expectation. It's been said we humans always live out the plot of an inscrutable tale. That certainly holds true for me. Whether to attend or not leaves me torn between wanting to improve myself and the desire to enjoy life as it naturally unfolds. I'm also curious to see if the love between Irene and me is still operable. The answer can't be rationalized, it must be experienced. My father taught me the only way to conquer fear is to climb the high diving board. Until now, I suffer little compunction over my previous conduct. I guess Ovid got it right when he is quoted as saying, "I see the good and I like it, but I do wrong anyway." Enough pondering, my work is a jealous mistress so I better get back to it.

I've come to the conclusion the only way for Liberty Battery to attain industry standard quality requirements is substituting litharge for ball milled oxide. Doing so will dramatically change positive plate performance.

Basically, I am referring to the present tetragonal lead crystal structure and residual hard lead particles. Litharge is produced by the Barton pot technique. The lead oxide is composed of orthorhombic crystals and minimal residuals, which are better for humidity curing growth. By incorporating a temperature controlled humidity curing oven the resulting crystal morphology can reach desired density, strength, and chemical reactivity.

This claim can be tested before any capital expenditure is considered or debated. And, since the proof of the pudding is in the eating, I'll suggest mixing a test batch of paste using litharge and pasting enough positive grids to assemble six industrial cells—designed for either 450 or 600 ampere hour capacity. After the grids are pasted, the normal Liberty processes are to be followed.

My contact in the engineering department is Paul Mueller, a lad with hands on field experience. Even though he lacks a college degree, his know-how is perfect for my needs—someone to follow the process from start to finish. While there will be those who have their noses bent, the fact Frank Turner endorses the idea puts an end to the grumble.

By dealing directly with Paul, I learned Liberty had a small pony-mixer in their equipment warehouse. He felt the only thing wrong with it was electrical—an easy fix for a handyman.

The test procedure was e-mailed to Paul with a copy to Frank Turner. Figuring, since we need to purchase a drum of litharge, it might expedite matters with Frank on the mailing list. Finally, I asked Paul to keep me updated on progress since I plan to be present at the start.

Now, with the project safely on its critical path, I can give proper attention to the convention. It opened on Monday; however, given people were still arriving, no important events were scheduled. I plan to attend persona non grata. With Chicago just a little over an hour away, I could drive up on Wednesday morning and make an appearance. Then, that evening, beg off any dinner invitations and meet Irene at Miller's Pub around eight.

The more I thought about it, the more I decided it would be best to book a room at the Hampton motor lodge, in case a return was incapable on the same day. The Hampton is fifteen miles west, yet, only twenty minutes away.

As luck would have it, all single rooms were filled; however, they did have one of their suites still open. I got a deal for only fifty dollars more than the price of a single room.

Arriving at lunchtime and parking my car in the hotel basement garage allowed me to walk directly to the lobby restaurant. While most conventioneers were upstairs eating lunch provided by the organization, there were a few members seated here in the luxurious lobby luncheonette, conspicuous by their nametags. Acknowledging them with a nod, I was led to a table and handed the lunch menu. Peering over the bill of fare, I observed those previously recognized had their heads together, no doubt explaining who I am.

A turkey sandwich and a cup of coffee fit the bill. Reaching across the empty table next to me, I borrowed the morning paper. It served as an adequate prop for excusing my absence from the goings on upstairs. The room was practically empty when I finished; and, without adieu, the paper was placed back on its previous table and I took the elevator down to the vendors display room. Spending a little time at each station would wrongly identify my attending the convention. Relieved, when I found the Spartan Chemicals booth attended only by one salesman, whom I did not know, I stopped for a quick chat. After the short visit, my tour continued. When encountering old friends, the discussion centered on my old company and new job. Most were of the opinion Ramesh Patel was failing, to which I carefully remained neutral.

From the vendor display room I took the escalator to the main floor lounge, fashioned by its stately and sumptuous motif. There are enough priceless paintings hanging on the walls to fill a small museum. Speaking of hanging, the laughter being heard can be no other than Harvey Finefield, hanging at the bar.

"Steve Baker, let me buy you a drink," he joyfully shouted. "I was beginning to think you weren't attending the convention. I saw Frank Turner and he wasn't sure you'd be here."

"I kind of made up my mind at the last minute. I went down to the vendors display room but couldn't find you," I said.

"Yeah, I don't hang around the booth very much since we have some new people," Harvey confessed. "Irene still has booth duty. Did you see her?"

"Nope, I only met one of your new salesmen. He seemed to be doing a good job," I replied. "Did Frank mention my project?"

"Yes, but was rather closed mouth about what is entails."

"Well, I won't elaborate, but, it involves his motive power business."

"Would it mean more business for Spartan Chemicals?" Harvey quizzed, while handing me a scotch and soda.

"Could be, could be," I replied between sips.

"Are you gonna make my dinner?" Harvey asked.

"Thanks anyway but I need to get back. It's the housekeeper's day off and nobody is chaperoning the kids," I lied.

Harvey and his coterie moved to a table and I joined them. They seemed set for the remainder of the day or at least until the time of his dinner. Hearing jokes both old and new helped pass the time and skipping each round was accepted considering my drive home. When the clock reached seven thirty, I made my excuses and departed. Miller's Pub is just a short walk from the hotel and the Chicago's winter wind helped clear my head.

When frozen microscopic projectiles began striking my face, I realized a Chicago city block is a lot longer than first thought. Reaching Miller's Pub with squinting eyes and turned up collar was thankfully, not a minute too soon.

Finding a table facing the door I sat and ordered my usual libation. Occasionally, the crowd at the bar blocks my view, nevertheless, I trust Irene to negotiate through the assemblage, at which point, and she will see me.

Finally, she appeared after doing just that. She wore a dark winter coat with a fur collar and kept it on until the first daiquiri did its job.

In the beginning, they were clumsy and only made glancing eye contact, as if ignorant of how to properly act. Their previous relationship had become a tiring repetition, wearing away the excitement of newness. Their love was also forbidden to which they made their own law. Accordingly, they did not stain themselves with guilt. Being apart had created a chasm. The adage, "Absence makes the heart grow fonder" had faded into "out of sight out of mind," proving proximity is needed for true intimacy. Over time you forget what the other feels like, smells, and tastes like. On this cold autumn night they were sensing the chasm between them was beginning to close. Emotions had traveled full circle and met again.

Now, with every refill of their beverage, the custody of self-control began to dwindle. In the subdued lighting they touched hands. Both were fully aware of the others burning cheeks and pounding heart.

Irene's eyes fell upon her hands and she uttered, "Do you want to come to my room?"

"There's nothing I desire more but the situation is different. I no longer run the show. It would be embarrassing for both of us to be seen under intimate circumstances. But, I have a solution. Twenty minutes away is the Hampton motor lodge which is holding a suite in my name."

Flashing her familiar white grin Irene said, "I need to get back no later than five in the morning."

Steven caught the waitress's eye and called for the check.

The Hampton suite consisted of a living room, kitchen, bedroom, and bath, all surprisingly ample. Irene was the first to use the toilet having held her water while in Miller's Pub. Steven had more practice at being a diplomat and could last longer. Nevertheless, he was pleased to be only second in line. While sitting on the sofa, waiting his turn, a melodic voice, in a lower pitch, echoed from the convenience chamber, "I'm going to take a bath."

"Wait, let me take a leak first," Steven expressed.

"That won't bother me. You come on in," she replied, amidst the sound of a filling tub.

Irene had always been immodest in his presence. A trait taking time to get used to. He walked into the lavatory and did his business, but not before the view of Irene's nakedness caused an involuntary shy bladder pause.

Steven was the first to crawl into bed, leaving his clothes draped on a nearby chair and, also, leaving the night table illuminated. He laid back with his hands behind his head listening to the bathing sounds drifting from the lightened bathroom. Anticipation obscured any other thoughts other than the pending fulfillment.

Irene appeared in the faint light of the living room and scurried to the bed.

"Please turn out the light," she implored.

Steven was reminded that Irene preferred to make love in the dark, while he favored a little light in order to witness the attributes of her naked beauty. The reading light was turned off.

"It embarrasses me to be stared at in such a steadfast manner," she admitted.

In the darkness there was no need to avoid each other's eyes. They could finally relax and the anxious, uneasy, and rigid feelings were soon gone. When love reaches its highest point it is a mistake to try to put it into words. Quietly the exhausted couple lay face upward in ebon tranquility, with each bearing an unseen smile of satisfaction.

Reluctantly, the next morning, they returned to the hotel at five o'clock. Pulling up at the hotel-parking garage, Irene disembarked and hurried to the open doors of the elevator. He watched the elevator doors close and then pulled into the sparse traffic.

On the highway back to Kirksville, all thoughts of anything other than the night before were erased.

CHAPTER TWENTY-SIX

S TEVEN RETURNED TO WORK WITH heightened spirits. A renewed sense of energy compelled him to dig into the Liberty Battery undertaking. Nonetheless, his concentration was frequently interrupted by reflections of the night at the Hampton motor lodge. Mystified somewhat about how appropriate the sensuality when, heretofore, Irene had faded from retrospection.

The buzz from his fax machine alerted him of an incoming message. Impatiently waiting for it to end, he noticed it was from Spartan Chemicals. There was only a short sentence, "Have you recovered from the other night?"

Unaware of Spartan's fax machines location, he felt it prudent not to reply in the same method. Instead, he confessed via a phone call.

Later that day, while the family was having dinner, Virginia commented, "Ever since you got back from the convention, you're like the cat that got the bird. You need to do that more often."

Steven smiled in agreement thinking, "If she only knew."

November is a gray month. The crowning glory of autumn color has come to an end and only a few frazzled remnants remain on the ground. Soon floral life will be hidden beneath the earth and covered with a white mantle.

Because of extremes, from balmy days to those well below freezing, the month often is disagreeable. Saved only by Thanksgiving and consumer discounts, the harbinger of cold, chilling weather and its monotonous overcast, promotes a great deal of languor. On the brighter side, I do enjoy the taste of cinnamon and pumpkin pie.

As the year began drawing to conclusion, the general public could no longer frolic in warm sunlight, picnic, or play baseball. Now, in view of the fact days were becoming listless, more attention was given the newspaper headlines. France and Great Britain performed nuclear weapon tests— France at the Mururoa atoll and Britain, by virtue of an agreement with the United States, at the Nevada test site. Margaret Thatcher resigned and President Bush signed the Clear Act. Finally, Saddam Hussein refused to withdraw from Kuwait saying he was prepared to fight a dangerous war.

The result of a world loaded with consequential activity sometimes encourages introspection. We, as individuals, play only a bit part in this endless movie. Correspondingly, many of us face the hard fact the world doesn't revolve around us. Our protagonist in this story, while yet displaying egocentric behavior, is slowly beginning to correspond to having one woman in his life. (Many a loyal reader is not convinced and holds a wait and see attitude.)

Once Paul Mueller reported that the pony mixer was operable and a drum of oxide had arrived, the trip to Cleveland was scheduled. Upon arrival at Liberty Battery he found everything set in place for mixing a batch of litharge paste. Quantities of acid and water were scaled down to match the weight of oxide. Even though the acid was added slowly, a garden hose was used on the outside of the mixer preventing temperatures from becoming too high and burning the paste. As it so happened, the garden hose wasn't needed. Once the paste density gave the desired "crunch" when squeezed by hand, a cube weight was measured and the batch loaded in a metal cart and pushed to the pasting machine. One of the hourly workers shoveled the paste into the hopper, Paul Mueller fed positive grids, and pasted plates were removed at the end of the process.

Steven, satisfied thus far, directed those removing pasted plates to stack them separated from each other using racks designed by Liberty.

When the pasting job was completed the aforementioned racks were trucked to a humidity curing room.

"How long do we hydroset them?" asked Paul, unfamiliar with litharge paste.

"They actually don't require a hydroset since they have no free lead," Steven replied. "As yet we don't have the equipment to properly humidity cure so we now should be concerned not to dry too soon. By keeping the racks covered should serve our purpose. In a couple days they may be suitable for plate wrapping. Have you documented the test so far?"

"Yes sir. I'll make a full report of the data and give it to you tomorrow."

"Paul, I prefer you keep this test confidential and strictly between us. As I understand, Liberty Battery makes major decisions by committee. That might work well for Liberty but it's been my experience it creates a platform for politics to influence judgment. A camel is a horse designed by committee; therefore, I want all out ducks in a row when I make my presentation. Keeping our findings secret prevents the preparation of negative argument," I cautioned.

"They're going to pressure me," Paul stated.

"I expected they would. Just refer any questions to me, and play dumb," I replied. The look on Paul's face told me how difficult it's going to be for him to comply, but, I get a gut feeling he'll enjoy it.

"We'll use ball mill oxide for the negative plates. You probably have some in inventory. Take a sample out of the lot and have the lab run a free lead analysis. It's good to know, plus, it will tell us how reliable our hydroset process is performing.

The next day, the young associate was true to his word. He mounted the steps carrying the promised information. Passing the open door of Frank Turner's office brought his mission to a temporary halt.

"Come in son and spend a minute," Frank proscribed.

Paul felt like he was back in high school and called before the principal. Nervously, he obeyed, and edged into the rare territory of unfamiliar circumstance. He was relieved somewhat when asked, "How do you like working with Steve Baker?"

"I like it very much," was about all Paul could muster, self-conscious over the alien situation. His uneasiness slowly lessened after Frank stated, "I'm glad to hear it. When it comes to the motive power industry, he is one of the leaders. Before retiring, he founded Baker Battery and had a good portion of the industrial battery market. We're lucky to have him with us and sharing his knowledge so our company can make a better product."

By now, Paul's heartbeat was nearly normal.

Frank continued, "Learn everything you can from him and in a couple years, when Steve retires, you will be able to manage our industrial side of the business. That's all I wanted to know. I'm glad everybody's on board and happy," Frank conferred, indicating it was time for Paul to leave.

Leaving the room, walking on air, and with an increasing positive attitude toward the leader of his assignment, he couldn't wait to relate, word for word, the previous encounter.

"What you tell me is certainly good news for our project. Honestly speaking, I'm very concerned about your boss, Jim Price. If body language means anything, he's not very happy with me being here, especially on a program affecting product design. Unfortunately, I believe he has the temperament of a pedigree poodle. I'll take a crossbreed any day. Having faced the 'not invented here' syndrome before, what we're doing, temporarily excluding his input, must flip his pancakes. He operates under a mindset favoring internally developed products even when those externally developed are superior. We may not get a second bite of the cherry so let's make sure no detail is overlooked," Steven instructed.

When it came to his engineering supervisor, the word fear replaced the expression of respect. Hearing the opinion of someone highly regarded by Frank Turner make Paul's loyalty grow deeper roots.

Two days later the positive plates were dry enough to be wrapped. Each plate received a fiberglass insulator, bottom boot, and perforated retainer mat. After which, the wrapped plates were assembled with their corresponding negatives and stacked in a burning box. From there the conducting strap and posts were burned in place. The last step prior to formation was to sink the element into a polyvinyl jar and position the cell cover, sealing it to the jar. The covers have holes with lead inserts to allow the posts to protrude, facilitating the final operation, burning the buttons.

The test cells were of the 450 ampere hour design. Six units were filled with weak forming acid and tied into the electrical formation current along with three cells of those having ball milled oxide—the present product design.

The formation process usually takes about four days or 96 hours. Afterwards, the specific gravity of the operating electrolyte is adjusted. Test cells, and the three control units, will be discharged at their 6 hour rate until they reach 1.75 volts cut off. Total voltage, specific gravity, cell voltage, and both plate voltages will be taken and recorded each hour.

Although Steven had confidence in Paul Mueller, he felt the importance of this project decreed his being present over the weekend. He was a firm believer in Murphy's Law.

Assigned to the task of doing nothing was an unfamiliar burden. Even though he stopped by the factory a couple times over the weekend, during the remaining hours, unoccupied, he felt at sea. He turned down an invitation to play golf primarily because he wasn't in the mood for the embarrassment—he never got the hang of hitting the ball straight.

A phone call to Kirksville reassured that everything was under control. After the obligation to telephone Irene, he was back twiddling thumbs. Finally, he couldn't tolerate the idleness any longer and drove back to the factory and an atmosphere more conducive to his weekend character.

A similar routine took place Sunday and, by Monday the cells in the test circuit were completely formed and prepared for the critical measure of initial capacity. The standard requirement for industrial lift truck batteries was at least 90% of its rated capacity after three cycles and 100% after ten cycles. Up 'til now, Liberty cells hadn't reached more than 87%, no matter how many times they were cycled.

While confident the oxide changes would do the trick, it was only normal for a little apprehension to exist. Proof of the pudding will happen on Tuesday when the first measured discharge takes place; and, if things turn out okay, Steven plans to fly home Wednesday morning and working with Paul Mueller over the phone and fax machine.

The next day at exactly 8:00 a.m. the test circuit was opened and the discharge began. Voltages held steady for the first three hours, and then, the control cells began to weaken. After four hours they started to deteriorate rather quickly. The first control cell hit 1.75 volts at 305 minutes (84.7%) with the other two lasting only three minutes longer (85.6%). The weakest litharge test cell lasted 332 minutes (92.2%) and the strongest 340 minutes (94.4%). It was obvious the litharge oxide outperformed the in-house ball milled product. What's more, additional cycling will not bring the control units up to the 90% threshold, let alone 100% after ten cycles. On the other hand, having reached over 90% on the first cycle, almost guarantees compliance after ten.

Satisfied with the results, Steven made copies of the data, instructed Paul to continue cycling all the test cells, and repeat taking the proscribed measurements. Once convinced his instructions would be scrupulously followed, he returned to the motel and packed his travel bag. The next morning he was on his way back to Kirksville.

When Steven opened the front door he was met with warmth, peace, and comfort. He recognized the fact that domesticated children and the dulcifying ambience was the result of Virginia Prouder. She had become an irreplaceable treasure and also growing concern. Would Virginia accept another woman in the house? Considering Rosemary's position, it's not a quantum leap to think Virginia would harbor similar feelings. Loyal to the prescription of his former attitude, it's something to worry about later. He accepts the fact that the past is gone forever and the only meaningful time is the present. You can get back most everything you own but lost time is never retrieved. The future is unpredictable even though a portion of it is preserved for two women, Irene Jones and Coralee Smallwood. If he could make time stand still, he would keep both waiting in the wings.

Presently, when returning from his weeks in Ohio, he found himself anxious to be in the moment with Virginia Prouder. Without forethought, time has changed friendship into fondness, appreciation into affection, and stopping just short of changing affection into passion. That's not to say Steven hasn't visualized a theoretical relationship guided by reckless indulgence. Fear that his emotion is not shared keeps him from moving forward. Alas, the light of his desire is kept under a bushel and may never see sunshine. The risk of disclosure might ruin present circumstances, therefore, muffled by trepidation, his true feelings may never be revealed.

The month of December opened with unusually high temperatures, overcast skies, and a steady rain. The children were especially disappointed having anticipated December as signaling the advent of Christmas. Naturally, warm weather in December is an anomaly and holds on for a very short spell. In fact, only two days later, when the Baker family awakened, they were greeted by a different world. During the night Kirksville had its first major snowfall—up to six inches. Like a magnet, the sound of a snowplow drew Ashley and Kristen to the living room window. With their noses pressed against the glass, they cheered for the blanket of white covering the front lawn. Excitedly they ran to the kitchen where they found their Aunt Virginia at the stove and their father sitting at the table with a cup of coffee.

"It's Christmas time. When are we putting up the tree?" they chimed.

"Simmer down a little. We will put it up this weekend," their father said. Placing a platter of pancakes on the middle of the breakfast table, Virginia announced, "Breakfast is ready. Ashley, go tell Michael to hurry up." Just as soon as she finished, Michael said, "I'm here."

"We're going to put the tree up this weekend," Ashley repeated.

Breakfast eating sounds tinkled as the family was engrossed with pancakes and bacon, their favorite.

Finally Virginia asked, "What kind of Christmas tree do you have?"

"We have a large artificial with white flock already on it. We've had it for years."

"Then these children have never had a real tree," Virginia uttered. "You have a very large home and an excellent living room. I will only decorate a real tree."

The children's banter stopped quickly and all eyes turned to their father. He felt he noticed a frinking smile behind Virginia's sober face. There was no escape. Virginia had set him up and, more importantly, he liked it.

"We'll get a real Christmas tree this weekend."

"I'll go along to make sure you get the right one," Virginia confirmed, as the children ran about cheering between hugs for their Aunt Virginia.

When the joyful noise subsided, Steven reminded her that he had to be in Ohio the following week. Virginia replied, "Just set up the tree in its stand and I'll do the rest. You might have to make the stand."

It was past lunchtime on Saturday before they finally found a tree that was approved by Virginia. She agreed to a seven-foot Scotch pine with dense needle clusters and a few small pinecones scattered about. After a short argument over price, the tree salesman added a heavy wooden base.

The tree was eventually positioned where it could be seen from the street, giving enough room for walking around it. Virginia added a box of her own favorite ornaments and, together with the Baker's, decorations were in ample supply. Scotch pine, not like other species, is noted for its faint aroma; however, the pleasant smell was enough to keep the children excited and for Steven to remember on the plane ride to Cleveland.

The snowstorm traveled on an eastern path and reached Cleveland, Ohio before Steven's plane landed. Snowplows crisscrossed the landing strips in order to aid incoming flights. He, dressed for the occasion, rented a car and was soon on the highway heading for the motor inn. All in all, he was running about an hour and a half late. Too late for lunch at the country club, he decided to eat at the motel and go to work the next morning. A phone call will alert the factory that he was there and alleviate any concern.

The restaurant was crowded with other likeminded guests hunkering down until the morning.

The meeting was scheduled for 10:00 a.m. in the Liberty Battery conference room. Traditionally, at 9:00 a.m. refreshments rested on a side table and consisted of Danish pastry, donuts, coffee and juice. The hour difference allows for consumption of the treats, a little non-specific chitchat, and use of the lavatory located at the left of the meeting room. Eventually, when those in attendance had taken their seats, Paul Mueller distributed the bound documents containing the performance results of the litharge oxide test. In addition, an overhead projector was set up to enhance the presentation.

Because those conducting it performed the test in semi-secretness, final results were hidden from curious eyes. As a result, interest was piqued much more than usual, resulting in a full house. Besides Frank Turner, his personal secretary, Maxine Reynolds, was there primarily to take notes. Also, nearly every component of Liberty's operation was represented, including, the projects' nemesis, Jim Price with two of his engineering cohorts; Darryl Booth, sales manager; Wade Evans, quality control; Fred Carr, plant manager; Herbert Morgan, time study; and Derrick Gardener, office manager. With such a mixed crew it makes you wonder if the lavish breakfast layout might have influenced some for being there.

Frank Turner made a short introduction and turned the meeting over to Steven, who began by giving an overview of the electric lift truck battery market during the past three years. Next, drawing attention to the projector screen, he presented competition and market apportionment. While the major manufacturers held the lion's share, smaller companies divided what was left—approximately 15%. It was here that Liberty Battery could grow over the ensuing years depending on two controlling factors—aggressive sales and improved battery design.

Sales should have an advantage due to Liberty's name recognition. However, at present, it is a dubious task because of the appearance of lesser quality. Inability to meet current quality standards is a negative sales tool used by the competition. No doubt the competition has tested our product and broadcasted the results, primarily the failure to meet 90% of the rating in three cycles. It's in this area, failure to deliver required initial capacity, that my analysis was centered.

The industry uses litharge oxide and the manner in which it is processed is the difference. (Timed with the presentation, Paul Mueller placed the test result transparency on the projector.) Pointing to the screen, Steven continued, "The improved results were achieved by using litharge oxide in the positive plates." (He moved the pointer to negative half-voltage readings.) "The negative plate readings indicate their ability to support until the 1.75 volt cut-off. Better said, we can wait awhile before addressing the negative plate process. Now, if you turn to the last page of the document, you find my recommendations." (The appropriate transparency gave a full view.)

"First, use only litharge oxide in positive plates for industrial motive power applications. In the past, Spartan Chemicals has installed a bag house silo under a two-year agreement for exclusively using their oxide. The cost of piping and labor to bring it into the paste mixer can also be negotiated.

Second, while obviously meeting initial capacity requirements, it is only one part of the equation. Lift truck batteries are warranted for five years under normal operating conditions. Most of the competition offers their warranty on a three full and two years on a pro rata basis. With knowledge that the end user will not maintain their batteries according to the manufacturer's proscription, the customer accepts the pro-rata aspect. Considering misuse or customer abuse, a few manufacturers offer a full five year warranty stipulating, no over watering, one eight hour shift in a single day, properly matched chargers, and complete records on each battery. With such stringent requirements, I doubt if they ever had to honor their warranty.

Subsequently, battery life and crystal structure becomes a concern. At the end of our typical hydroset the litharge oxide plates are composed of large crystal structure. Over the years, a great deal has been learned about the importance of crystal structure. Larger lead crystals give less battery life while smaller extend the life. This is where a humidity-curing oven comes in. By raising the temperature, in 100%

humidity, about twelve degrees each hour until approximately 180 degrees Fahrenheit, maximum life is achieved. This usually takes eight hours, the rest of the time is primarily just drying the plates and, the total process takes one day. Several members of the battery association make suitable equipment. At this time I'm prepared to answer any questions."

As expected, Jim Price raised his hand. "What you claim may be true but the expense doesn't pass the cost/benefit test."

"Please explain."

"We won't sell enough batteries to cover the cost of equipment," Jim flatly stated.

"I would hold off any disparagement of the sales department before making such judgment," Steven replied. "With proper product and good literature, Darryl Booth and his staff will do a fine job."

"I didn't mean anything against the sales department," Jim Price disclosed.

"Don't apologize to me, tell Darryl. Are there any other questions? If not, my meeting is over and I turn it back to Frank Turner."

Frank closed the meeting with a twinkle in his eye. Later that day he made a phone call to a close friend who makes humidity curing ovens.

The moment he opened the front door, Steven was welcomed by the fragrance of the Scotch pine. Bedecked with elegant ornaments, tinsel, and soft colored lights, the Baker Christmas tree was dazzling. It was an exhibition of beauty and can only be attributed to Virginia Prouder.

The children were still in school, as she appeared from the kitchen wiping her hands on a dish cloth. A harmless peck on the cheek greeted his arrival. Leaving his luggage in the entryway, Steven followed her to the kitchen.

"How did the presentation go?" she asked while pouring a cup of fresh coffee.

"I think it went very well. I even got a shot at my nemesis without causing a riot, using only repartee."

"Are they going to follow your suggestions?"

"I'm not sure. They have to if they want to take part in the industrial battery business. I do know that Frank Turner wants to grow his company. That alone will make him give serious thought to my recommendations," he postulated while blowing on the coffee.

Virginia poured herself a cup and sat across from him. "What do you think of the tree?"

"I don't have words to describe it. It's the most beautiful Christmas tree I've ever seen."

"The holiday season is my favorite time of year," she declared. "I've always thought the tree ornaments tell a story, not only of Christmas but also about you. A great deal of history clings to those long pine needles. They hold pieces of our life reacquainting after being put away for a year. Some are magical and tell the story of our past. Children understand. Ashley had a story to tell about nearly every one of them, and I related the history of those belonging to me. Now, they all belong together becoming one family on the tree. Our Scotch pine is enchanting, bringing joy, memories of Christmas past, beautiful sadness, cheer, and hope for the future."

Virginia's duende easily broke through any resistance of indifference Steven could muster. Struck dumb for a second, he came out with, "What would you like for Christmas?"

"The best gift of any Christmas is the family around the tree sharing memories and love."

The racket in the entryway could only be the children home from school. With supper, homework, bath and bedtime, it will be hours before the adults can resume their conversation. A discourse equally desired. It all rested on when the children decided to go to bed. At the same time the mahogany grandfather clock struck ten with a chorus of harmonious chiming, Ashley lay prostrate in front of the fascinating tree, lolling in fairyland. Her trance ended when her father said, "Time to go to bed sweetheart."

Alone at last, the drowsy couple was nodding. Half asleep they gave up the ship but agreed to resume their tête-à-tête at a better time.

The ensuing week was highlighted by undistinguished routine. Steven was kept apace of activities back in Ohio through phone calls from Paul Mueller. The family coffer increased significantly with the lawsuit settlement and insurance payoff, even so, wealth has yet to alter

Steven's inherent frugality. He has come to the conclusion, seducing Virginia will take longer than originally hoped for. Consequently, on Friday morning he called Paul Mueller to learn the state of affairs, "Is Jim Price still looking for a dog to kick?"

"Yeah, he's mad as hell, but scared to death of Frank Turner," Paul replied. "I haven't heard any more about the project."

"Well, maybe no news is good news. You take care this weekend and I'll talk to you on Monday."

His next call was to Irene telling her he planned to travel there for the weekend. Even dutiful sex is good until it is over. Before leaving, he drove downtown and bought her a Christmas gift. It mainly served as a peace offering, since, once again, he won't be with her on Christmas.

CHAPTER TWENTY-SEVEN

URING THE NIGHT, ON CHRISTMAS Eve, Mother Nature delivered a quiet soft snowfall. It became an object of wonder to gaze through the frosted picture window at the sparkling sheet of white, still flawless at daybreak. It also was an impeccable beginning for this blessed day, a day where children's wishes come true.

Kristen was expected to be the first to awaken. She didn't let them down. Hesitating to be the leader downstairs, she woke Ashley and coaxed her sister into bolding hands and descend the steps together. Sounds of jubilation brought the rest of the family to the festive scene, while Virginia went unnoticed to the kitchen to make coffee and prepare breakfast. By the time she called them to eat, a mountain of holiday wrappings covered the floor. "Save the bows," she directed Ashley. "We can use them again."

Once they were finally corralled at the table, they were like worms in hot ashes. Too excited to eat, Virginia gave them absolution and released them back to the tree. Catching her subtle smile, Steven realized how much he appreciates this woman. Unaware of what was happening to him, Virginia has gradually broken through the deterrent to his heart.

Getting up from his chair, Steven grabbed his coffee and said, "Let's go in with the children. I want you to open your presents."

"You didn't have to get me anything," she mildly protested, at the same time, taking the cup from his hand. "I don't want you spilling coffee on our beautiful clean carpet." She placed it on a tray, and said, "I spent half a day using the steam cleaner just following the spoor of coffee drops. If you must take your coffee to the living room, use a saucer and be careful."

He took three big gulps and then returned the cup to the table.

"Aunt Virginia, I put all your gifts together," Kristen declared. "Do you want me to hand them to you?"

"If you wish."

The first gift handed to Virginia was Kristen's favorite, a stuffed animal with a pendant hanging around its neck. A Nikon camera was next, followed by an haute handbag with her initials fashionably etched on a hanging charm. The remaining gifts were purchased by the children and governed by their limited funds. Virginia was speechless. It was the first time in her life to be given such expensive gifts. The handbag alone had to cost in the hundreds let alone the gold jewelry.

"I hope you're pleased," Steven voiced sincerely.

Wiping tears from her eyes, Virginia disclosed, "This is the first time in my life to receive such gifts."

"Is daddy crying?" Kristen asked innocently.

As the daylight hours began to dwindle, the panorama through the living room window was spoiled. Squirrels and rabbits had left their tracks while vigorously in pursuit of food. Nevertheless, the first impression set the tone and will last forever.

When all the excitement settled down, appetites increased. Homemade pizza did the trick. It also served to give the children's high-spiritedness a temporary rest. Sitting around the dining room table all agreed that this was the best Christmas ever. It could only improve by having Rosemary and David in attendance. Unfortunately, that couldn't be arranged this year.

Natural light had finally surrendered, compelling Virginia to turn on the hanging chandelier and adjust down the illumination.

Now dwelling in low light prompted Ashley to suggest that they all go to the living room and watch the tree with only Christmas lights turned on. Passing through the archway leading from the dining room to the living room, Michael looked up to make sure the sprig of mistletoe was still pinned where he put it. He planned for his girlfriend to walk beneath it so he could demand a kiss. Pleased that everything was as he staged it, he joined the rest of his family in the living room darkness.

For at least an hour the family sat entranced by the grandeur of rainbows reflected against the ivory-colored walls. It had been a wonderful, but, tiring day and, when the yawns began to increase, the children accepted that it was time for bed. Virginia and Steven, the last to retire, shut off power to the tree and crossed the archway to the dining room and kitchen. Steven drew attention to the mistletoe and Virginia became a willing partner. Their embrace lingered a few seconds longer than the traditional kiss required. That scintilla of time was easily recognized by Steven, and did not escape his rapacious thoughts. As his hands lowered down her back, Virginia whispered, "There will be none of that until, if, or when, we are married so guide your actions accordingly."

All that was left for Steven was a cold shower in order to let his blood redistribute.

The holiday season has come and gone and Kirksville finds itself immersed in a deep freeze. The temperature, mired in the teens, shows no indication of winter thaw. Not everyone is complaining. A pond near the Baker residence has frozen solid, presenting a great opportunity for the children to try out one of their Christmas gifts, ice skates. With red cheeks and runny noses, all three become proficient for their ages. A bonfire, located a safe distance from the ice, affords the opportunity to warm up and, when their father and Aunt Virginia appear with a thermos of hot chocolate, that finishes the job. The adults settle in on a bench near the fire and take part by watching the skaters. Soon, visibility is provided only by the fire, which begs for more logs in order to witness activity on the ice. For the sake of the children, who have been out nearly three hours, and the image of a standing rib roast residing in a warm oven, Steven determined it was time to go home. His children offered no argument.

The Scotch pine had been stripped of its decorations and unceremoniously dragged to the front street only to be thrown into the back of a city truck loaded with a few of its relatives. Ashley and Kristen witnessed this municipal offense while standing at the large picture window of their rearranged living room. The incident was saved since Aunt Virginia had taken copious photographs with her new Nikon camera.

All the while, the two adults carried on with a fawning attitude and performed like inadequate actors in a B movie. Fooling no one, the children saw through the imposters immediately; however, they couldn't decipher why. Between the adult intellects roiled the turmoil of not exactly knowing each other's thoughts. Would she ultimately dismiss? Would he lose his desire? No answers were forthcoming. It was he who blinked first.

"Have you given more thought to our discussion?"

"Have you?"

"Yes, under a pretense of a business trip, we could secretly be married. Unless, of course, if your mind is set on a big wedding."

"I've already had one of those and you know what happened there. I'd be happy to be married by a justice of the peace as long as the certificate is legal."

With children around, whenever adults speak in a low voice it works like a magnet. Inquisitive ears tend to probe closer and closer until the conversation is easily heard. Alas, that also becomes the time when adults speak in normal tones. Kristen, acting the scout for Ashley, came to nothing on her mission.

Confines of a stubborn winter have begun to loosen its grasp. While skies are still overcast and bleak, a chilly wind signals the promise of spring and more favored days. Youngsters were playing basketball on the schoolyard blacktop even though obstinate snow had to be scooped away. Baseball, the personal game of choice, stood on the sidelines waiting as an eager replacement. The wait won't take much longer since trees are starting to sprout their incipient flower and daylight begins to linger.

The adults in the Baker residence have been reticent to discuss the Yuletide agreement. Taking the pact as certain, they conduct each day like the one before and only their glance gives them away.

Mrs. Murphy, the neighbor next door, has agreed to tend the children the week Steven must be in Ohio (Coincidentally, Virginia Prouder also has personal business that week). While the children are disturbed over the change, they've been appeased by the fact the week will go by fast.

And so, on the Ides of March, another important event transpired. Steven Baker and Virginia Prouder were married. Just across the Indiana state line the couple took part in an elopement special and was married two hours later. For only two hundred dollars they avoided the pomp and notoriety of a public church wedding. And, as they continued to Ohio, Virginia had her legal marriage license safely tucked away in her purse. Steven was numb.

Earlier in the week, lodging was reserved at a popular bed-and-breakfast, a restored nineteenth century home. Their temporary residence was located within walking distance from upscale shopping and elegant restaurants, plus, just a skip and a jump from Liberty Battery. The rustic home featured other amenities, such as, library, sitting rooms, and formal dining room. Steven had booked a suite within the home. In addition to the bedroom, a large modern bath and living room went with the deal.

Upon arrival they noticed a wrought iron fence surrounding the property and an arrow indicating free parking for guests. Finding the gate open, the newlywed travelers took an empty space and removed some of their luggage. At the registration desk they were in awe over the restored vestibule. It was like being taken back a hundred years, boosting Virginia's desire to see their accommodations. She was not disappointed.

Legally they have every right to be there together, yet, they suffer under unexplainable guilt. It goes beyond newlyweds facing the first night coexisting as man and wife. Each has experienced that before. It was a strange and frightening sensation as if they had just met. They were entering into the realm of the unknown, unsure of each other's assiduousness.

Steven was worried about his history while married to Virginia's sister. Did she know all the steamy details? Probably not. True, he had become more involved with his family since Elaine's passing, but even then, found time to visit Irene. Like the chains of Jacob Marley, he has forged his own, Sharon Lezotte, abetting a murder, Irene Jones, and to a lesser degree, Coralee Smallwood. He knew for certain, if he had confessed it all, they wouldn't be together in Ohio, let alone married. Steven's hope is he doesn't talk in his sleep. Virginia's hope is to be acceptable to her new husband. She will spend tonight with her bible closed.

That evening, by all accounts, was awkward, clumsy, and hilarious as they got to know each other better. With regards to Virginia's concerns, only one word will suffice, successful. So much so, they couldn't make it to the first breakfast. Those attending knew the reason why. Later, descending the stairs, the contended couple found many guests enjoying the luxurious living room ready to greet them with an insightful and welcoming smile. The courtesies were repeated as the pair headed for the front door leading to the sidewalk.

While the weatherman predicted a cold day, brilliant sunshine begged to differ. Our protagonists ambled along with an uplifted gait. Everything appeared as though for the first time. The couple was exceedingly pleased at their image in the storefront windows, holding hands. Between wind gusts, the sun did administer subtle warmth, so much so, they unbuttoned their winter coats, but soon realized that was premature once a cloud blocked the springtime rays. The brisk walk had amplified their hunger. Accordingly, they turned into a crowded restaurant. Many of the customers were also under the spell of a sunny day, gleefully sipping coffee while waiting for the shops along the boulevard to open for business.

After consuming a generous morning meal, the twosome agreed they had enough outdoor exercise and headed back to their cozy retreat. Both felt taking a nap after breakfast looked to be a good idea. After all, remembering the previous evening had whetted their appetite for a repeat performance. It's going to be a while before the duo accompanies others, in the B&B, for free breakfast.

On Monday morning, Steven walked into the battery factory bright and early. Frank Turner had endorsed nearly all of his recommendations. As previously suggested, Spartan Chemicals did, in fact, erect an oxide silo outside the pasting department. The conditions for the construction were not revealed. The humidity curing oven, likewise, found its appropriate position and was in the final stages of debugging. At Steven's suggestion, Paul Mueller was graduated to manager of motive power batteries, and took the promotion like a fish to water. Darryl Booth was still boasting about his samples of motive power sales literature and anxiously awaited final approval.

Frank had invited Steven to lunch at the country club—this time just the two of them. He wanted to express his personal appreciation. "I've received a couple phone calls from your former dealers, one in New York and the other from Tennessee. They both confessed it was at your urging."

"They're good people and pay their bills on time." Steven replied. "Together, they could sell over two million dollars in batteries."

"That would certainly jump start the business, but, I will need your guidance as to how it's handled. Darryl is a good man except he knows no more about motive power than I do."

"I'll have a talk with Darryl this week and work out some details on protected territories. If there's one thing that keeps a dealer awake at night it's someone selling in their territory."

Frank chuckled, took a sip from his martini glass, folded his hands on the table, and leaned forward, "I know I'm increasing your duties, over our original agreement, however, I'm more than willing to compensate by raising your salary. Just let me know how much more you want."

"Thank you, I appreciate the offer. Let's wait a while before we get into that. I think Darryl will get the hang of it sooner than you think."

"Okay, but keep it in mind. I don't want you retiring on me," Frank stated. "By the way, when did you get in? I had Maxine call the motel and they said you hadn't registered yet."

"This time I'm not staying at the motel. I'm staying at a bed-and-breakfast with a guest."

"Why you rascal you, just send in the receipt and we'll reimburse you."

"Don't get it wrong. I was remarried last week. We're sort of on our honeymoon."

"Well congratulations, when will we meet the new bride?"

"Right now I can't say. It will probably be on the next trip."

"Bullshit, plan on having dinner with Margaret and me Thursday at our house," Frank insisted. Taking Steven's silence as tacit approval, he ordered another martini and asked the waitress to bring the menus. Later, after lunch, Frank dropped Steven off at the factory entrance.

"Aren't you coming back in?"

"No, I've got to tell Margaret were having guests on Thursday, and help her clean up the dog hairs," Frank joked. Obviously, he had another meeting downtown. They don't own a dog.

The week progressed perfectly with testing the first humidity cured positive plates, working with Darryl and his sales crew, and the B&B at night. Taking stock, Steven has never been happier.

It came as no surprise that Margaret Turner fell in love with Virginia. They hit it off from the start. Virginia's maturity and female acumen stood out compared with the other Liberty wives. Margaret insisted he bring her along on every trip. They could go shopping together and have tea with some of her girlfriends. In other words, she promised to keep Virginia busy and entertained.

On Friday morning, the newlyweds actually took part in the free breakfast, and then, the groom made one more visit to the factory, making sure all questions were answered. His bride stayed behind and packed for the return trip to Kirksville.

The whole trip seemed like a dream. To the best of their knowledge, nothing went wrong. Most times such a visit leaves one with a sense of an entity amiss. Possibly it's a discord you can't actually put your finger on. Maybe a regret of a stumble, social miscue, or conflict. Today, however, nostalgia rules the roost.

The sound of voices coming from the driveway caused Kristen to run to the front room window and exclaim, "Its Daddy and Aunt Virginia, their back!"

Michael and Ashley, standing nearby, burst through the doorway to help carry the luggage in. The bouncing mood changed abruptly once they reached the foyer, giving a clear view of the parlor. Thereupon, they noticed, sitting in an overstuffed chair, their daughter Rosemary, conspicuously with her dander up. She was angry enough to chew iron and spit nails.

"I see you're still up to your old tricks," she directed to her father.

"What are you talking about?" he replied. "And what are you doing home?"

"I'm talking about another one of your immoral trysts and with Aunt Virginia to boot. I'm ashamed of both of you." Turning her glare to Virginia, "Mother was your sister. Have you no scruples?"

Before Virginia could answer, Steven interrupted, "You're jumping to conclusions and this time you are dead wrong. Before we explain, answer me one thing, why aren't you still in school?"

"I've dropped out for a while for personal reasons." (Too personal to be repeated in front of her siblings and Virginia. More than likely, it has to do with a romantic breakup, which she will divulge sooner rather than later.) "I can teach grade school for now and finish my master's degree anytime."

"You can make more money with a master's degree," her father commented, for lack of something else to say on the subject.

"There are more important things than money," she affirmed.

"Not if you don't have any," he quipped.

Temporarily changing the subject caused Rosemary's tirade to slightly subside. Still fuming, she asked for an explanation. Virginia took the lead, "Last week, before traveling to Ohio, your father and I were married. For many reasons we both wanted a quiet ceremony."

"How could you? My mother was your sister. Don't you have any scruples? We still have grief."

"For how long have you known your mother, twenty years? I've known my sister for over forty. I know her better than you will ever know your mother. Elaine would not want your father to be alone. She would be pleased for him to have married me," Virginia attested. "You will eventually move out and start a family of your own. There will be enough on your plate just to make it work. Be thankful your father won't be part of your worries. At the moment, a peaceful and happy home depends on you. Give some thought to it. As for my part, I'll do everything in my power to make certain it is just that."

Knowing Aunt Virginia will live with them forever gave Ashley and Kristen broad smiles. Both were puzzled over their older sister's objection. The tension needle, which had been pushed off the scale, now is within readable measures, yet nowhere near the normal zone. That will take more time. The remaining productive hours were used to rearrange bedrooms. Rosemary had her own room again and Virginia united with the master suite. For the rest of the day they all agreed to hitch a ride on the vehicle of civility and hang on. Wisely, Virginia stayed the effort to cook a balanced meal. Instead, she ordered pizza, much to the merriment of the youngest Bakers.

Over the weekend it was like walking on eggshells. The adults made every effort to prevent a flare up. Rosemary still remained the fuse to a keg of dynamite. Fortunately, she chose to be confined to her room. Reposing on her bed with the curtains drawn, the soft sound of crying reached her father's ears.

Steven gently tapped on her door and opened it part way, "What's the matter sweetheart? Are you ready to talk to your father?"

She ran to her father's arms and sobbed aloud, "Oh Daddy, Carl and I have broken our engagement."

"I never knew you two were engaged. Why did you end it?"

"I didn't, he did."

"What did he say?"

"He said I was too opinionated and assertive. I'm not that way, am I Daddy?"

"Not in the least, sweetheart. Some men are afraid of a strong woman. Do you let him have his way sometime?"

"Maybe."

"That's what I thought. If he's worth his salt, he'll come back and when he does, tell him he is right."

"About what?"

"Everything."

"Everything?"

"You want him back don't you? You can take over after your married. Now, dry your eyes and join your family."

With behavior under control, the family moves one step closer to domestic bliss. Such euphoria, an unattainable goal, must have every individual, under the same roof, in a state of tranquility—impossible. Perhaps, the best one can hope for is just curtailing the shouting. Men tend to relax more when the women are busy with household chores. It's the other way around should roles be reversed. Role sharing is a modern concept but a pipe-dream for the average family, especially those on the lower end of income. They continue to be guided by Biblical proscription.

Financially, the Baker family is considered well off. I was once told having a million dollars doesn't make you rich. You need to have ten million dollars to actually be wealthy. With Steven still working, and a seven-figure savings account drawing good interest, the Bakers have no worries about money.

Steven Baker, one time self-proclaimed male chauvinist, finds himself married to a woman of stern values. Without question, should he stray even an inch off course, or commit one indiscretion, she would divorce him in a heartbeat. Doing so would be a costly affair in which he could lose his house and half of his estate—not to mention the humiliation going with it.

Certain happenings have recently taken place making his new life somewhat easier. Coralee Smallwood has eloped with her art instructor. A 'Dear John' letter lies hidden in his home office files.

Sharon Lezotte has disappeared from the face of the earth. Her friends at Kroger's told him she sold her house and purchased an airline ticket to California.

And finally, Irene Jones heard of his marriage through the trade journals, most likely due to Frank Turner and/or his associates. It left her with only memories and the one link that binds them together—Miller's Pub.

Hardly attritional, Steven confesses, "I loved my wife but I've known other women. I try to be kind to my children, but my rule is firm. I guess I'm like other men, part good, part bad, but never what could be termed evil.

Regrets, I have a few. Right or wrong most of my transgressions received ablution during my reflective fantasies. Nevertheless, as we grow older the masculine allure gradually diminishes. At that point, we come to the realization new memories are few and far between. We tend to rely on those previously created. With each new year the past grows closer and closer until it seems like only yesterday those things happened.

Basically, I can't say I'm a changed man, but, I've learned homegrown tomatoes are always the best. Virginia wins this blue ribbon. I've also come to learn all men love a girl who doesn't exist. It's after they are married when the real girl appears. Only the lucky ones still love when her true identity is revealed. They learn to love what they have. It isn't the same with women. They marry a man confident in their ability to change him. This never happens. Virginia lays her true identity on the table. There are no surprises where she's concerned. I would describe our relationship as satisfying. We all dance to the same tune when it comes to the music of satisfaction."

The New Beginning